THE
WONDER STICK

Grumgra confronts Ru

The
Wonder Stick

by Stanton A. Coblentz

Illustrated by S. Glanckoff

Cosmopolitan Book Corporation
New York • MCMXXIX

CONTENTS

v

Contents

ILLUSTRATIONS

THE
WONDER STICK

CHAPTER I

Grumgra the Growling Wolf

A HUNDRED thousand years have passed since
a certain memorable twilight in the forest of
Umbaddu. Beyond a long ragged ridge of spruce,
the sun went down in forlorn crimson precisely like
the suns of a later day; across the winding valley,
with its shaggy woods and age-battered buttes and
cliffs, an enchanted calm had settled, as though time
had ended and there were no other days to come.
Only the Harr-Sizz or Long-Snake River, foaming
in tumultuous serpentine along its deep rocky cañon,
persistently broke the silence of the great wilderness; though now and again the call of some belated
bird, or howling of hyena, or long-drawn, mournful
plaint of some lonely wolf, would sound weirdly and
from far away like a voice from another world.

Yet birds, wolves, and hyenas were not the only
inhabitants of those houseless solitudes. Down by
the brink of the river, where the waters had widened
for a space to a smooth-flowing glossy expanse, a
curious creature was threshing its way among the
dense reeds and bushes. At the first glance one might
have mistaken it for some monstrous beast, a cousin
of the orang-utan or the gorilla; but a second
glimpse would have shown one that it belonged to a
more advanced race.

Walking with a pronounced stoop on two massive legs, it reached a height only slightly below that of a modern man. At its side was slung a rabbit-skin pouch filled with pebbles, and in its huge right hand it carried a rough-hewn club the size of a table leg; while its great barrel-like chest, its short pugilistically thick neck, and enormously developed arms gave proof of a strength that few moderns could equal. For clothes it wore only a rudely cut strip of deerskin, which hung loosely from the broad, curving shoulders not quite to the knees; and over all the exposed parts of arms, legs, and breast there spread an unbroken mat of dense black hair.

But most remarkable of all was the creature's face. In features more beastlike than human, the savagery of the jungle seemed to be warring with something that was not quite of the jungle, and in spite of the heavy jowls and apelike jaws there was just a hint of a miracle to come. The head was large and powerful, the forehead broad but low and receding, the eyebrows perched on prominent bony ridges that went far toward giving a brutish aspect. The nose was flat, and the nostrils broadly dilated, the ears round, protruding and movable, the chin weak and almost non-existent; the mouth was wide and the teeth ground down almost to the jaw, while the cheeks, like the rest of the body, were covered with a wilderness of black hair. And as for the eyes —they were small and black, and yet keen and brilliantly lighted; and they burned and sparkled with alert intelligence as their possessor pushed his way warily through the thicket.

Arriving at the edge of the dense brush, he was confronted by a wall of rock that shot precipitously upward for hundreds of feet. Even a mountain-goat might have hesitated before attempting the seemingly impossible ascent; but the hairy-limbed one did not so much as pause, though handicapped by the weight of his pouch of pebbles and of his club. With an air of absolute assurance, he turned a few paces to the left, then began to scramble up an almost imperceptible little path that twisted in and about among a jumbled pile of boulders. It was a sort of natural stairway, though frequently there was a gap of five or six feet between steps and the man had to lift himself from rock to rock with much straining and pulling of his huge arms. Sometimes he stood on ledges so narrow that one misstep would have plunged him to destruction; sometimes it was not his feet but a powerful clinging hand that preserved his balance, and one would have expected to see his fingers slip and his huge form reel and stagger into the abyss. Yet all the time he betrayed no fear, and continued on his way with the apparent carelessness of a tight-rope walker.

The last gray of twilight was merging into the blackness of night when at last the climber paused on a little shelf of rock two-thirds of the way to the top. Out of a long irregular fissure in the cliff a dim light was shining, a strange flickering light that might have brought visions of goblins or ghosts. But the climber was neither surprised nor alarmed; and after halting for a moment to give his panting heart time to subside, he uttered a loud, thick-voiced grunt. Instantly, from some unseen recess in the wall, dozens of responsive voices were raised in a hoarse, excited chorus; then, after a second or two, the fissure began to widen, and by the pale, eery illumination the watcher could distinguish three or four grinning, apelike faces, and six or eight curving hairy arms that tugged and tugged at a huge, slowly moving boulder.

Meanwhile the shouts continued, louder and louder, growing and growing in volume and excitement, until it seemed that hundreds of wildly agitated voices were clamoring all at once. At the same time, the tumult grew stranger and stranger, with hollow reverberations as of men calling from some subterranean grotto; nor did the uproar diminish before the straining arms had opened a cleft the size of a man's body. Then suddenly, with a swift contortion of his limbs, the new arrival slipped through the aperture; and once again the tugging arms were to be seen, pulling, pulling the boulder back against its fellow rocks.

Soon, on that deserted terrace of the cliff, only the weird, wavering light was visible through an opening as narrow as when the climber had arrived. But, from within, a multitude of voices could be heard, clamoring not quite so tumultuously as before, but chattering steadily and excitedly, like enthusiastic children who have no end of things to say.

And just beyond the replaced boulder, in the cavern whence the grinning faces had appeared, a

grotèsque spectacle was in progress. To the modern
eye, it would have looked more like a scene from
another planet than of this world—and more striking, perhaps, than the scene itself would have been
the stage on which it was erected. Imagine a long,
curving, irregular gallery, roofed and paved and
walled with smoke-stained rock, in places so low
that a man would have to stoop to pass beneath it,
in places arching to an ample vault from which slow
waters eternally drip and drip; imagine the dusky
walls adorned with strange-colored pictures, pictures of animals long extinct, of cave wolves and
cave bears, of mammoths and woolly rhinoceroses;
imagine curious trophies hung side by side with the
paintings, and above them, the skulls and antlers
of huge stags, the horns of aurochs, the hides of
wild boars and of mountain-sheep, the teeth of bears
and the fangs of serpents slung into great hideous
chains; while at one end a tall heap of bones,
hundreds of which have been split and splintered
for the marrow, bears evidence of many a greedy repast. And picture the whole scene illuminated from
a single source, a great blazing pile of logs near the
mouth of the cavern, so that for a few yards the
cave stands forth clearly revealed, while for its
greater length it is obscured in a vague smoky
twilight that gradually gives place to the blackness
of utter night.

Within the cave, all was tumult and confusion.
Every shadow seemed to be populated; and out of
every dark recess crawled some hairy form, with

excited voice raised to greet the new arrival. That he was one of them would have been apparent at a glance; they too were mantled in furs and skins, whether of the deer, the wild horse, or the bison; they too were stooping and brawny and covered with hair, with the same retreating forehead, the same thick neck and powerful jaws, the same bony eye-ridges and glittering black eyes.

As the newcomer entered, half a dozen long stout arms were flung about his neck and shoulders, and half a dozen sinewy hands seized him in a fierce grip of friendship. Then so closely did the swarm press about him, so furiously did they squeeze and struggle to be near, that one might have expected him to be crushed or suffocated.

"Welcome back!" they chorused, in a tongue crude as that of a mid-African savage. "Welcome back, Mumlo the Trail-Finder!"

And in the confusion of voices that ensued, one might have distinguished little more than a series of guttural clucks and grunts—"Gru ghra, gru ghra, gru ghra!"—like the murmurings of a bewildered mob.

Yet that throaty tumult was in reality a pandemonium of joy. "Welcome! Welcome! Welcome!" rang out the voices—which is as near as the primitive words can be given a modern equivalent. And mingled with the greetings, there came a storm of questions: "Where have you been so long? What have you done? What have you seen? Why are you alone? Where is Grop the Tree-Climber? and Wamwa the Snake-Eyed?"

So insistent were these inquiries, and so determined was each questioner to be answered, that
the newcomer could only turn in bewilderment from
one to another, mumbling a monosyllable here and
a monosyllable there, but apparently saying nothing
to satisfy anyone, since for some time the confused
jabbering continued unabated.

Then with lightning suddenness the tumult ceased.
One of the mob uttered a single frightened monosyllable—and all tongues stopped short in mid-
sentence. A look half of awe, half of actual fear,
came across the grimacing faces; the sharp glittering
eyes were all fastened upon the farther recesses of
the cave, from whose midnight fastnesses a huge
shambling form was emerging into the nearer twilight.

"Grumgra the Growling Wolf!" muttered one
or two under their breath; and all drew back as if
by instinct as the newcomer sullenly approached.

His great form, in the wavering shadows, seemed
truly monstrous and redoubtable, perhaps more
monstrous than the clear radiance of day would
have shown it to be. As compared with his fellows,
he was of enormous build—not less than six feet in
height, with gorilla-like chest, thick-set sinewy limbs,
and the solid stocky aspect of one whose excess
weight runs to muscles. His head was large, even
in proportion to his immense frame, and his broad
forehead was not quite so low as those of his kinsmen, although the glowering, ferocious aspect of his
long hairy face, with the exceptionally prominent
jaws and high, tapering cheek-bones, made him even

more savage-looking than the majority. Armed with an oaken club almost as tall as himself, clad in the hide of a black wolf and adorned with a crown of wolf's teeth, he was truly a figure to strike terror to the hearts of the timid.

Majestically he stalked toward the firelight, while at his coming his tribesmen retreated as far as the walls would permit. Within a dozen paces of the flames, he paused; then, lifting his club ceremoniously above his head, he uttered a single deep-voiced sound, more like the bellowing of a bull than the speech of a man. And, at this command, the cowering mob began hesitatingly to approach him, though all were careful to keep beyond range of the club. But one of their number—he who had that evening scaled the cliff and been received so tumultuously—made bold to step almost within arm's length of the scowling one, and, without waiting to be bidden, launched into speech.

"O Grumgra, O great chief," he said, "I have done as you have ordered. I have been many days' travel toward the land of the noonday sun, and have seen wonderful things and met with queer adventures. And I have entered a strange bright country, fairer than this country, a strange and glorious place for our tribe to live. But evil spirits dwell there and have done wicked things to my companions, for Wamwa the Snake-Eyed was caught by the deep waters, and Grop the Tree-Climber was caught by a wild beast—and none of us shall ever see them again!"

At these words a low moan issued from a far corner of the cavern. But, disregarding the interruption, Grumgra burst out sonorously, in tones more thundrous than those of his fellows: "Let us thank the gods of the wood that brought Mumlo back, although he bears us sad news. But what does the fate of a few men matter? Mumlo has saved us from the bad spirits that try to destroy us. For a longer time than any man can remember, our fathers have lived in this cave; but now, my people, the day comes when we must leave. You know how the winters have been growing longer and colder; how the sharp winds blow, and the snow piles thick for many moons, while the great sheets of ice, in the direction of the storm-wind, creep nearer and nearer every year. And our game gets scarcer and scarcer, for the mammoth is huge and terrible and hard to hunt, and the reindeer is wary and fleet, and the woolly rhinoceros and the wolves and bears are ferocious and kill many of our people. Yet there are stories in our tribe of a time when great warmth-loving beasts bathed in our rivers, and when mammoths without hair roamed in the woods. If we are wise, we may follow these creatures to warmer lands. And that, as you know, is why we have sent Mumlo the Trail-Finder to learn what sort of country lies under the noonday sun."

"Let Mumlo tell us what he has seen!" came the voice of one of the men. "Let Mumlo tell us—"

But instantly the rash one regretted his words. An angry flash came into the black eyes of the chieftain; with a resounding thud, his great club smashed against a projecting spur of the cavern wall.

And while the splinters flew in a hundred directions, Grumgra bellowed, "Mumlo will speak only when I bid him to!" And perversely he added, "I do not bid him to speak now!"

For a second he paused, as if uncertain of his own intention; then followed with the growling admonition: "Let him now be fed and given sleep and rest after his long journey! And let none question him more! Tomorrow, when the sun is awake again, we shall all gather here and listen to his story—and then I shall tell you whether we shall leave the cave or stay!"

And, having issued his ultimatum, he made a sedate about-face; and, swinging his club commandingly, slouched away into the shadows.

CHAPTER II

Ru the Sparrow-Hearted

THE first gray of dawn had barely begun to widen above the eastern ridges when the people of Umbaddu were once more astir. Great brawny hands applied themselves again to the boulder at the cavern entrance; and, through an aperture barely large enough to admit a man, the inhabitants emerged one by one, each armed with a club, yet each making his way with apparent ease down the perilous slopes to the river. Reaching the bank, they flung themselves down at full length and sucked in long draughts after the manner of thirsting beasts; following this they fumbled about among the brush for roots and berries, and at length, having satisfied their appetites, pulled themselves once more up the precipitous stairway of the cliff.

Meanwhile, within the cavern, all was activity and life. Several of the younger men were strenuously hauling in great dead logs through a rear entrance, which gave directly upon the forest; several half-grown lads were disposing of the refuse of yesterday's meals by the simple process of casting it outside the cave door; and scores of the women—who were clad precisely like the men, and were most easily distinguishable by their smaller stature and relatively hairless faces—were absorbed in what might be termed the household pursuits of the time. A few sat sprawled about nursing hairy infants in full view of all the tribe; a few were undertaking the vigorous chastisement of unclad urchins of five or six, who seemed too energetic in flinging flint chips about the cavern; one or two were casting fagots upon the great roaring fire, which had to be kept alive both night and day; while a majority were engaged in culinary duties. One, holding the flayed body of a rabbit above the flames on a long sharpened stick, was cooking according to the conventional method; another, busily grinding up nuts between two flat unpolished pieces of stone, was preparing a sort of gruel which, when seasoned with crushed grasshoppers and grubs, was regarded as delicious; still others, equipped with rude mallets, cleavers, scrapers, and knives of flint, were ripping off the skins of slaughtered deer, or pounding various edible herbs into a pulp, or smashing and softening a certain small beanlike seed until it came within the range of a hardy digestion.

For more than an hour these activities continued without interruption save for the snorts and snarls which marked the not infrequent disagreements between tribesmen. Then suddenly, as on the preceding evening, a portentous hush, almost a paralysis, came over the people; and out of some hidden recess stalked the great glowering figure of Grumgra, his club swinging menacingly, his shrewd little eyes glittering and sparkling like an evil threat.

"Let all our people come here!" he roared, in tones that rang and echoed angrily in those narrow corridors. "Let them stop whatever they are doing, and come! Go, call those that are outside! And if anyone wants to stay away, let him do so—if he dares!"

Here Grumgra twirled the club above his head as if to acquire practice in swinging it; and his people, needing no second warning, hastily abandoned their various tasks, and scurried in all directions in loud-voiced haste. It was not fifteen minutes before the stragglers had all been called back from the river bank and the entire tribe had gathered in a semi-circle about the fire.

A weird assemblage they made, those two hundred men, women, and children, with their heavy-featured, bestial faces, their sinewy, hide-mantled bodies, and alert, staring black eyes; while the fire-light cast fantastic wavering shadows about them, and in their midst, dominating them as a cock dominates a flock of hens, a great apelike figure stood with battered club uplifted in command.

With the abruptness of a thunderclap, the deep bellowing voice burst forth: "Listen with careful ears to what I say, my people! Many days ago—more days than the fingers on the hands of three men—I sent Mumlo the Trail-Finder to the country of the noonday sun. I told him, and also Grop the Tree-Climber and Wamwa the Snake-Eyed, to look for a better cave for our tribe. Now he has come back, and we will hear what he has to tell us."

While the voice of the chieftain still roared and

echoed through the cave, several stout hands seized the unwilling Mumlo and thrust him toward the firelight.

Standing in front of all his tribesmen, his face illuminated fitfully by the flames, while two hundred pairs of eyes regarded him solemnly, he had no choice but to obey Grumgra's command, "Speak, Mumlo! Speak!"

"What would you have me speak of?" he pleaded, gazing with fascinated interest at the chieftain's club. "There is too much to tell! Wamwa and Grop and I traveled for days and days through dark forest, and along green river cañons and over rocky hills. Sometimes we came out upon wide meadows, and sometimes the land was covered with brush and stones and was very hard to pass. But we kept on and on, and lived mostly on roots and berries and the bark of trees, though now and then we feasted on some small creature we slew with stones or clubs. At night we lit a fire with our flints to keep the wolves away, and in the day we watched and watched for wild things, since great and terrible animals filled the forest, and often we had to climb the trees in a great hurry. And it was a huge animal that took Grop away from us, for once we came upon a herd of buffaloes in an open field, and before we could get back to the woods a mad bull had rushed upon him, and—"

Horrified exclamations interrupted the speaker; but Grumgra, apparently unaffected, brought his club down warningly upon the floor.

"We are not here to learn what happened to Grop!" he grumbled, with a foreboding scowl. "We are here to learn about the country you found. Tell us that, and nothing more!"

"The country that we found," resumed the Trail-Finder, taking care to put a few additional inches between himself and Grumgra's club, "was all overgrown with grass and deep forests. It was much warmer than our own land, and even on the tops of the mountains there was no snow. But deer and bison and wild boars and horses and cattle browsed there in large herds; and there were many berries and fruits and nut-bearing trees. And up among the cliffs above a great river I thought I saw the entrance to a cave like ours. In crossing this river, Wamwa slipped and was taken by the bad spirits—"

Again the great club was lifted in a silent threat; and the angry eyes of Grumgra warned the speaker to keep to his story.

"It would be a very good land for us to live in, O great chief," Mumlo hastened to add. "When the cold days came, we would not find it so hard to kill game enough to keep us strong. We would not have to shiver all the long winter moons, not having fires or furs to make us warm. Our babes would not die, and our women would not moan and cry for meat we could not give them; but it would be summer always, and there would always be warmth and plenty for us all."

And into the eyes of Mumlo for an instant came a contemplative glow, a half-dreamy light that seemed to belie the heavy jowls and brutish features, and to foretell the visionary who—a hundred thousand years later—would still be conjuring up Utopia.

But almost instantly that light died out; the thick lips were curled into a snarl, and a hoarse growl rumbled from the speaker's throat. Across from him, in the further rim of the firelight, a bull-like shaggy form had sprung up with menacing fists upraised, and there came the muttered challenge: "You lie! You lie! There can be no such land!"

"Quiet, Woonoo!" yelled the chieftain, with an oath. And the club swung in such deadly earnest that only the extreme agility of Woonoo saved him from being mangled. As it was, the crash with which the club struck the cavern floor served as a warning to the overdaring; and the attempted chastisement was followed by an appalled silence, broken only by the murmurs of the more audacious: "Just what Woonoo deserved! Woonoo the Hot-Blooded always is getting into trouble!"

Meanwhile the offender had slunk away into the shadows to the rear, and, having once tempted destiny, was apparently resolved to take no further chance.

"Tell us more, Mumlo," encouraged Grumgra, in milder tones than before. "Tell us more. You think—you think we should all go to the land of the noonday sun?"

"O great chief, I think we should all go," pleaded the Trail-Finder. "We hear nothing now but the cries of the hungry, and the groans of those whom the demons of sickness have taken. You know how our people are growing fewer and fewer each year. Our old men can tell of a time when we were many as the days from one spring season till the next; but for every two that walked in our cave then, there is only one that walks in it now. And you know, O chief, where the rest are—how many are sleeping with their women and babes in the burial grotto at the cavern's end—and how many have left their bones to the cave bear and the hyena. You know, O chief, so why should I try to tell you? A few more ice-cold winters, and the wolves will be crunching the ribs of the last of our tribe!"

The speaker stopped short, and a horrified silence—broken only by the crackling logs in the great fire—settled over the entire assemblage.

It was Grumgra's voice that next made itself heard. "Mumlo speaks well," the leader acknowledged, leaning meditatively upon his club, as though he had forgotten its aggressive purposes. "Mumlo speaks well—it is true that we are getting fewer and fewer, for the great frosts are more than our people can stand, and when the winter comes the wild beasts seize us, or else some evil spirit creeps near, and we sicken and die. We do not wish to leave this cave, where our fathers and their fathers and their fathers before them have lived—but is it not better to go from our home than to perish?"

Having reached a bellowing climax, Grumgra paused as if to allow his words time to penetrate.

There followed a frightened silence, broken now by a whispered exclamation of dread, now by a muttered oath of horror; and this awed speechlessness continued even after Grumgra had shouted his last words, "What do you say, my people? Tell me, what do you say?"

For a moment no one said anything at all. And, after a few seconds' silence, Grumgra lifted his club in a fresh gesture of command.

But at this point, interruption came from an unexpected quarter. Out of the shadows to the rear a slender form drew forward; and one of the younger tribesmen—scarcely more than a boy, he seemed—raised his voice in a manner that compelled attention.

"Let me speak, O chief," he cried, in deep tones almost musical beside those of his fellows. "Let me speak a very little!"

A scowl came over the dark face of the leader. His right arm drew back as if to wield the club and crush the intruder.

"What? You speak, Ru?" he roared, derisively. "You, Ru the Sparrow-Hearted?" And into the jet-like eyes came a hard light as of disdain tinged with anger and hatred.

"Yes, O chief, I ask to speak," affirmed Ru, coming forward with a boldness that seemed to belie his name. And placing himself directly before the chieftain, well within range of the club, he stood like a deliberate challenge between Grumgra and the people.

A greater contrast than the two men presented could hardly have been imagined—at least, not in those primeval days. Physically Ru was slight as his opponent was gigantic; he stood scarcely over five feet in height; and his frame, while well knit and evidently equipped with strong and flexible muscles, had none of Grumgra's gorilla-like amplitude, but was slender as a sapling and had apparently been designed for grace rather than for power. At a single stroke, Grumgra might have crushed and mangled him like a fly—yet the difference between the two men was not wholly physical. For there was something about Ru's face which seemed to atone for that which his body lacked. Like Grumgra, he had the characteristic hairy features, the characteristic eyebrow ridge, tapering cheek-bones and massive jaws of his tribe; but, unlike Grumgra, he seemed to possess some indefinable quality that tempered his inherent brutishness. His forehead did not recede like those of his tribesmen, but was straight and high as that of a modern; his face was long and sagacious-looking, and his head unusually capacious; while his eyes—queer anomaly among that dark-pigmented race!—were not black like those of all the other Umbaddu, but gleamed shrewdly with a steel-gray glint!

And with a courage unique among the Umbaddu, those gray eyes firmly met the black ones of the chieftain. Perhaps it was the very audaciousness of their gaze that restrained Grumgra, for his club, though half uplifted, did not descend upon the dar-

ing one; but in tones of irritation and contempt he
muttered: "Then tell us, Ru! Tell us what you have
to say! But tell us very quickly!"

And while Ru turned to address the multitude,
derisive hisses sounded from dozens of voices; and
in tones half of laughter, half of mockery, some
of the more garrulous murmured: "Ru is going to
speak! The Sparrow-Hearted is going to speak!
Listen to the Sparrow-Hearted give advice!"

But above the cackling of the audience rose the
clear voice of Ru:

"It is true, my people, that we must leave this
cave, where our tribe has lived since the beginning
of things. But it is not true that we must leave
without knowing where we are going. Mumlo the
Trail-Finder has been to a land which he says is
fairer than this—but that does not show us that our
whole tribe can follow. Two of our companions
have already been lost, and many more may go the
same way unless we are careful. For we are not very
strong after all, my people. Remember the huge
mammoths and the bears that roam the land; the
storms that beat about us with cruel clubs; the torrents that race down upon us and bear us away; the
great cold of winter, and the famine that is worse
than the cold. If we are to live at all, we must be
wiser than our foes. We must—"

At this point a low undercurrent of hissing, gradually becoming louder, compelled the speaker to
pause. And a score of hostile, curling lips snarled
the question: "What are we to do? Tell us, Ru,

what are we to do? Shall we stay here and starve?"

Simultaneously, a half-suppressed, contemptuous laughter broke from some unseen spectator. And it was with difficulty that Ru could lift his voice above that of the gibbering, chuckling mob, and continue:

"It may be that Mumlo has not seen all the land he has visited, or that he would not know how to find his way back there again. Or it may be that there is some other land much fairer—some land where we could all grow strong and happy. And why should we not do everything we can to find out?"

Then, turning to Grumgra, who loomed before him with a hostile frown, Ru pleaded: "Let us not act like foolish children, O chief. Send out some other men—as many as the fingers of one of my hands. Let them look at the country Mumlo saw, or try to find some better place. I myself will go gladly, if only you will say yes."

"No!" thundered the chieftain. "I say no!" And the great club came down with an echoing thud, and sent the dust of the cave floor flying.

Hastily Ru withdrew, lest a second blow wreak greater havoc. And as he pressed back into the shadows, derisive murmurs filled the air; and many a pair of black eyes, glistening in malice and scorn, followed him with proud, superior gaze.

"The Sparrow-Hearted has had his say!" came the amused roar of Grumgra. "Now let me have my say. We will not let the bad spirits take any more lives on foolish journeys. And we will not waste any more time—the gods of the spring season have been here a whole moon already. After the sun has come up and gone down and then come up once more, we will all set forth into the land of the noonday sun. What do you say, my people?"

Since there was none that dared to say a word, but all merely gaped and gaped in stupid bewilderment, the most momentous question in the history of the Umbaddu had apparently been decided.

CHAPTER III

A Daughter of the Cave

RU THE SPARROW-HEARTED did not remain to hear Grumgra's final words. Hurt in a manner that he himself could hardly understand, he shambled away into the farther darkness, picking his course along winding, coal-black passages with a certainty that only perfect familiarity could have made possible.

At length, out of the dusky distance, there shone a feeble light, flickering uncannily as a phantom. Gradually it brightened, until by the dim radiance Ru could distinguish the curving low-roofed outlines of the cavern, whose walls were irregular and misshapen as though carved by some egregious blunder of nature. But he kept on without paying any heed to those well-known formations; and finally, after rounding a sudden turn, he found himself face to face with a log fire—a much smaller fire than that at the farther end of the cavern, and yet large enough to shed a comfortable light and warmth.

With a thankful sigh, Ru flung himself down into a little hollow in the rock across from the fire. And there, curled up like a cat basking in the sun-

.light, he lay motionless for many minutes, staring with wide, contemplative eyes into the writhing flames.

Strange thoughts kept trailing through his mind —thoughts that stung and tortured and would leave him no peace. Why must he always call forth his people's raillery and jests? Was it only because his limbs were small and his eyes were gray? Had he not done that which none of them could do? Had he not, as the reward of many days of labor, hewed out this hollow in the cavern wall, where he might lie in comfort while his tribesmen lay on the rocky floor? And had he not built his own fire, and even made a chimney in the rock above, that he might have warmth and light while his fellows had only the dark and cold? And had he not made a club more powerful than any other of its size, by tipping it with flint while they used only wood? And had he not shaped and sharpened his flint knives and cleavers till they worked twice as easily as those his tribesmen used? And was he not even now planning that which no man had planned before— a weapon that would strike like lightning, and slay at a great distance?

As the thought of the new weapon came into his mind, Ru reached meditatively for a long, slender shaft of wood that lay concealed in a crevice between two rocks. It was little more than the thin, wiry trunk of a young tree, denuded of branches and leaves; but a crude perforation at each extremity showed the clear mark of human workmanship; and the dried tendrils of a fibrous plant, stretched loosely between the two ends of the shaft, gave evidence of what the young artizan was attempting.

Forgetting his resentment at the injustice of his tribe, Ru began to apply himself to his invention. First he stood with one end of the shaft pressed against the cavern floor, and strained and pushed with his right hand until the wood was bent outward in a wide curve; then he strained and pulled with his left to draw the tendril of the plant tightly from end to end of the shaft.

He had almost succeeded, when the tendril snapped and the wood shot out and straightened with a force that sent him reeling against the cavern wall.

Less bruised than angered, he was picking himself up, when a low merry giggling rang out of the darkness behind him. And even without turning he recognized the voice of Yonyo the Smiling-Eyed.

"So the Sparrow-Hearted is still playing his pranks?" laughed the newcomer, in tones that betrayed as much of malice as of good-natured gaiety.

And there stood before him, in the smoky firelight, she who of all women in the world was for him the most beautiful, the most tantalizing, and the most wrath-provoking. To the eye of a later age, she might not have proved seductive—but to the untrained eye of Ru she represented the acme of all things desirable and unattainable. Clad in a glossy robe of horsehide, with her full, well-rounded breasts and her muscular legs exposed, she bore on every feature the impress of her tribe—the massive head, the low, wide forehead and bony eyebrow ridges, the large, flexible ears, the powerful jaws and huge flat nose. But in her wily black eyes— somewhat larger than those of her kinsmen—there gleamed and glittered a strange, alluring light that set her off from all the other women of the tribe. When she smiled, Ru felt that a wonderful fire shone over her whole face, so that he would forget that she was a mere human like himself, but would think of wild flowers unfolding in the spring fields, and blue lakes twinkling beneath blue skies, and rainbows and stars and the song of birds.

Ru did not know why he had such thoughts on seeing Yonyo, for he had never heard any of his brothers speak of like feelings. Nor did he know why the very sight of Yonyo made him tremble as the sight of no other woman could do, so that he was often sad when she was away, and was filled with strange, disturbing longings when she was near. All this Ru did not understand, but he did understand very well that Yonyo would never be his woman— for did she ever seem glad when he spoke gentle words to her? and did she ever smile upon him except to mock? Besides, was she not coveted by Woonoo the Hot-Blooded and Kuff the Bear-Hunter?—and could he swing a club so well as these great rivals of his, and win his bride in an open fight?

With the anger of the baffled, he turned upon

Yonyo; and there was no gentleness in his voice
as he met her taunting question: "Yes, Yonyo, I
am still playing my pranks. And there will come a
day when the tribe will beg to play them with me!
You, too!—even you, the tormenting and the Smiling-Eyed!"

A low burst of scornful laughter came as her
reply. And pointing toward the shaft of wood, which
he still held in his hand, she demanded contemptuously: "Is it with that stick that you will make us
play your pranks? Tell me, Ru, is it a wonder
stick?"

"Yes, it is a wonder stick!" flung back Ru, choking down an impulse to seize his bright-eyed tan-
talizer and force her to her knees before him, until
she cried for mercy and the tears came.

For a moment he stood confronting her in a
glaring silence, while the sparks danced about her
and the flames fitfully illuminated her tanned hairless face.

And then, seized with a longing to make her
understand, to make her share his own enthusiasm,
Ru reiterated: "It is a wonder stick, Yonyo! Listen,
and I will tell you about it!"

"Yes, tell me," she murmured, somewhat subdued by his earnestness, although ridicule still shone
in her eyes.

"Have you never gone roaming among the bushes
and shrubs, Yonyo?" he demanded, speaking with
a fury born partly of the bright appeal in her face,
and partly of the breathless interest of a great dis-

covery. "Have you never noticed how one may twist
and bend the small shoots, so that they will swish
back with terrible force? I was wondering, Smiling-
Eyed, if I could stretch a stout fiber between the
ends of one of those shoots. Then I could bend and
hold it so that it would swish back whenever I
wanted. And it might throw a sharp stick through
the air like a rock, and make a weapon that would
strike from far away—"

"And strike those foolish thoughts from your
head!" derided Yonyo, bursting again into laughter.

Ru, cut short at the climax of his discourse, felt
a renewed impulse to seize and throttle her.

But perhaps she divined his intention, for with a
scornful, "The Sparrow-Hearted has need of new
weapons!" she went darting down the shadowy passageway, and in a moment had disappeared around
a bend, her mocking laughter ringing merrily behind her.

Within Ru's breast a choking anger arose; and
her flight was like a challenge to follow. With
furious eyes and fast-heaving heart he set off in
pursuit, filled by a blind desire to seize the elusive
one and crush her madly to him.

But she was swift of foot, and in those dark corridors he could not even see her flying form. Only
her laughter, echoing merrily through the gloom,
told him that she was not far beyond; and such
was his frenzy that he had little thought of possible
danger, but dashed ahead despite the risk of stum-

bling over some unseen rock or depression in the cavern floor.

Yet not until he had approached the great fire at the cave entrance did he see her again. Then, still with a smile upon her taunting face, she stood gleefully awaiting his arrival. But she was not alone—just ahead of her, overshadowing her like a protective tower, stood Woonoo the Hot-Blooded!

And from the ugly thick lips of the giant there issued a menacing snarl; and the bull-like form advanced with powerful arms outspread to seize and strangle his adversary.

Knowing better than to risk a conflict, Ru merely answered his opponent's challenge growl for growl, while backing away at no inconsiderable speed. Then, when suddenly the Hot-Blooded tired of delay and started toward him with a swift ferocious lunge, Ru turned and raced furiously back into the shadows.

And merry was the tittering of Yonyo, as she witnessed the rout of the weakling. And merry was the laughter of the tribespeople as they watched Ru's hasty retreat, and murmured: "See the Sparrow-Hearted run! How well the Sparrow-Hearted runs!" But dark indeed was the gloom within the heart of Ru when at length he had outdistanced his rival and slouched sulkily back to his lonely fire in the loneliest, farthest corner of the cave.

CHAPTER IV

The Hunt and the Fire

ON the day preceding the tribe's departure for the land of the noonday sun, two important preparations were made.

First of all, a mighty hunt was arranged. All the able-bodied men—and they numbered nearly a hundred—set out together for their favorite hunting-ground, where they stationed themselves at intervals in a rude circle about a strip of field and forest two or three square miles in extent. Then, at the signal of the chieftain's shout relayed from man to man, the hunters started at a trot toward the center of the circle, meanwhile yelling and clamoring at the top of their lusty voices and raising a hullabaloo that might have awakened the dead.

Needless to say, any animals roaming within the chosen area would take alarm. Some, wild with fear, would endeavor to dash past the huntsmen, and not a few of these would offer a target for clubs and stones; a majority, driven toward the center of the enclosure, would find themselves hemmed in by an ever-tightening ring of their foes. If they could not save themselves by a desperate flight through the encompassing lines—as many did, in fact, save themselves—they would be forced irresistibly toward the four or five pits in the center of the closing circle. And since these had been dug with careful forethought and shrewdly covered with concealing branches and grass, the victims would topple headlong into the ten-foot depths; and there, bellowing with fear or howling with pain, a mass of convulsive, twisting forms and broken limbs, they would present an easy mark for the clubs of their persecutors.

On this particular day, the Umbaddu hunters were unusually successful. Two wild boars, a wild horse, four wild cattle, half a dozen rabbits, a score of squirrels, a doe and a fawn of the giant deer, a half-grown moose and a young rhinoceros—these constituted their trophies of the chase. Now they would have meat in plenty for days and days to come! And the penalty for this gigantic haul had been exceptionally small—not a man had been killed, though the shoulder of Kuff the Bear-Hunter had been ripped open by an infuriated wildcat, and Ru had earned the mirth of his fellows by taking to the trees and saving himself by the bare fraction of an inch before the charge of a maddened aurochs.

The victims, once dispatched, were skinned and cut up on the spot; and this was a long and laborious process, for the flint knives and scrapers worked slowly and clumsily and with a vast amount of wasted effort. Much of the booty, indeed, had to be left where it lay as an offering to the wolves and vultures; yet when the hunters at last set off homeward, each was weighed down to capacity with the flesh, hides, and marrowbones of the slaughtered.

And with what a tumult they were received when, having scaled the cliff walls, they stood once more at the cave entrance! One would have thought they were warriors returning from the conquest—the women greeted them with screams of delight; they shouted with childish glee at sight of the fresh stores of food; their great broad faces grinned with ape-like grimaces, and their heavy lips smacked with anticipatory joy. And every returning huntsman was welcomed by some particular woman, who smiled admiration at him from her beady black eyes— every huntsman, that is, with two exceptions.

The first exception was Grumgra, who was greeted by a circle of three or four congratulatory females. And the second was Ru, whose return seemed not to be noticed at all, but who stood by sullenly and alone, while his boisterous fellows shouted loud stories of their exploits, and the Smiling-Eyed pressed healing herbs to the wounded shoulder of Kuff the Bear-Hunter.

After the tumult had begun to die away, the women busied themselves in holding great sizzling joints above the fire and in laying out smaller joints to smoke. And now the tribe began its second preparation for the departure.

This event was signalized by the arrival of Zunzun the Marvel-Worker. While the returned hunts-

men sprawled in ungainly attitudes about the fire
or crouched upon their haunches with heads bent
motionless above their knees, a flutter of excitement
stirred the farther recesses of the cavern, and a
squat, sinewy form slowly emerged. At first sight
there was nothing to distinguish the newcomer
from his kinsmen, except that his stoop was extreme
even among this race of stooping men—he bent
forward like an anthropoid ape, with long arms
dangling before him from sloping shoulders. But
as he shambled into the firelight, one might have
observed another point of distinction; for while his
massive face and gorilla-like features were not less
bestial than those of his fellows, his black shaggy
mane was interspersed and mellowed by hairs of
gray. For Zunzun was quite old—he had more
years, some said, than the month had days—and it
was rumored that his memory reached back to the
time when the eldest among his living tribesmen
was a babe suckling its mother's breast.

As he approached, the onlookers automatically
ceased their chattering; and in unconscious unison
they all sat up, with eyes fastened upon him.

When within a few paces of the fire, Zunzun
paused, flung his hands upward, and launched forth
upon a prayer to the fire-god. In deep, bellowing
tones, which resounded uncannily through those dim
rocky corridors, he begged the spirit of the flames
to take care of his people and protect them from
wild beasts and the storm-wind. And the blazes,
which flashed and crackled gustily, seemed to be

signaling an encouraging reply; the flickering sparks
gaily spoke a bright message; and the glowing faces
of the people, obscurely seen in that smoky gloom,
were overspread with a light and a fervor like that
of worshipers in a temple.

On and on Zunzun rambled, on and on in tones
constantly more charged with emotion; and he told
the fire-god of all that his people had suffered, and
how they languished and grew thin in the long
months of winter, and how they craved a warmth
and plenty they had never found, and how they always begged the god of the sunshine to beam upon
them with more light and heat—but how the god of
the sunshine had never heard.

Before Zunzun had finished, his gleaming black
eyes had grown soft and moist, and his plea was
no longer a solitary one, but rather was spoken in
chorus. At first singly, and then in groups, his hearers joined him, all shouting their appeal to the
fire-god, and all taking care to shout their loudest,
so that the god must pause and listen. For a while—
so intense was the fervor of the people—one could
have heard nothing but a din of discordant screams
and yells, in which no single word was distinguishable. But after a time, sobered by something
domineering in the tones of Zunzun, the straining
voices were modulated and blended together, so
that they clamored in a sort of rude rhythm, almost
a chant of entreaty; and, following the lead of the
Marvel-Worker, they chorused: "Hear us, O fire-
god, hear us! Light us the way to warmer lands!

Fill our days with feasts and make them comfortable! Let your great heat singe and kill our foes, the wolf, the bear, and the wind from the snow-land! Help us, O fire-god, for we are in need of you!"

And after the voices had stormed and pleaded for many minutes, at times wailing in anguish and at times rising to a sobbing crescendo, Zunzun finally snapped into silence—and the tumultuous mob followed his lead, though now many eyes were tear-stained, and many eyes shone with an unwonted brightness.

But grave were the tones of Zunzun as he eloquently beckoned toward the flames, and murmured: "Now surely, my people, the fire-god has heard us. So let us ask him if he is of a mind to do as we wish."

In contrast to the pandemonium of a moment before, an absolute stillness had come over the assemblage. A hundred pairs of black eyes were staring questioningly at Zunzun; a hundred mouths were agape with wonder, but uttered no word. Even Grumgra the Growling Wolf stood as if transfixed, and had nothing to say; even Woonoo the Hot-Blooded and Bru the Scowling-Faced watched meekly as babes and ventured not a grunt, while the awe in their gaze was equal to that in the gaze of a child.

Meanwhile the Marvel-Worker was performing a curious ceremony. Bending down to the ground, he scooped a half-burnt oaken limb out of the flames; then, having beaten out the last trace of fire, he began to examine it with slow and painstaking scrutiny. Just what there was to observe was more than any onlooker could have said, but Zunzun apparently saw plenty to inspect, for he regarded that charred bit of wood with the furrowed brow and intent expression of one who reads some puzzling but important document. And at length—while his fellows still stood gazing at him in silence— he nodded his head as if satisfied, rose slowly to a stooping position, and opened his mouth to speak.

"The fire-god says he is here with us," he declared, reassuringly. "He has heard our plea, and will go with us to help us on our long journey."

At this a thankful tumult burst forth; and many were the murmurs of gratitude and relief. Some of the hearers, in their joy, threw congratulatory arms about their neighbors' necks; others literally howled with delight; one or two attempted a sort of rude, sidling dance; and more than one voice was uplifted to praise the name of Zunzun the Marvel-Worker.

But amid that happy demonstration, there came a single dissenting note. "How do you know? How do you know, Zunzun?" rang forth a clear voice— the voice of Ru. "Just what did the fire-god say? And how did you find out?"

But his words were drowned amid a chorus of hisses and jeers; and the Marvel-Worker, casting a disdainful glance in the direction of his challenger, did not deem it necessary to reply.

Instead, turning to address the people, he directed: "Let us show our thanks to the fire-god. Let us all make him an offering."

And every man, woman and child snatched up dried fagots and twigs and flung them into the flames, with fervid cries of "Thank you, fire-god! May the fire-god burn forever!"

And the fire, as if in gratitude, flared and crackled more vigorously than ever; and all the assembled people joined hands in a mighty circle about the flames, and began to swing back and forth, back and forth, and leap and caper like children, while shouting with religious zeal, "Thank you, fire-god! We will always serve you and bear you offerings! May the fire-god burn forever!"

CHAPTER V

The Migration Begins

THE day of the migration had dawned. The last rites had been performed; the Umbaddu people were leaving their ancestral dwelling-place. Some among the tribesmen had paused to look with sadness at those dark and picture-littered walls that they should never see again; some had gone to place flint weapons and chunks of meat in the burial grotto at the cavern's end, where lay the bones of loved ones; some had cast the horns of bison, the teeth of bears and patches of bearskin about the cavern floor, as an offering to the cave-gods whom they were deserting; some—and these were all members of the milder sex—had made themselves objects of ridicule by indulging in orgies of tears; while a majority—particularly of the younger tribesmen—shouted in sheer exultation, since before them lay the open world, the unknown, and adventure.

It was a curious procession that made its way down from the cliff-dwelling and out along the wilderness trail. Women with babes in arms and tenacious two-year-olds clinging to their shoulders; men laden with trailing limbs of deer and cattle, and with pouches bulging with roots, herbs, and berries; scrawny children that released themselves like acrobats from rock to rock, and from time to time screamed and howled as they slipped upon the boulders—such were the leading members of that little army of migrants. Owing to the mass of provisions, of weapons and flint implements that had to be transported, many of the men and women had to ascend and descend the cliff three or four times; and so many were the delays, the minor mishaps and altercations, that the morning was half done before the tribe was actually on its way.

Led by Grumgra, who wielded his club imperiously, the people straggled in single file on a little trail made long before by huntsmen along the cañon of the Harr-Sizz River. Like their leader, all the men carried clubs, though Grumgra's was by far the largest; and not a few of the women likewise bore clubs, and moreover swung them in a manner that indicated some proficiency in the art of self-defense. But the women, for the most part, were impeded by the weight of the heavy tools and provisions, which the men had thrust upon them following the descent of the precipice; and these were slung in great masses about their shoulders, exaggerating their natural stoop and making their gait slow and laborious. Only a few of the younger women—such as Yonyo the Smiling-Eyed and Lum the Twittering Bird—were exempted from such duties; and this was because, not being subject as yet to any man, they were not compelled to share any man's exertions.

But in spite of the burdens that weighed them down, most of the people were in a merry mood. Some, in voices deep-toned and rude and yet with the trace of a pleasing rhythm, improvised snatches of song, which their comrades caught up in a riotous chorus; others would go meandering carelessly away from the trail to examine any curious insect, rock, or weed; and a few of the younger tribesmen engaged in uproarious games of hide-and-seek, and even in good-natured but quite energetic scuffles and wrestling bouts.

Meanwhile several men designated by Grumgra went scouting ahead of the party, to both sides of it, and behind it, to discover if there was any sign of dangerous beasts. With a keenness of eyesight rivaled only by the savages of a later day, they would scan the river bank and the underbrush for the footprints of wolf and bear; and with a keenness of scent that their successors might have marveled at and admired, they would occasionally put their nostrils close to earth and sniff appraisingly. Only once—when the alert senses of Mumlo the Trail-Finder told of the recent passage of the woolly rhinoceros—was a word of alarm flashed to the tribe; but the beasts had evidently gone their way in peace, and before many minutes the people had entirely forgotten the danger.

Mile on mile they plodded, on and on with scarcely a stop, in and out and in and out along the bank of the deviously winding Harr-Sizz River. In places the cliffs shot perpendicularly above them to

The migration

an unscalable height; in places the hills rolled
toward them in a long graceful grade, dark-green
with an impenetrable growth of pine or spruce; in
places they lost sight of the river and the river bluffs
in forcing their way through thorny thickets of
the wild rose, or in hewing a path through an en-
veloping wilderness of creepers and vines. Now and
then, through some cleft in the hills, they would
catch glimpses of far-flung and majestic panoramas,
with chiseled snow-peaks jutting in the distance; and
once, when an entire mountain stood unbared at the
far end of a long, deep-cloven ravine, they could
see that the ranges were more than half cloaked
in glittering bands of white.

Yet such spectacles had small effect on the minds
of the migrants. All their lives they had known
these scenes—and they thought no more about them
than about the blue of the skies or the white of
foaming waters. Only one of their number—Ru the
Sparrow-Hearted—peered at those snowy summits
with contemplative eyes; and into the mind of Ru
came strange and perplexing thoughts. He wondered whether the spirits worshiped by his tribe
were big enough to rule this world of wind and
cloud and crag; somehow, in those gigantic slopes
and forest-draped solitudes, he felt vaguely the
workings of forces vaster than he, and recognized
hazily the presence of a Mystery he could never
explain, a Glory of which he was part and which
enveloped him.

For many minutes he had been walking soberly

by himself, not taking notice of his tribesmen that trailed ahead of him and behind, not taking notice even of his own club that dragged in the dust, nor of the gap in his rabbit-skin pouch, through which from time to time some implement would drop noiselessly to the soft grass and be lost. He had forgotten for the time about the migration, forgotten that he was following a perilous trail; into his mind had come faint glimmerings of enigmas that would still be vexing his kind a hundred thousand years to come. . . .

A sharp prodding in the neck aroused him abruptly to an awareness of himself. And, wheeling about in anger as fierce as it was sudden, he was confronted by the sparkling, roguish glance of Yonyo.

Then, while he stood glaring at her in speechless rage, she waved a pointed twig derisively in his face, and exclaimed: "The Sparrow-Hearted has need of something to wake him up! What was the Sparrow-Hearted dreaming about?"

For a moment he did not reply. His impulse was to strike back as one strikes back when dealt a brutal blow—to seize her in furious arms, and crush her till she begged for mercy. And no doubt it was thus that Kuff the Bear-Hunter or Woonoo the Hot-Blooded would have disposed of her; but Ru, alas! was not Kuff or Woonoo, and could do no more than glower ineffectively at her.

"What was the Sparrow-Hearted dreaming about?" she repeated, growing impatient at his silence.

"About things you could never understand!" he declared, fiercely.

"What is there I could not understand?" demanded the incredulous Yonyo. And seeing those large black eyes bent upon him half laughingly and half inquiringly, he felt his wrath slipping from him and an old strange emotion returning.

As his anger died away, it occurred to him to try to make her share that which he felt.

"Shall I tell you, Yonyo?" he asked, while side by side they began to jog along the forest path, their feet noiselessly pressing the carpet of dead leaves. "Shall I tell you?"

Receiving a mumbled affirmative in reply, he launched straightway into his explanation.

"I was wondering," he continued, slowly, while reflecting how marvelous was the light in the gaze of the Smiling-Eyed, "whether, after all, the wise men of our tribe can know all things. I was wondering whether the world was really made by the magic of a fire-god that lived in a cave as big as a whole mountain, as the old stories tell us; and whether there may not be other gods than the fire-god and the sun-god and the gods of the caves and woods and winds. Why were we born, Yonyo, and why do we live, and why—"

"And why ask foolish questions?" broke in the puzzled Yonyo. "What are you thinking about, Ru? Why worry about such things?—Let the wise men settle them for us!"

Then, seeing that Ru remained sullen and silent,

she bent down and plucked a weed from the way-side, and began to prick him prankishly upon the cheek. And when, annoyed, he tried to snatch the weed from her, she eluded his grasp and darted away with eyes that flashed a challenge to follow.

Without knowing why, except that she drew him on irresistibly, Ru let his club slip to the ground and dashed after her.

Strangely enough, she was not hard to overtake. In a very few seconds, he had come up to her, and had flung his arms about her in a crushing grip.

"Yonyo! Yonyo!" he murmured, with a bold-ness that surprised himself not less than her. "I want you! I want you! Oh, will you not be my woman, and share my fire with me, and—"

But, with the agility of a young leopard, she had struggled free of his embrace.

"I?—be your woman?" she demanded, standing proudly before him, her nostrils distended with anger. "Who are you—Ru the Sparrow-Hearted? Who are you? The man whose woman I am must be a real man! He must be a hunter of wolves!— not of earthworms! He must have slain his bears, his wild boars, his aurochs! And he must not be a dreamer of silly dreams!"

And, with a scornful laugh, Yonyo started away again.

Stung to fury, Ru raced after her once more— but he had gone scarcely ten paces when there came a warning rustling through the bushes ahead, and a massive hairy figure burst menacingly upon him.

It was Kuff the Bear-Hunter, who, even with his wounded shoulder, made a formidable antagonist. His little black eyes gleamed with evil wrath; his enormous thick lips were curled into a snarl that displayed the white glistening teeth; his great arms were outspread as if to mangle and destroy.

With a hasty glance at his onrushing foe, Ru turned and fled. And, as he scurried into the shelter of a thicket of reeds, the laughter of Yonyo was flung after him like a blow.

For the rest of that day, Ru kept to himself. He did not seek to join the chattering, frolicsome groups of young folk; he did not trudge side by side with any of his elder tribesmen in amiable fellowship; he plodded in morose silence along those gaily echoing forest lanes. Only now and then, when some small boy or girl would approach and coax him to some playful tussle, would his intense gravity relax; but it would relax only partially, and after a minute he would again succumb to gloomy reveries. Why had he been made so small of stature, so frail of limb? he asked himself over and over again, as he had asked time on time before. Why could he not stand face to face with his rivals, and fight them as any but himself would have done? Must he always be like the slinking hyena, which keeps at a distance and disdains equal combat? Must he be powerless to control even his own will? and, having decided to face his persecutors, must he find himself racing away ratlike at the first hostile scowl?

Such thoughts were still filling Ru's mind when at length the day's march ended. The sun was just beginning to dip its head beyond a dark, distant ridge of forest when Grumgra, bellowing at the top of his voice, gave the order to halt. At first he did not seem certain what camping-place to choose; and there was manifest indecision in his tiny black eyes as he scanned the broken line of woods that paralleled the stream, the green flowery meadow that stretched between the forest and the river bank, and the jutting cliffs perhaps half a mile down-stream, where forest and meadow gave place to a rocky cañon through which the waters foamed tumultuously.

Then, while scores of his kinsmen stood regarding him speechlessly but with anxious eyes, the chieftain suddenly decided: "We shall camp here in the open fields. And build a ring of fire to keep away the wild beasts."

In silence the people received this command—in silence, with only one exception. For while Woonoo and Kuff and the others heard and prepared to obey, he who was known as the Sparrow-Hearted strode forward, and in loud tones requested, "O chief, may I speak a little?"

For reply, Grumgra merely snarled. His little eyes gleamed with angry fires; he grasped his club with ominous firmness.

Although the distance between them was hazardously narrow, Ru seemed to assume that the Growling Wolf's snarl was consent. In a voice loud enough for all the tribe to hear, he demanded: "Are the fields safe, O chief? Would it not be wiser to camp under the cliffs? Then it would be easier to keep the wild beasts off—"

But he could proceed no further. Howling with rage and swinging the club as if to do instant murder, Grumgra strode toward the impudent one. And once again Ru had to save himself by means of his feet. And once again the tribe laughed loud and merrily.

Now came the most trying of all the day's exertions. While the men went off into the forest in groups of three and four to gather firewood, the women busied themselves with pieces of flint which they hammered laboriously together time after time until at last the eagerly awaited spark kindled a pile of dead leaves. Many minutes were passed in this pursuit, and twilight was settling down, before at last half a dozen fires, fed from the limbs of fallen trees, were blazing with bright and heartening gusto.

Within the line of the fires—which were arranged in a rude circle—were assembled all the men and women of the tribe, who lay sprawled on their robes of bison and deerskin, chattering contentedly and noisily consuming huge chunks of smoked venison or newly roasted morsels of boar's flesh. Now and then one would leave to go down to the river bank for a long draft of water, which he would suck in animal-like; but as the darkness deepened, such departures became less frequent, and at length ended entirely, for all knew better than to venture away from the fire into the perils of the night.

Twilight had not yet fallen when a loud sobbing, from the extreme end of the encampment, aroused the attention of the curious. One of the younger women was weeping as women in those days seldom wept, her whole frame shaking convulsively, her dark eyes a blur of tears. And to those who questioned her she could not give coherent reply. She could only blurt out disconsolately, "My Malgu! My Malgu!" and return at once to her stormy grieving.

But there was little need to explain. It was known that Malgu was her three-year-old son; and as there was no sign of him now, it was assumed that he had been lost on the way to camp. And this could mean but one thing. Considering the wolves, bears, hyenas, and other carnivores that infested the woods, there was little chance that anyone would see Malgu again.

So the people merely shrugged their shoulders, as sensible people do when told of some regrettable incident. And since there was nothing to be gained by lamentations, they turned straightway to more pressing affairs. After a few minutes, only a low, half-stifled moaning told of the bereaved mother's grief; and two hundred voices were prattling as gaily as though Malgu had never been.

As night settled down, a great weariness overcame the people. One by one they wrapped themselves in their furs and hides, placed themselves

as near as possible to the fire, curled up snail-like
so as to retain all possible warmth, and surrendered
themselves to slumber. And it was not long before
a series of hearty snores replaced the garrulous
voices of the early evening.

But there were some who were not permitted to
sleep. Six men, designated by Grumgra to keep the
fires alive and at the same time watch for prowling beasts, were to do duty until midnight, when
they would be replaced by six of their kindred.

Among the earlier group of sentinels, the first
to be named was Ru—who clearly owed his choice
to his presumption in questioning Grumgra's wisdom. There had been a howl of derision when, in
the presence of the entire tribe, the chieftain had
assigned him to the hated duty; and it was the
knowledge of his comrades' mockery and chuckling
glee, far more than regret at the loss of dearly
needed repose, that angered Ru when he took his
place beside one of the fires and prepared for the
long, lonely watch.

Certainly, his task was not an enviable one, for
he had to keep close to his own particular fire,
and there could be no communion between him
and his fellow sentinels. Through the intervening
shadows, he could hardly recognize them as human
at all; they looked like ghosts as they watched beside the uncanny yellow fires at distant ends of the
encampment; and, like ghosts, they kept elusively
away from him.

As though to make his vigil more difficult, Nature as well as man seemed to be conspiring against him. While the day had been blue and clear, the night turned out to be dark and starless; and a cold wind, which came howling out of the north, had shoved a black mantle of clouds across the sky. Not often had Ru seen so wild and bleak a night. Except for the light of the fires, which quivered and tossed and darted out lean orange lips like distracted things, there appeared to be no illumination in the world; and, except for the dark, slumbering camp and a narrow and fitfully lighted circle of the fields, he seemed to be standing in the midst of a gigantic void. Yet from that void there issued strange and disquieting sounds—not only the moaning and soughing of the gale as it plunged through the limbs of unseen trees, but the voices of night prowlers occasionally lifted in growls and grumblings and long-drawn wails that brought no consolation to the heart of Ru. Once, indeed, the void did seem to be pierced by something other than sound, for out of the distance he could distinguish two close-set phosphorescent orbs staring at him like menacing phantoms—then, in an instant, they were gone, and there was only the darkness again, and the chilly wind whirling and sobbing past.

"Evil spirits are abroad in the world!" thought Ru, as he piled fresh logs upon the fire; and he pictured the streams and the air and the clouds as alive with savage monsters and still more savage men, some of them made in the image of Grumgra, though scowling even more ferociously than he, and with clubs ten times as long; and some of them in the likeness of the wolves and hyenas that might even now be prowling within a stone's throw of the camp.

He was occupied with such gruesome thoughts, and was wondering whether the wicked spirits might not be tempted to leap in a plundering band upon his people and smite them with bearlike teeth and claws, when his attention was distracted by something moist and cool settling upon his palm. It was only a drop, but after a second it was followed by another, and then by another still—and with a sinking of the heart Ru realized that it was raining. This in itself would have been no occasion for alarm, since the people were used to getting wet, and moreover were protected by their thick, hairy manes—but as the downpour began to come faster and faster and the wind began to screech and scream like some triumphant marauder, Ru glanced with growing anxiety at the fires, and piled on the fagots with desperate speed in the hope of reviving the flagging flames.

But the wood was wet, and would burn but poorly; and the shower waxed heavier and heavier until it came down in torrents, and Ru, dripping from head to foot, could make out the lively little streams that rippled everywhere through the camping-place. Then once again he caught a glimpse of phosphorescent eyes through the howling gloom; and amid the roaring of the plunging, falling waters he could distinguish now and then another roaring that was still more sinister.

By this time all the camp was awake. Aroused

abruptly from their slumbers, men, women and children came surging in all directions like a rout of
distracted shadows; and, literally tripping and
plunging over one another in their frenzy, they
clamored and yelled as if to match the tumult of the
elements. Suddenly, amid the rushing and rioting
of that panic-stricken mob, Ru felt himself being
pounced upon, shoved aside and trampled; and as,
in confusion, he picked up his bruised body and
slipped hurriedly away, he saw that the multitude,
in its terror, was heaping log after log with insane
haste upon all six fires—with the result that all, already sputtering feebly, were stifled utterly by the
excess fuel, and after a last weak flutter or two,
gave up the struggle and delivered the camp to darkness.

It would be impossible to picture the confusion
that now reigned. Women were shrieking, babes
screaming, men pleading and praying to the fire-
god or bawling terrified, panicky orders that no one
heeded. One, in a trembling voice, would beg all
to be calm; another, in piercing, blood-curdling
tones, would call out that he saw a wolf, a bear,
a mammoth; now and then there rang forth a wail
as of the most terrible anguish; and once, after a
particularly hair-raising cry, there came the grumbling of some predatory beast, followed by a rending and a crunching of bones.

And all the while the whole world remained
black, deathly black as though there could be no
such thing as light. And all the while the rain came

down in drenching sheets, and the wind snarled and blustered, and ominous growling things were sneaking through the gloom. Every man stood with club poised, ready to strike—though who, if need be, could strike fast enough?—and thus the long weary hours of the night dragged by, until at length the rain ceased, and the wind, like a weary beast, subsided, and a faint glow came into the sky and showed the hills and woods in shadowy outline, and then at last, after agonies and agonies of waiting, a pale gray streak above the eastern bluffs gave promise of another dawn.

CHAPTER VI

The Wrath of Grumgra

IT was a doleful band of migrants that stood revealed in the first dreary light of morning. Shivering and drenched, with soggy fur-mantles and rain-soaked skins from which the slow water dripped and dripped, they looked like beasts just returned from a perilous plunge; and little trace of their usual energy was apparent as they mournfully wandered across the miry soil, or lugubriously eyed their disheveled fellows. More than one bruised arm or gashed thigh or wrenched shoulder bore witness to the panicky scuffle of the night; several of the people were nursing blackened eyes or feeling sullenly at jaws that displayed new-made gaps; while one of the most woebegone of all was he who exhibited an enormous swelling on the head—due to the terror of a kinsman who, mistaking him for a wild beast in the dark, had struck him with a club.

But these were the least of the casualties. In the soft soil at the edge of the encampment, ill-omened five-clawed footprints were to be seen; and in one or two places a new-made crimson patch caused even the most hardy to tremble. Too well the people read the dread meaning!—but at first they had no idea

54

who the victims were, nor even how many victims there had been. In loud-voiced anxiety, each man and woman began to search and cry out for those nearest to him—so that for a while the pandemonium was as great as during the storm. Half-crazed mothers raced about calling stray children; stray children screamed and bawled for missing mothers; great brawny males went searching with angry eyes for their unseen mates, and frenzied women begged for word of their absent men; friend stared into the turbulent mob for lost friend, and wild-eyed striplings for vanished maids; and now and then there would be a scream of exultation as two who had given up hope were reunited.

As time went by, most of the missing were found, for some had gone unobserved amid the blatant mob, and some had taken to the trees in their terror and one by one had returned. But after two or three hours, there were still several who remained unaccounted for; and these included two men, a woman, and three children.

Although it was not the nature of the Umbaddu to give themselves up to orgies of lamentation, still the loss of six persons—particularly when these included two able-bodied men—was recognized as a matter of importance. It was regarded, indeed, almost as a public misfortune, and, in accordance with a custom handed down from remotest times, had to be investigated before a council of the entire tribe. For it was the belief of the Umbaddu that no full-grown man ever came to his death ex-

cept through the agency of evil spirits: hence, whenever a man died unaccountably, the evil spirit had to
be discovered and his human agent appropriately
punished.

No one was surprised, therefore, when, instead
of ordering the migration continued, Grumgra began the day by giving instructions for a tribal conference. There was not so much as a thought of
protest—and when at length the excitement of the
night had died away and all hope had been surrendered for the missing ones, the survivors gathered
in a wet and bedraggled and yet eagerly chattering
group on the damp grass of the meadow.

Just a trace of apprehension, however, flitted
across the frowning faces when the stooping form
of Zunzun the Marvel-Worker was observed beside
the bearlike hulk of Grumgra. And no pleasure
lighted the scores of staring black eyes when, after
crushing some grass-stalks between his fingers and
scrutinizing them speculatively, Zunzun turned to
the chieftain and slowly announced: "O Grumgra,
I can see from the green color of the grass that
evil spirits are abroad. We must find out who it was
that caused the rain to fall, and who it was that
put the blood-fury into the claws of the wild beasts
—and him we must punish!"

"Yes, him we must punish!" echoed Grumgra,
with malevolent relish.

And every man turned to eye his fellows fearfully—for who could say that his closest friend
might not have harbored the evil spirits? or who

could say that the wise ones might not make a mistake and punish the wrong man?

"Someone has angered the fire-god and made it go out!" roared Grumgra, in the tones of an accusing judge—and all his hearers quailed and instinctively withdrew. "Someone has angered the fire-god! Who can it be?"

For a moment there was silence, while the audience gazed furtively at the trees, at the grass, at the river—at all things but the terrible eyes of Grumgra and the bewitching eyes of Zunzun.

"Then if no one will speak, we will find out!" shouted the chieftain. "Zunzun the Marvel-Worker will ask the spirits of the woods, and they will tell him!"

Whereupon Zunzun began to bob up and down, up and down, as though in prayer to some unseen divinity. First he would touch the grass with his outstretched palms, then he would rise as far as his stooping posture would permit and fling his grizzled arms heavenward; then he would bow down again and repeat the ceremony time after time, all the while mumbling and muttering, "Nunc, nunco, no, nuncu, nunco, no," in a jargon unintelligible even to his hearers.

But the spectators, although they did not understand, were immensely impressed. The scores of ferret eyes were riveted upon the Marvel-Worker; the powerful jaws gaped wide with wonder; now and then a tremor of fear crossed the furry countenances.

At length, apparently feeling that his antics had sufficed to appease the wood-gods, Zunzun sought rest from his strenuous exertions, and, turning to Grumgra, whispered a few words that none of the tribe could catch.

But whatever it was that Zunzun confided, Grumgra was evidently well pleased. A broad smile softened his brutish face; into his gleaming little eyes there came a light as of sly enjoyment.

Not a murmur flitted through the assemblage as Grumgra strode sullenly forward, and lifted his club in token of command.

"Zunzun has found out the evil one's name!" he snapped; then he stopped short to give his announcement time to penetrate.

"The evil one is sitting among us now!" continued Grumgra, in portentous tones; then once more he stopped short, while each man peered at his neighbor suspiciously.

"Shall I tell you who the evil one is?" he proceeded, with the manner of one who anticipates a pleasant announcement. "Shall I tell you?"

"Tell us! Tell us!" came an eager chorus.

"Listen then, and I shall tell!" assented Grumgra. And, after another pause, he thrust his left hand out accusingly. "There is the evil one! There he is! There he is!"

Dozens of eyes, straining to see, observed that the condemning finger was pointed straight at Ru.

"It's a lie!" shouted Ru, springing furiously to his feet. "A lie, a lie—"

But before he could complete his denial, powerful hands had seized him, and he was struggling,
kicking, tearing and biting, all to no avail, in an
overmastering grip.

And while the crowd cackled and gibbered in glee,
Grumgra scornfully announced: "I have found out
all that the Sparrow-Hearted has done. He made
wicked magic last night. He does not fight before
our eyes like other men—he runs away, and then
works his evil like a crawling serpent behind our
backs. While we were all asleep, he spoke with the
wind-god and the gods of the clouds, and told them
to put out the fire-god. Also, he called to the bad
spirits of the woods, and told them to catch and
eat our people. This the bad spirits did—and for
this Ru must suffer!"

Here Grumgra paused again, while breathlessly
the people awaited the sentence he was to pro-
nounce, and Ru, heavily panting and more than half
exhausted, still strained uselessly in the arms of his
persecutors.

"If it were anyone but the Sparrow-Hearted,"
Grumgra resumed, tapping his club significantly, "I
would have him slain—no, I would slay him with
my own hands! But who wants to wring the neck
of a sparrow? And so I will not kill him this
time—"

Murmurs of disappointment were beginning to
be heard from several quarters; but Grumgra, with
a ferocious frown, hastened to reassure his people.

"I do not mean that we shall not punish him. I

shall not hit him with my club, for do we not need all our men to help us in the hunt?—but until he lies down for his last sleep he shall bear the marks of his bad deeds. He has put out the fire-god by making the rain come—and so the fire-god must take vengeance. Go, my people, gather new fagots and light the fires again; then let us scorch black marks upon the Sparrow-Hearted's throat, that all men may see and know of his shame!"

Delighted titters expressed the approval of the audience; and at the same time a growl half of rage and half of agony issued from the throat of Ru. But a huge mud-caked hand, thrust savagely across his mouth, stifled his protest in mid-career; and while he squirmed and struggled ineffectively in the arms of his captors, he could see several of his tribesmen darting about with great zest to gather fagots and flints.

But it proved to be no easy matter to make a fire —the wood was wet, and would not burn. And while the delay prolonged Ru's torments, it gave him a vague hope and a bitter satisfaction to watch his fellows sweat and toil to no avail, pounding the flints furiously together and kindling spark after spark that invariably vanished in thin air. Hours went by, and no fire was made; by degrees his persecutors wearied of holding him, and their oaths became terrible to hear; while the dismayed people began to murmur that Ru had bewitched the fire-god.

As time wore on, it became apparent that the

migration could not be resumed before the following morning—the punishment of Ru had cost an
entire day. But Grumgra seemed determined that,
regardless of the waste of time, Ru should be punished; and as he strode pugnaciously from group
to group, swinging his club and snarling at the unsuccessful fire-makers, it seemed likely that if Ru
did not suffer someone else would. Once, indeed, the
chieftain went so far as to lunge viciously at the
skull of a particularly careless handler of the flints;
and, after the intended victim had escaped by the
fraction of an inch, his fellow workers applied
themselves scrupulously, but none the less with one
eye furtively upon Grumgra.

Time was to lend their labors success. The sun
had come out somewhat hesitatingly that morning;
but though he worked slowly he worked surely; and
after a few hours, some of the fagots had become
reasonably dry. Thus it happened that, when the
afternoon was already old, the people saw the bright
flames once more leaping and crackling in the center
of their encampment.

And now came the eagerly awaited event. With
the excitement of spectators at some rare entertainment, the tribespeople gathered to see the punishment of Ru. All eyes gleamed and glittered in greedy
pleasure, and all lips uttered exclamations of joy,
when at length the culprit was dragged and shoved
toward the flames. Despite his small physique and
the strain and exhaustion of the last few hours, Ru
was fighting like a wildcat. Some new and almost

superhuman strength seemed to have come into him,
now that the fires flashed so near; four of his
larger kinsmen were needed to hold that furiously
writhing, squirming little form; and the blackening
eyes of two of the men showed the marks of his
outthrust fists and feet, while on the arm of another
was a gaping red gash where the captive's teeth
had wrought angry vengeance.

But the vehemence of Ru's resistance only
whetted the enthusiasm of the mob. Added to the
anticipated delight of the burning, there was the unexpected pleasure of a fight—a spirited fight, with
all the zest of reality! Hence the people crowded
close for a glimpse of the wild-eyed, convulsed form
of Ru; hence they jeered and gibed in raucous glee
when, in the unequal scuffle, he was hopelessly on the
bottom; and they held their breath and gaped when
at times he wriggled free of some encompassing arm
and appeared about to escape altogether. No hint of
pity for him issued from those tense, thick lips,
no murmur of encouragement, or of admiration
at his desperate struggle; the women looked on as
intently and as cold-eyed as the men; and the children—whenever they could squeeze close enough for
a glimpse—stared at the condemned one as dis-
passionately as their elders. Even when crimson
patches appeared on his face and his nose spouted
blood, there was not a tremor of sympathy or regret; even when, in the frenzy of the combat, his
deerskin robe slipped off and he was left with only
his hairy natural covering, there was not a murmur

of revulsion or horror. But with the sporting aloof-
ness of men who watch two cocks tearing one
another to bits, the tribespeople saw Ru gradually
beaten and bruised into a bloody submission.

At last, having put forth all the effort of which
human flesh is capable, he lay sweating and panting on the ground, while a bulky kinsman sat across
his outspread legs, and two others held his hands
pinioned. About him, like voices in an evil dream,
he could hear the expectant gibbering of the multitude; above him, he could view a blur of faces,
evil faces gleaming with a cruel joy; to his left, when
he turned his bloodshot eyes aside, he could see
Woonoo the Hot-Blooded holding a long pointed
stick in the flames.

But he was almost past seeing or caring. His
senses were deserting him; he hardly knew who he
was or where; the world seemed to be whirling and
whirling around, and he was as though floating
somewhere far away in a fog that would not lift.

He was aroused to full consciousness by the sight
of a glowing something dangled just above his eyes.
It was the red-hot stick, which Woonoo had thrust
meaningly before him; and just above it shone a multitude of fiery eager faces, disdainful and com-
passionless as the glaring brand itself.

And as once more there surged across him the
frenzied desire to escape, he was stabbed by sight
of that which was more cruel even than the searing
flames. Two well-known eyes, enticing and distract-
ing eyes, were isolated suddenly amid that con-

fused throng, beaming upon him as if in pleasure, in ridicule, in amused contempt. . . .

Some there were who afterwards claimed to have heard him murmur, in wounded tones, "Yonyo! Yonyo!" But they could not be sure; perhaps it was but the fumings of a crazed mind. At all events, his words were drowned instantly by the hissing of scorched hair and flesh, and by a scream so horrible that even the most bloodthirsty quailed and shuddered.

And while the victim lay moaning on the ground, writhing and twisting like a worm that has been trodden upon, the curious pressed forward and observed a huge black mark upon his neck and chest— a black mark which took the form of a rude cross.

CHAPTER VII

The Fire-God Speaks

THAT evening Grumgra chose a camping-place at the base of the cliffs several hundred yards down the river—the very cliffs he had roared at Ru for suggesting. Here, in little hollows and recesses of the rocks and under the protection of the beetling precipice, the people had no difficulty in lighting their fires and keeping them burning; and though once again a strong wind and rain came up, the storm did not beat directly down upon them, and they slept undisturbed until morning.

But there was at least one of their number—even excluding the sentinels—who could know but little sleep that night. Exhausted to a point almost past fatigue, Ru lay wide-eyed through the long hours, while all about him sounded the heavy breathing of his fellows, and to both sides the uncanny yellow fires wavered and blinked like the eyes of malignant giants. He was so stiff and sore that he could scarcely move; even to turn upon his bruised side caused him many a half-stifled groan; yet a continual torment of burning in his mutilated neck and breast made him writhe and twist incessantly.

But the anguish of his body was less excruciating

than that within his mind. His physical injuries
would heal and be forgotten; but deep within him,
walled from contemptuous eyes, there was a wound
that would not heal and would not be forgotten.
That searing brand, so greedily applied by Woonoo,
had scorched more than his skin and flesh; it had
withered away at a stroke his very feeling of kin-
ship with his people. Previously, when scoffed at or
taunted, he had seemed to be cut off from them
only for a moment; now it appeared to him that
he was an alien—for all time an alien in the midst
of his own people. There was no longer anyone
in whom to confide, anyone in whom to seek refuge;
even she of the dazzling eyes could see his misfortune and laugh; and neither she nor the others
would care if he should vanish into the river or
down the throats of the wolves.

But as he lay there in the firelight, moaning and
moaning in unheeded agony, a furious resolve came
into his mind, gripping him with such vehemence
that for the moment he forgot his pain. It was a
thought that was not new to him, yet in its present fury it seemed wholly new. As his people had
mocked and derided him, so they should one day
worship and applaud; as they had made him grovel
at their feet, so they should one day grovel before
him; and where Grumgra stood in club-wielding
might, he should walk in power more absolute even
than Grumgra's! Strange thoughts for one so beaten
down and humiliated, for the outcast and the cull
of the tribe! But even in this moment of despair

he knew that he was master of that which his fellows could never command, for he could think while they could only act—and his thoughts should win him the world!

Nor were his plans confined merely to vague hopes. With the shrewdness of the practical dreamer, he was scheming for the hour of his triumph even in this hour of his defeat. First of all, there was the weapon which would strike at a distance, and which sometime, surely, he should learn how to make. Then again, there was the might of the fire-god—that very fire-god who had burned and tortured his flesh. If he had been able to master this great spirit, his troubles would have been spared him; if he could still learn to master it, he would have an ally more powerful than any club that was ever brandished. Just how to tame this elusive force he had no idea; but he promised himself that he would wait and watch until sometime, unexpectedly, the secret would open before him.

Several of Ru's fellows, awakening in the early dawn, thought they heard him mutter something that sounded suspiciously like an oath of service to the god of fire. But they only laughed at what they deemed the Sparrow-Hearted's ravings; and they amused themselves by prodding the puny one lightly with the points of sticks in order to see his anger.

That morning, when Grumgra gave the order for the march, Ru was scarcely able to stagger along with the tribe. His aching limbs were matched by his aching head; his body felt strangely hot although a cool wind was blowing; his trembling legs seemed in danger of collapsing. Like one in a nightmare, or like one suddenly grown old, he tottered through the gloomy forest aisles, feeling as if each step were to be his last. How he endured the long miles he never quite knew, nor how he withstood the mocking gaze of his fellows and the inquisitive eyes that constantly explored his throat and breast, as though his scarred flesh were an inviting sight. Only the fact that the tribe was burdened with many children, whose pace was slow and who could not be left behind, enabled Ru to keep within sight of his kinsmen. Even so, he had visions of being forsaken altogether, and of finding himself, in his helplessness, suddenly face to face with one of the fanged prowlers of the woods.

Perhaps eight or ten miles were covered that day —a good day's traveling, indeed! And when, in the late afternoon, Grumgra called a halt and chose a camping-place, Ru was so exhausted that he sank down with a thankful sigh, and began almost instantly to atone for the loss of two nights' sleep.

The following morning he awoke feeling much refreshed; and, having bathed in the stream, he helped himself liberally to chunks of dried buffalo flesh and of the venison that the women were roasting over the fire. This was his first repast in almost two days—and now, although his limbs were still sore and aching, he felt once more in an optimistic mood.

But as the tribe set out again through the woods by the banks of the interminable Harr-Sizz River, he became conscious that something was still lacking. His sense of exile had not left him; since his public humiliation two days before, scarcely a person had spoken to him; he could hear the people murmuring that he was in touch with evil spirits, and that a word from him might bewitch them. Even when the children, drawn to him by the force of old attraction, would approach with the smiling request for another tale of aurochs or bears, their elders would scowlingly order them away. And so Ru was lonely, more lonely than he had ever been before. He was filled with sadness to hear his fellows chattering merrily ahead of him or behind, while he trudged on and on all by himself; he longed vaguely for some companion, some particular companion all his own; and his craving, although he could not understand why, seemed always to settle about Yonyo—even she, the scornful and the heartless one, whom he was trying his best to forget.

But he could not forget her. More than once, when she passed him on the trail, it stung him through and through to see that she went by without even a disdainful glance; and more than once, when he saw her strolling gaily with Kuff the Bear-Hunter or Woonoo the Hot-Blooded, he was filled with an almost uncontrollable fury to rend and destroy. Had he but possessed the strength, he would have sprung pantherlike at these great tribesmen of his, and struck and struck till they lay stiff and lifeless before him.

But the feebleness of his limbs was an effective bar to his murderous impulses. Day after day went by, while Yonyo seemed to have forgotten his existence and Kuff and Woonoo openly vied for her companionship. Meantime he seemed to be still under a cloud, for no one would speak to him, even though, in his loneliness, he made repeated advances to his former companions. At night he was forced to sleep by himself in a solitary corner of the encampment, and by day he had to glide ahead of his tribesmen or behind them through the interminable lengths of the wilderness.

And now his only solace came from watching the bewildering and ever-changing panoramas—the tumbled ragged-white vistas of far-off snow-peaks, the dark, steeply curving slopes of the spruce and pine, the tumultuous blustering river with its bank of reeds or rocks, the tiny blue lakes that dotted the valleys like inverted bits of the sky, the massive cliffs and crags and the boulder-littered plains, with now and then a waterfall that came foaming from the heights with a crashing and roaring as of a god's voice. At times Ru's quick eyes would catch the flash of some moving thing, and he would stop short to watch the queer inhabitants of the wilds: the huge brown mammoth, with its grave high head and long curling tusks; the golden yellow double-horned woolly rhinoceros; the enormous, swiftly gliding red deer; or even the wild horses, bison, and cattle

that browsed upon the river grass in peaceful bands.
Somehow, although he could not say why, Ru was
glad merely at sight of these creatures; and in his
interest in them, and in his glimpses of the great
hills and rushing waters, he found relief from that
anger and despair with which his people had filled
him.

After ten days had gone by, and the wounds in his
body were almost healed, but the wounds in his
heart were festering more painfully than ever, there
occurred a series of events which brought a sudden
end to his career as outcast.

Those events began with a curious discovery of
Ru's. One evening he chanced to observe a woman
cast a bit of bison tallow into the fire; and he noticed how the fat sizzled and sputtered with bright
yellow flames much more brilliant than the normal
wood fires. Like all his people, he had seen such a
spectacle time upon time before; but always he,
as they, had watched without eyes, and no thought
of possible utility had ever occurred to him. But
now, in a flash, it came to him that the fire-god
loved tallow, fed upon it greedily, and would serve
anyone who made him an offering of it. What if,
in place of wood, one should try to burn old and
dried-out fat? or, rather, wood prepared with a
coating of fat?

No sooner was the thought in Ru's mind than he
had begun to experiment. Selecting the long straight
limb of a fallen tree, he greased it with a heavy layer
of tallow he had cut from a recently slain bison.

Then, cautiously and not without some fear of the fire-god, he thrust the end of the stick into the flames.

Two or three of his tribesmen, who were squatted idly on a mound of earth some paces away, grinned in apish amusement to watch this new antic of the Sparrow-Hearted. They were preparing to leap up and seize the greased stick from his hand by way of pleasant sport, when they fell back in amazement to see a brilliant deep-yellow flame spring up at the end of the pole. And, the next they knew, Ru was striding toward them waving a flaming brand that seemed like a threat from the fire-god himself.

They did not wait to learn more about that threat. With terrified squeals, they took to their feet, while Ru followed at his leisure with a smile of amusement and triumph.

Wherever he went, he was greeted with frightened screams and cries. The children ran howling from him; the women pressed back with shrieks and yells; the men stood growling and threatening at a distance, but drew hastily away whenever he strode too near; while many a fever-ishly moving lip framed prayers to the fire-god. From end to end of that camping-place—a wide glade in the heart of the forest—Ru stalked like an avenging demon. It filled him with a wild, exultant joy to see even the great Grumgra hold his dis-tance, even Grumgra, the dreaded and the growling one; and his heart sang with fierce glee when Zunzun the Marvel-Worker—he who professed to be the fire-god's nearest friend—went tottering hurriedly away before the sputtering menace of the torch.

Rapidly and vigorously the brand continued to burn, with an energetic crackling and flaring, until it was less than half its former length, and the molten, scorching grease began to flow along Ru's fingers.

He was just about to throw down the brand and beat out the flames, when he beheld that which filled him with sudden madness. At one corner of the glade, shielded behind a mountainous boulder, sat Woonoo the Hot-Blooded; and in his huge hairy arms lay one whom Ru recognized all too well— Yonyo the Smiling-Eyed!

With a roar of murderous rage, Ru was upon them. His torch gleamed and wavered wrathfully; he forgot for the moment the torments of the melting fat; he was bent only on singeing and branding his rival. And Woonoo, taken off his guard, was aware only of a fire-brandishing fury that came dashing upon him out of the void, waving the yellow flames as if to sear him to cinders.

Without taking time for a second glance, time even to recognize the mad apparition as Ru, Woonoo squealed with terror, cast the startled Yonyo from him, and fled for the woods. Ru, pressing close behind, was forced to be content with flinging the torch after him and scorching the hair of his back.

A few moments later, Ru returned from the chase with a triumphant grin. Yonyo was still standing, as if dazed, beside the boulder from which she had been so rudely thrust; and, as Ru passed, she turned toward him with a smile that was almost friendly. But he seemed not to see; and, without so much as a glance in her direction, he strolled resolutely toward the center of the encampment.

Seeing that he was without the burning brand, the bolder tribesmen now came forward to meet him; and it was not long before even the more timid had ventured near. From their excited way of crowding about him and chattering, one might have thought Ru exceedingly popular. But he was not to be deceived by their effusiveness; resentment still rankled within him. And so he did not respond to their advances; he did not reply to their questions, did not explain his power over the fire-god; he seemed not to hear their friendly jests, their praise, their offers of companionship.

On the following evening, there occurred an event which added still further to Ru's newly won prestige.

It happened that, at the close of the day's migration, one of the men curiously explored the hollow of a tree-trunk, and there discovered that rarest of all treats—a bees' nest filled with honey. Regardless of the stings of the infuriated insects—which, after all, were much impeded by the hairy natural covering of the people—some of the doughtiest of the tribe contrived to capture the entire treasury of sweets; and, laden down with their booty, which consisted of a mixture of wax, honey, squirming grubs and dead bees, they hastened away to camp to enjoy the feast.

So eager were all the people not to miss their share of this delicacy, and so greedily did men, women, and children swarm about the possessors of the prize, that all other pursuits were momentarily forgotten. Clamoring and shouting for a portion, smacking their lips hopefully or gustily licking long dripping fingers, the people pressed in a furious rabble about the fast-disappearing dainty, so rabid for a taste that one might have thought them engaged in a riot—and few remembered that no other food was being prepared, that no precaution had been taken against possible danger, that no fires were being kindled for the night.

Yet, while the tribal fires had been neglected, it would not be quite correct to say that no fires at all had been lighted. Screened from the gaze of the multitude behind a slight rise in the land, Ru sat patiently preparing a little fire of his own. And when at length the flames sprang forth with gusto, he began to ignite sticks of various kinds and sizes, all of which had been liberally greased. . . . But of this his kinsmen knew nothing. Like hungry vultures quarreling over a bit of carrion, they were still squirming and struggling about the honey.

Suddenly, when the pandemonium had reached its loudest, the participants were startled by a growl more savage even than of the dispossessed honey-seekers. In deep-voiced tones, half like the grumbling of an angry dog, half like the bellowing of a bull, there sounded a challenge so terrible that the blood of all ran cold and their paralyzed legs seemed limp and useless beneath them. And out of the forest there trotted a thick-set furry beast as large as a grizzly, with little brown eyes gleaming evilly, gigantic paws and large curving claws outspread, and monstrous glittering mouth gaping wide.

After the first glance, the people's paralysis left them. "A bear! A bear! A cave-bear!" they cried, mad with terror. And where, but a moment before, there had been a maggot-like, convulsive throng, there was suddenly nothing but a mound of honey-drenched earth. In a wild mob the fugitives raced for the trees, shrieking and crying in dread, dashing one another aside in their fury to reach shelter, then literally climbing over one another as they mounted into the protecting branches.

But his Majesty the Bear, having caused all this consternation, took little note of the results. With long greedy tongue he began to lap up the spilled honey; and, as befits a conqueror, he was so absorbed in consuming the spoils of victory that very soon he had quite forgotten the vanquished.

But the vanquished had not forgotten him. From their perches in the tree tops, they watched the marauder feasting; and, while they watched, they chattered angrily, made hideous grimaces, and shouted furious names at the enemy.

In the midst of their tumult of hoots and howls, an astonishing spectacle distracted their attention

Ru frightens the bear with his torch

from the bear. Suddenly, as if from nowhere, a
short, slender figure flashed into view beneath
them, waving a burning brand and striding toward
the redoubtable beast!

The spectators gasped. Some muttered in amazement, some in alarm; one cried that Ru was out
of his wits; others screamed that he had bewitched
the monster, or that the bear would crush him
like a rabbit. But all eyes were fastened steadily
upon him as, still brandishing his torch, he pressed
straight toward destruction.

In a moment he was well out in the open field,
too far from the trees to seek safety in flight.
And then it was that the beast became aware of
him. With a snort of anger, Bruin turned to confront his foe; but his wicked little eyes burned with
a light that was not altogether of menace.

Swinging his torch round and round in enormous
circles till the flames hissed and sizzled threateningly, Ru strode on and on without a pause. In
another moment, he was so near that the bear
might have been upon him with a leap.

But the bear did not leap. Instead, he reared upon
his great hind legs, looming taller than the tallest
man and stouter than five men. Ominous mutterings
issued from his cavernous throat; his huge lips
curled in a defiant snarl; his gigantic paws were
outspread as if to strike and crush.

Then, when Ru could feel the hot, foul breath
upon him, he started forward with a shout and a
rush, as if to throw himself upon the monster, as

if to thrust himself straight into those powerful gaping jaws.

But the furry one did not wait for the onslaught. With a howl of terror, he turned and lumbered away into the woods; while Ru, pursuing him with the firebrand, at the same time motioned to his people to come down from the trees.

CHAPTER VIII

A New Misadventure

FOR three days following the bear-chasing exploit, Ru was as much sought after as he had previously been shunned. It was as if his people now felt him to be the possessor of some unique and supernatural power; as if they believed him to be in league with unseen but mighty spirits, whose friendship was at all costs to be won. And since the obvious way to court such friendship was through courting Ru, he was showered with attentions where of old he had met only neglect. Four or five of his kinsmen were at all times ready to go chattering at his side whether or not he desired their company; and, when he sat down to rest at the end of the day's migration, there was always someone to approach with flattering words and seek either to wheedle out of him the secret of the firebrand, or else to beg some charm that would give protection against the fire-god. Even the young women of the tribe—Mono the Budding Tree, Sizz-O the Serpent-Tongued, and others—cast admiring, half-inviting glances toward him from beneath their high-ridged bushy brows; while more than once Yonyo the Smiling-Eyed approached with jests and laughter that scarcely availed to break down his sullen silence.

For he was still disdainful of his people—as disdainful of them as they had been of him. Brooding upon the wound on his breast, whose cross-shaped ghastly scar was as a mark of shame, he distrusted their vows of friendship; he suspected that at heart they loved him no better than before. And so, although at times in his loneliness he longed to dash down the barriers at a stroke and be one with his people as of old, yet his pride and wounded sensibilities combined to keep open that rift which his own peculiarities and Grumgra's hatred had created.

But after three days, he suffered a fall at once sudden and disconcerting. And the indirect cause of the misfortune was a lack of that caution which, had he been but a little wiser, he would surely have exercised. One evening he was seated in a lonely corner of the encampment, experimenting before his own little fire with some long sticks and a mass of tallow, when suddenly he became conscious of two gleaming black eyes peering at him from amid the shrubbery. At the instant of his discovery, the eyes disappeared, and he could not be sure whose they were nor how long they had been watching; but an hour later the unhappy sequel told him all that he desired to know.

It was late twilight, and he was seated in the midst of the tribe, chewing eagerly at the roasted ribs of a wild horse, when Woonoo the Hot-Blooded came strutting from behind a clump of shrubbery, waving a brilliant yellow torch—almost precisely like the torch of Ru's invention! And behind Woonoo towered Grumgra, wielding a similar but very much larger torch! They both moved without a word to the center of the encampment, while scores of gaping men and women paused between bites to stare at them in awestricken wonder.

At length, mounting the recumbent trunk of a huge dead tree, Grumgra began to speak in his usual bellowing voice.

"One of our people," he commenced, without formality, "has just done a great deed. He has learned how to make the fire-god work for us. He has given us these fire-sticks you see now." Here Grumgra swung the torch about his head in scintillating circles. "After this, we may all have fire-sticks to help us in our hunting. Is it not strange magic, my people? This magic was made by one of our bravest men—one of the wisest and biggest of us all—Woonoo the Hot-Blooded!"

Grumgra paused, and a tumult of excited gibbering signified the applause of the audience. Ru, trembling with anger, noted an admiring gleam in the eyes of Yonyo as she glanced toward the Hot-Blooded; and at the same time Grumgra continued in words that scorched him to the heart.

"There is another of our people," resumed the Growling Wolf, in tones that justified his name, "who would have us think him a friend of the fire-god. But this man is really like a worm; he is not strong at all, and did not make the fire-stick. For the fire-god is mighty and would not help a half-man like the Sparrow-Hearted—"

"Lies! Lies!" screamed Ru, springing to his feet in a quivering frenzy. "All lies! I was the one that made the fire-stick! I was the one—"

But his words were drowned by a chorus of hisses and hoots. He felt someone seizing him from behind; he was thrust brutally to earth; while on all sides rang the jeering laughter of his fellows.

Released from the bruising hands, Ru crawled away like one in a nightmare. As he reached the outer fringe of shadows, he could still see the monstrous form of Grumgra waving the flaming brand, and just beneath him the huge but smaller fire-wielding shape of Woonoo; while dozens of grimacing hairy faces, shining with apelike grins and contortions in the unsteady light, seemed to burn and glow maliciously as the taunting faces of imps.

And thus ended the three-day reign of Ru. Thus ended that power which he had won by his wits, and lost by his carelessness. Henceforth he was to be again the despised, the outcast, the butt of derision, the solitary wanderer; henceforth he was to hear that hated appellation, "Sparrow-Hearted," dinned again and again into his ears, and was to be shunned by his people, and most of all by her, the tantalizing, the Smiling-Eyed.

All the rest of that night no one came near him; and all the following day he roamed by himself, no longer sought by the gay, chattering groups; and the merriment that rang about him from the forest re-

cesses burdened him with melancholy thoughts. A
feeling of sadness and of desolation was upon him
and would not be shaken off, a sense of frustration,
of anger and of futility. He would scarcely have
known how to laugh even had he had someone to
laugh with; and in the brooding silence of the woods
and the overshadowing gloom of the hills and crags
he found but little compensation for the scorn in
the eyes of Yonyo and the sneer in the eyes of his
kinsmen.

But if he had fallen from his momentary high
estate, his present troubles were as nothing beside
those which awaited him after another day or two.

Having kept close to the Harr-Sizz River for
scores of miles, following its innumerable twists and
turns and serpent-like convolutions, the tribe was unexpectedly confronted with the necessity of crossing
the stream; for the waters turned abruptly north-
ward in a long, unbending line, and Mumlo the
Trail-Finder insisted that the land they sought lay
toward the mountains in the direction of the noonday sun.

While a tumultuous throng clung to the bank
shouting directions, several of the men began to
wade into the stream, seeking a suitable spot for
fording. The river at this point was fairly wide,
and seemed to be correspondingly shallow; yet its
current was rapid and angry, and gurgled past in a
steadily moving muddy torrent. As a result, not a
few of the men were buffeted off their feet; and, except for the fact that they were unimpeded by

clothing, they would hardly have been able to force their way back to safety.

But despite innumerable setbacks, they persisted. And at length Mumlo, moving some distance downstream, found the point where he claimed to have crossed before. The stream here was perhaps double its average width and much more shallow than in most locations; yet it was not quite so shallow as the more timid might have desired, and in places the waters came well over Mumlo's shoulders.

But there was little chance for hesitation. Straight into the stream plunged the men, their shoulders bent beneath the weight of the rapidly diminishing provisions; and straight after them followed the women and children in a shouting, splashing rabble. Some—particularly among the younger folk—seemed to take the crossing as a pleasant sport, and leaped and pranced in the waters like aquatic animals; others screwed up their beady little eyes into an expression of extreme gravity, and peered out across that broad flowing expanse with no sign of relish. Toward the center of the stream, the shorter tribesfolk lost connection with the bottom and had to trust to their swimming ability; and this they did with invariable success, although one or two of the children seemed in danger of being washed away and were saved only by the timely outthrust of a parental arm. As for the infants, of whom there were well over a score, they were carried on the shoulders of the tallest men, where, screaming with terror and clinging with a grip that showed no sign of relaxing, they were perhaps safer than their older brothers and sisters.

One of the last to attempt the crossing was Ru, who had been loitering near the bank examining a shrub whose flexible stem seemed well fitted for the long-distance weapon he was planning. It was only when he feared being left behind that he tore himself away; and when at last he plunged into the water, he was in a great hurry to make up for lost time, and recklessly swam almost the entire distance.

Half exhausted, he was about to clamber up the opposite bank, when he saw two pairs of familiar eyes peering at him in malicious glee. At a glance, he realized that Woonoo the Hot-Blooded and Kuff the Bear-Hunter could mean him no good; but he could not imagine what evil design they might have. And, at all events, he had no choice except to attempt to pull himself up the moist, slippery rocks as though nothing were amiss.

But he very speedily learned what was in the minds of Kuff and Woonoo. With one accord, as though following a prearranged plan, they reached out their powerful arms, seized Ru about the neck and shoulders, and flung him back into the river. And, as he descended with a splash and felt the flood racing above him, their guffaws rang loud and heartily through the startled woods.

Panting, and half choked with the water he had swallowed, Ru rose to his feet and started unsteadily back to the bank. He did not suppose that his fellows would repeat the prank—the first time, it might be excused as a joke; but, if continued, it would turn into something more serious than a friendly bit of sport.

So, although both exhausted and angry, Ru tried to take the little game in the proper spirit and to grin. But his effort was a feeble one, and failed woefully. . . . With renewed guffaws, Kuff and Woonoo ran to meet him as he struggled up the bank; the next he knew, he had felt the irresistible arms gripping him again, had gone flying through space, and had splashed once more into the strangling flood.

Recovering himself with an effort, Ru stood for a moment breast-deep in the water, staring furiously at the impish, grimacing faces of his persecutors. He was now convinced that they were ready to repeat their pranks time after time; consequently, he sought to elude them by swimming to a little projection of land about a hundred yards down-stream. But, upon arriving, he found to his dismay that they were there awaiting him. And, not content with merely waiting, they were wading after him into the stream, forcing him to retreat hastily toward the center.

By this time, half a dozen spectators had gathered to watch the sport. With titters and chuckles of raucous mirth they encouraged Kuff and Woonoo, meanwhile joining in boisterously by jeering the Sparrow-Hearted with every evil-sounding name at their command. And after a minute one of

the more audacious spirits, not to be satisfied with
mere words, picked up a pebble and ostentatiously
flung it at Ru, who was now standing waist-deep a
dozen yards from shore, undecided how to attempt
another landing.

With a splash, the pebble disappeared in the
water just to Ru's rear. And a chorus of gleeful
shouts broke forth as Ru turned with a start to see
what had happened. Immediately several of the
men, quick to seize upon ideas, profited from the
example; and in another instant Ru was the center
of a little shower of missiles. Most of them vanished
into the water without effect, but one of them struck
his arm with a painful thud, to the immense amusement of his tormentors; and so many stones were
whirling through the air and splashing in the water
that Ru took the one obvious course, which was
to make with all possible speed toward the center
of the stream.

But his withdrawal lent additional zest to the
amused chorus on the bank, as well as additional
speed to the stones that pursued him. So insistent
was the bombardment that he had to press on and
on through the deepening torrent, until at length
the bottom slipped from beneath him and he had
no choice except to swim.

But his tribesmen did not seem to know when they
had had enough of a joke. Although by this time Ru
was so exhausted that he could barely keep afloat,
the mood of entertainment that possessed the spectators was far from satisfied. Not realizing or not

caring what grave results threatened, they continued to pelt Ru gleefully, following him along the bank as he drifted down-stream, and all the while jeering him to their hearts' content.

Ru meantime was engaged in what promised to be a life-or-death struggle. Again and again he felt the powerful swirling torrent breaking over him, and only with an effort lifted his head for a reviving breath. Again and again he swallowed huge gulps of the muddy water, and heard a muffled roaring like a death-threat in his ears; while, in his terror, he had visions of huge strangling arms reaching out for him from the depths and dragging him down as he had once seen a stag dragged down by the quicksands.

He heard no more the gibes and taunts of the mob on the bank, heard no more the splashing of the stones; he was waging a desperate fight against the current, which was narrower here and much swifter than where his tribe had crossed—and the current was winning the battle. His panting heart was straining in vain, his tugging muscles pulled feebly against the gigantic body of the water; his bulging eyes were staring in a last agony at the vague, rushing shore; louder and louder dinned the drumming in his ears, more insistent the force of that pounding, suffocating fury that broke over his head; he floundered and lunged, rose again and sank, slowly rose again and sank, while over him came a maddening, baffling longing for air. . . . Then strange lights and shadows were wavering

about him, something dark and formless was bearing down upon him—and, the next he knew, his
fingers were clinging to some great and solid object.

Opening his eyes, he felt himself returning by
degrees to life, and realized that he was gripping
the floating trunk of a dead tree, which was bearing him swiftly down-stream toward an unknown
expanse of blue water.

CHAPTER IX

Lost!

NOT yet recovered from his shock and exhaustion, Ru climbed with difficulty onto the gnarled upper surface of the drifting tree trunk and lay there at full length, his hands clutching a projecting broken-off limb, his feet trailing behind him more than half in the water. He was still too weak to think of swimming to the bank; and while he lay on his new-found craft, gradually regaining his strength, the current was carrying him steadily toward the unknown blue expanse.

Almost before he was aware of his new peril, he found himself on the surface of an enormous lake—a much larger lake than he had ever seen before. Its rippling indigo expanse spread far, far away, out of sight and to vague infinities; and Ru could make out only dimly the ragged lines of the snow-peaks that fringed the farther shore.

By this time the motion of the log had almost ceased; and, at a barely appreciable speed, Ru was drifting toward the center of the lake. At first he perceived in this no cause for alarm; then, as he observed that hundreds of yards separated him from the bank and that the distance was still widening, sudden terror filled his mind. . . .

How was he to regain the shore? Was he to float out to the middle of the wide waters, far beyond swimming distance of the land? and was he to be there when the sun went down and the darkness dropped over all things? and then again when the sun came up and lighted the world? And would he stay there even till the hunger pain came and the bad spirits flew down and took him beyond the last mountains, so that he would never again walk with his people among the rocks and woods? Or—most dreadful thought of all!—even if the water-god let him go and he could swim to shore, would he know how to find his way back again to his tribe?

Many times before in his brief career Ru had felt forlorn and forsaken; but never had he been oppressed with the same overwhelming desolation as now, when he gazed across the glittering waters to the tree-lined reaches of the land, and realized that somewhere in those impenetrable vastnesses his people had vanished, and were doubtless even now retreating on some undiscoverable trail. In one swift, cruel stroke, all the terrors of exile flashed across his mind; he felt as if he had been deserted; he felt deliberately trampled upon and thrust aside. And when for a moment he saw himself for what he was—an isolated mite adrift in an unheeding immensity—he had almost ceased to care, would almost have welcomed the smothering flood-waters.

But after an instant of inertia, the old savage desire to live came flaming back upon him. No matter what agonies he suffered, he must save himself; no matter what difficulties and dangers he had to face, he must face and surmount them—he must, for it was the law of life! And if for a while Ru had felt pitifully small, helpless, and abandoned, it was not long before hope had flashed into life again, and had brought his will to life with it, so that he began thoughtfully to calculate his chances of rescue.

First of all, how find his way back to the shore? Never in his life had he attempted to swim much more than the width of a river—would he then be safe in undertaking this far wider distance? Remembering his recent near-fatal experience, he could not persuade himself to take the chance; even the precarious foothold of the log was vastly preferable to the certain risks of the open waters.

But if he was not to leave the log, how return to land? For many minutes Ru pondered without avail, while in growing dismay he gaped at the dark, ragged lines of the trees, whose distance was slowly and yet perceptibly widening. Then, when the delay and the increasing cold and the dread of oncoming night were challenging his better judgment and he again considered hazarding the swim, chance suggested the remedy which his unaided wits could not provide.

Every once in a while, when for the sake of comfort he shifted his weight, the log would lurch and turn abruptly; and on some such occasions, while he was seeking to regain his balance, his feet or hands would fly out haphazard into the water, giving the log a shove that altered its position by a few inches or a foot. At first Ru did not recognize the possible importance of these accidental movements; but after he had observed them several times, it came to him on a sudden that his craft need not move only as the winds and waters dictated! He himself might push it in any direction that he desired! And as this startling thought invaded his mind, he thrust his right hand into the water and shoved with all his might—with the result that the log did actually swerve and turn much as he had surmised it would.

Thus the art of navigation had its beginning!

But the discovery was not without its drawbacks. Although he could indeed propel the log in any desired direction, he found his craft to be most ungainly; it responded with the utmost slowness to his will, and moved only by inches toward the too-distant shore. After the passage of an hour—an hour of most strenuous paddling, during which Ru several times lost his balance and fell into the water—his goal was obviously nearer, and yet still so remote that he almost gave up hope of reaching it.

It was at the moment of returning despair that a new idea occurred to him. And here again chance played a part. He observed the leafless dead limb of a tree floating barely out of reach—about as thick as his arm and perhaps twice as long. With a little cry of delight, he flung himself into the water and seized the prize; then, returning to his log-vessel, he promptly took his second step toward a mastery of navigation.

To his great joy he found that, seated astride the log with the long stick for paddle, he could advance much more rapidly than when he used only his hands.

Even so, his progress was still plodding and laborious—the most cumbrous raft of a later day could have offered him lessons in speed. Yet, to Ru's way of thinking, his rate of movement was encouragingly swift; and his mood became self-congratulatory when he saw that the shore was approaching, actually approaching, so that he should surely reach it before dark. And from his thankful heart there issued something like an unspoken prayer, a prayer of gratitude to the spirits of the woods and the waters that had given to him—to him, the despised, the Sparrow-Hearted—an almost miraculous control over nature.

But this joyous feeling had deserted him when at last he stood on the sandy shore of the lake. Except for the pole which had been his paddle and was now his club, he was without resources or defense other than nature had offered him. He had no food; he had lost his flint implements in crossing the river; his covering of deerskin had slipped from him. And these handicaps—although assuredly serious enough—were by no means the worst. How far he might be from his people he did not know, and of their general direction he had only the vaguest idea; but that they would send no scout to look for him was certain, and that days might be consumed in the return to them was probable.

Meanwhile he was alone in an unknown land, with neither landmarks nor trail to guide him. He would have to dive through forests where the sun-god could not penetrate, and dart across plains where the wind-god thundered and roared and bade the wolf and the wild bull roam like mad. What gigantic obstacles loomed before him, what ambushed perils lay in wait, was more than the gods themselves could say!

For many minutes Ru stood in a mournful reverie by the rippling lake waters, now gazing out across that imperturbable, unfeeling deep-blue expanse, now staring up into the quivering tops of the densely massed pines and the ampler towers of the oaks. He could not decide what to do or how to begin; he was thinking with anger of the brutality of his tribespeople—of how they had brought him to this pass, yet would not care, even could they know, but would only gibber and grin inanely. In imagination he saw one of them—her who was known as the Smiling-Eyed—and watched her grin and gibber with the rest; and at this fancy a great rage seized him. He was filled with longing to rush back to her, and seize her in his arms, and hold her with such passion that the insolent smile would vanish from her face and she would look up at him meekly and in wonder.

But even while such thoughts crowded through his brain, he did not forget that he was standing alone in a perilous country. Some subconscious protective sense—a sense far keener in those primitive days than in a later age—aroused him abruptly to a dread reality. Suddenly Yonyo and his people vanished from his mind; he was aware only of himself and of the little tree-encompassed patch of beach whereon he stood. A great fear went shuddering through his heart, fear swift and all-enveloping as at the stealthy approach of death. His breath came short and fast; his heart began to hammer ferociously; the hair along his back bristled, and his eyes were twin points of terror fixed upon a dark spot in the underbrush.

Yet all the while there was no visible cause for alarm. Nothing could be seen to stir among the dense verdure; there was no sound except for the distant cry of a bird calling to its mate, and the nearer sound of the wavelets lapping the shore; the breeze peacefully swayed the tall spires of the pines, and from along the lake a butterfly went zigzagging and spiraling happily.

Then suddenly, from the throat of the watching man, came a blood-curdling scream. And, as he screamed, he turned and went streaking toward the trees; while after him, with great feline leaps, darted a monstrous tawny form, with green eyes lustfully glaring, and saber-like tusks curving downward from cavernous jaws.

In an instant the contest was over. Barely in time to beat the spring of the lithe body and the thrust of the murderous fangs, the pursued dashed up the nearest tree and swung himself out of sight in the foliage. And the pursuer, with hair-raising

Ru hides from the sabertooth

screams and yelps of baffled rage, slid agilely about
at the base, at times rearing its massive form against
the trunk as if to dare the ascent, at times peering
upward with blazing, evil eyes as of a cat that covets
an inaccessible robin.

Never before had Ru beheld such a beast.
Wolves, bears, rhinoceroses, hyenas, he had learned
to fear and to fight; but never had he heard his
tribesmen even tell of a terror such as this which,
half lion and half tiger, was prowling at the foot
of the tree. Still wide-eyed with horror, as the
screams of the beast sent chill shivers down his
spine, he drew himself up into the highest branches;
then, although he knew that he was secure for a
time at least, he continued to shudder as if the
fanged one were even now springing at his throat.

For a long while he could still make out the
tawny form among the vague shadows beneath; and
when those shadows began to deepen and twilight
slowly settled over the world, Ru did not know
whether or not his foe still lay in wait for him.

But he did not desire to take any chances; he
held resolutely to his fastness in the tree tops, determined to remain there until morning. Even had
there been no sabertooth, he could not have en-
trusted himself to those perilous woods in the dark.
Here among the branches it was not likely that any
night marauder could reach him; and though it was
most uncomfortable to balance himself on his lofty
pinnacle, and though he was obsessed by continual
fears of falling, yet he found it possible to huddle up

safely in a crotch of the boughs and even to secure some sleep. He was surprised to find that the experience—although he knew it to be his first of the kind—did not seem exactly new to him; he felt almost as if he had come back to an old home, as if he had slept countless times before among the tree tops, had rocked and swung in the same wind-blown couch, had known that the same green leaves were above him, had stared down fearfully into the same blackness where shadowy terrors prowled.

But while he could not have explained why, Ru knew that every sound and sight of that interminable night seemed familiar. The tigerish scream from far off when some great beast pounced upon its prey; the shrill and horrible death-shriek of some slaughtered creature; the hooting of some owl-like bird, and the lonely plaint of some roaming wolf; the mysterious shadows that occasionally went streaking across the open space beneath, and the glowing, ghostly eyes upturned now and then as if staring malignantly at him—all these seemed as things known and feared in lonely vigils long ago, known and feared in some half-remembered dream. And lying in a clinging heap among the branches, with ears alert for every sound, and eyes searching the darkness for every flash and glitter, Ru thought of his people slumbering securely beside their camp-fires; and as he remembered how comfortably they rested on their earthen couches and how little they need fear slashing fangs and claws, the heart within him was envious and sore.

By the first dreary morning light, his eyes began to explore the ground for trace of his saber-toothed assailant. But there was no sign of the catlike monster. Was it lurking in ambush somewhere just out of sight? or had it wearied of waiting and gone off in search of easier prey? Ru had no way of knowing, and felt by no means certain that the beast had left; but after he had hesitated for many minutes, and the full light of day streamed from above, his hunger and impatience and sheer discomfort combined to decide for him.

Warily he began the descent, inch by inch, with motions so cautious that not a leaf was ruffled— still no sign of a possible foe. At length he had reached the lower branches and stood perched there in uncertainty, ready to fling himself back into the tree top at the first hint of danger. But no such sign appeared; only a few buzzing gnats and now and then a murmuring bee broke the stillness of the woods; and his senses brought him news of nothing threatening.

At last, choking down his visions of huge fanged jaws and ambushed tawny forms, Ru released his hold on the tree and slid silently back to earth.

But nothing happened, absolutely nothing—the motionless trees and the wide rippling waters and the clear blue sky alike seemed unconscious of his deed of daring. And though his limbs were trembling and his eyes were filled with dread and he stood long by the tree, still prepared to dash back to safety at the least suspicious rustling, the world

appeared friendly and serene as if it harbored no
saber-fanged marauders.

Finally, when he had convinced himself that his
persecutor had gone, not to return, Ru started
cautiously across the open space and regained his
club, which he had dropped in his precipitate flight.
Thus protected, he strode to the brink of the lake,
where he bent down and sucked in a long, refreshing draft, following which he was ready to set out
again into the unknown.

It seemed to him that there was now only one
possible course to pursue—to keep close to the lake
and the river until he reached the point where his
tribe had crossed. Then, guided by the tracks they
had made, by the scraps of food and clothing they
had cast aside, and by the damage they had done
to the vegetation, he should have little difficulty in
tracing their route and ultimately overtaking them.

But this plan was by no means as easy to carry
out as Ru had expected. In places the lake shore was
lined with bogs and swamps, around which he had
to tramp endlessly; in other places there were steep
bluffs to scale, rapid streams to ford, and thorny
thickets to penetrate; and all the while he had to
maintain a keen lookout for serpents and hostile
beasts, and had to keep near enough to the trees
to be able to reach them if necessary. Once, indeed, he did seek them in a panic when a suspicious
stirring of the foliage brought reminders of the
sabertooth; but it proved to be nothing more than
a wild horse, which went about its business without

disturbing him. On another occasion, his heart almost stopped short with fright when a tremendous crashing burst forth from a little clump of woods just ahead; but having sought his usual retreat among the branches, he observed the enormous, hairy light-brown bulks and immense curving tusks of two mammoths, and noted with relief that the beasts were evidently in a sportive mood, for they went ambling out of sight with trunks playfully waving, apparently oblivious to any creature so puny as man.

As he glided through the woods and along the shore of the lake, Ru stopped now and then to pluck berries from the dense clusters of bushes; or else to gather certain familiar roots, which he washed in the lake waters and then devoured without further preparation, masticating their tough fibers long and vigorously with his huge grinding teeth. Even so, he had difficulty to find sufficient nourishment; and though he lost nearly half his time in the search for food, he was conscious of an increasing hunger as the long hours of the day dragged wearily past.

So many were the delays, and so circuitous the route he had to follow, that twilight was descending by the time he had reached the Harr-Sizz River. To arrive before dark at the crossing-place of his tribe was now out of the question; and so, with renewed forebodings, he began to look about him for a suitable tree for the night's lodging.

But it did not take him long to decide. While he

was peering contemplatively at the serene blue lake and the plunging river and the long graceful lines of the forest, he was startled by a cry that suddenly broke from the depths of the wood. . . . Long-drawn and shrill, it shrieked and screamed with a savagery as of some challenging beast, an utter ferocity that made his blood run cold. Yet it was not the call of a beast; despite its demoniac fierceness, it was unmistakably and horribly human; and it rang and echoed at first with a fiendish menace, then with a note almost of triumph, of exultation, as of a devil rejoicing.

Following the cry, and blending with its final tones, there burst forth another and even more blood-curdling yell—a howl as of extreme terror, of hatred, of agony. Swiftly rising in a crescendo, it ended abruptly in a half-stifled moan; then came a series of moans and dreadful gasps, as of some creature writhing in torment; then once more the shrill challenging voice, followed by other voices screeching in wild glee or still wilder terror; then the sounds of scuffling and heavy blows mingled with a clamorous confusion of voices that chorused like a din of demons, but gradually and slowly died down, until the silence of the vast solitudes once more covered all things.

Long before those cries had ended, Ru was perched among the tree tops. Clinging to the upper branches, well out of sight of the ground, he sat as still as though he were a man of wood; yet his wide-open eyes were alert with wonder and fear, and his ears missed not one note or tremor of the mysterious tumult. Who might those strange combatants be? he inquired of himself; and he trembled merely at the knowledge that they were human. For a moment it came to him that—ferocious as they were —they were perhaps his own people; but he dismissed the thought instantly, for the voices had in them a savagery surpassing even that of the Umbaddu. But, if not his own people, who could they be? He had never been told that there was any tribe in the world except his own; but there were old legends—legends ridiculed by the wiser tribesmen —that other peoples existed, and that some of these were brutal and fierce as wolves.

While remembrance of these discredited legends was troubling Ru's mind, the twilight was gradually deepening, and utter darkness was stealing down about him. And through the gathering night, in the direction whence the voices proceeded, he was amazed to observe a faint glow—so dim at first that he could not be sure whether he had not merely imagined it, then by slow degrees brightening into unmistakable reality: a ruddy luminance that seemed to issue from beyond the tree tops, filling the spaces just above the black rim of the foliage with a flickering ghostly light, which wavered and rose and wavered and rose with uncanny fitfulness. And in the midst of that appalling radiance, whose pale red was of an indescribable ghastliness, there shot forth from time to time little yellow sparks, which leaped up brightly against the sultry background and instantly vanished.

By this time Ru had forgotten the legends about

strange tribes of men. He was remembering tales
that old men told on winter evenings beside the firelight—tales of red goblins that danced and sported
in the woods at night, with eyes of flame, which
could shrivel a man to ashes, and claws of flame,
which could strike through the trees like lightning.

As the slow, anxious minutes wore away, Ru
caught no glimpse of the dreaded ones, although
the weird, wavering light continued to trouble him,
and now and then, by straining his ears, he thought
he could hear that which sounded suspiciously like
a murmuring of voices. But he could not be certain; and, as time went by, the ruddy glow grew
dimmer, and at last only the far-off querulous calls
of bird and beast disturbed the profound silence of
the night. Then gradually the lonely watcher succumbed to the lulling mood of the woods; and forgetting his doubts and solitude and terror, he folded
his arms about the limbs of the tree as about a
dearly loved friend, and slipped into a delicious
dream that he was back again among the comforts
of the old familiar cave.

CHAPTER X

The Men of the Woods

WHEN Ru awoke, the mysterious light had disappeared; and in its place the first pale glimmer of day was newly revealing the world. The night's adventures now seemed so extraordinary that Ru wondered vaguely whether he had not merely dreamed them; and when the heartening morning light had filled all things, he could hardly understand why he had been so frightened.

As by degrees his courage returned, he felt the proddings of that slyest of temptresses, curiosity. What had been the meaning of that which he had seen and heard? Would it not be possible to find out, and find out safely? Might he not even make some marvelous discovery? learn of the existence of some people akin to his own? perhaps even find friends among that unknown people?

Realizing his danger, and yet resolved to tread so cautiously that he might seek refuge in the trees at the first suspicious sign, Ru descended from his leafy perch, regained his club, and warily set out in the direction of the night's terrifying sights and sounds.

At first, as he made his way through those

shadow-dim woods, treading noiselessly on the thick matting of dead leaves and scrupulously avoiding the dense clumps of underbrush, Ru observed nothing out of the ordinary. Here and there some little bird, rustling unseen among the shrubs and vines, made him stop short in quickly conquered alarm; here and there some squirrel would flash into view and out again, with bright beady eyes alertly glittering. But, except for such harmless creatures, there was no sign of life, and the great wilderness stretched before him, silent and undisturbed.

He was almost convinced that he should discover nothing—that he had taken the wrong direction, or that there was nothing to be found—when his keen eyes caught a telltale mark in the soft soil. Faintly traced in the midst of a narrow open space was the imprint of a foot—a human foot of gigantic proportions!

For a moment Ru stared in surprise and dread. Fearfully he glanced toward the trees, lest one of a race of giants be watching him unseen; then he began to inspect the ground on all sides, and speedily discovered scores of similar footprints! That they had not all been made by one individual was apparent from their difference in size; and that they had not been left by his tribesmen was evident from the fact that several of the unknowns were lacking in one or more toes.

Tracing the footprints toward what appeared to be their source, he forgot for the moment his own

possible peril. Curiosity still led him on blindly—
with every step he was finding fresh evidence of unaccountable things. He was appalled at sight of a
great blur of clotted blood at the edge of a fallen
tree, and at sight of numerous sinister-looking red-
dish spots and patches. In a secluded little pocket
of the glade, he observed that the herbs and grass
had been beaten down as though in some terrific
struggle, and here too were the same ghastly blots
of red; and finally, when an uncanny creeping sensation was running down his spine and his better
judgment was counseling him to flee, he beheld that
which stabbed his mind with such sudden and overwhelming horror that the memory was not to leave
him until his dying day.

Huddled in a cluster of shrubbery at one end of
the glade, was a gruesome apparition that seemed
half man and half beast—more beast than man, for
surely this great motionless hairy bulk could not be
human. It lay slumped among the bushes as though
it had crept there to breathe its last; an intermittent
trail of blood led from it to the open spaces; its
huge apelike head drooped almost to the ground,
with enormous jaws agape, thick lips slimy with
coagulated foam, and glazed little black eyes sight-
lessly staring. On its broad shaggy chest the crimson gore was matted, while its battered right temple
was little more than a clot of red.

With a low cry of alarm, Ru drew back. He did
not take time for a second glimpse; in a panic, he
raced away, raced straight across the open and

toward the farther woods—scarcely knowing where he was going, filled only with a mad desire to escape that bloody terror in the bushes.

But, in his impetuosity, he was to dash directly upon a still more alarming scene.

From the place of the strange footprints and blood-marks, he fled into an adjoining and larger glade. Almost in the center of this grass-covered opening, he stopped short in fresh terror; and his startled eyes surveyed the ground at first without full realization, but with gradually growing comprehension—comprehension of the most fearful deed that even those savage days could boast. The appalling fact was not that the ashes of a camp-fire lay before him, a few of the embers still dully smoldering—this he had half expected to find; it was not that the relics of a feast lay scattered among the weeds and grass, which reeked of the entrails of animals, discarded bits of hide and fat, and crushed and shattered bones. That which made Ru shudder and quail was that the feast had evidently not been confined to animal fare. From a recess between two rocks, a gaunt blood-stained skull leered at him, bits of flesh still clinging to the brow, the brain-cast battered as by a heavy blow.

With a gasp of revulsion, Ru recognized that it was the skull of a man! And on the ground beside it he detected scraps of reddened human skin and hair, split and charred human thigh-bones emptied of marrow, and severed human fingers and toes!

Slowly, like one half stunned by a blow, Ru

started to retreat. His horror-stricken eyes searched the borders of the glade for sight of the dread feasters; his limbs began to tremble uncontrollably beneath him. Fortunately, there was no sign of anything menacing; neither beast nor human challenged him before he had gained the bushes and vanished.

But as he stole away into the underbrush, he heard that which seemed to confirm his worst fears. From across the open space a renewed tumult startled him—a tumult as of voices calling. They were heavy and raucous, like the voices of his tribesmen, yet the accentuation was not that of his people—and they had in them a bestial note like that of prowling wild creatures.

But who they might be Ru did not seek to discover. At as rapid a pace as he could maintain without making a telltale noise, he picked his way among the thickets in the direction of the lake. Thorns pricked his hands, sharp stones cut his feet, bloodsucking insects alighted upon his unprotected skin—but he did not notice; in his mind was a ravening dread that drove him on like a goad of fire. Had the terrible unknowns discovered his presence? Hearing him, had they returned? and, observing his footprints, were they even now following on his trail? Were they—though built in his own form—hunting him as man hunts beast? And was there danger that they would overtake him, strike him down, and—

But here Ru's imagination reached a barrier that it would not cross. He recalled the scraps of human

skin and flesh scattered about the burnt-out camp-
fire—and at this abhorrent memory he shuddered,
thought of old tales of men that ate men, and
strained to quicken his gait.

From time to time, as he glided beneath the trees
and through the tangle of bushes and shrubs, he
paused to listen for the sound of possible pursuit.
At first he heard no more than the heavy pounding
of his own heart; a moment afterwards, he could
make out only the fussing and chattering of some
gossipy bird; but not much later he detected a suspicious crackling and rustling in the brush.

Was it only the noise of some browsing beast?
Ru did not take time to find out. Forgetting all
caution in his panic, he darted down the long
meandering twilight aisles at the speed of the
hounded wild thing, while the squirrels leaped from
his path with startled eyes, and frightened flocks
of wood-doves made way for him with a heavy
flapping of wings.

Somewhat to his surprise, he came out suddenly
at the shores of the lake. For a moment he halted
in confusion; then recognized the long sandy beach
that he had passed only yesterday afternoon.

Straining every muscle, he began to dash along
the shore toward the mouth of the Harr-Sizz River.
Several minutes passed; he had covered hundreds
of yards; all was silent again, and there was no sign
of approaching peril. He was just beginning to believe that he would elude his pursuers, when a sudden shrill shouting broke the stillness of the
woods. . . .

At that crisis his heart gave a terrific thump. His brain worked with lightning rapidity. If he took once more to the forest, his tracks would be found, the pursuit would be renewed, and, driven to exhaustion, he would probably be overtaken. His only refuge therefore lay in the waters. Not in swimming, for he could not swim far enough or fast enough; the one hope was in his new-found means of propulsion.

And good fortune favored him, for a little distance down the beach lay a fair-sized drifted tree trunk, resting more than half in the water. With an effort, he set the huge mass afloat; then waded in after it and pushed it as far as possible from shore; and finally, equipped with his club as paddle, he climbed to a precarious seat astride the log, and shoved and shoved until he was·well out in the lake.

He was perhaps a hundred paces from land, when an enormous shambling shape shouldered out of the woods and halted on the beach. At this distance Ru could hardly be sure that it was not one of his own people; like them, it was thick-set and stocky, with monstrously developed shaggy black limbs. But it was even more hairy than his tribesmen; it wore no clothes at all; and its great form was unusually bent and stooped, while its long arms slid down in front of it almost to its knees.

For an instant the creature paused on the beach, peering about it in all directions as if bewildered. Then, sighting Ru where he was struggling with his unwieldy craft, it let out a long-drawn ferocious bellow of rage; in response to which half a dozen of its fellows, all likewise stooping and unclad, came plunging and snorting out of the woods.

There followed a moment's silence, during which they all stared at Ru in obvious amazement, meanwhile pointing to him significantly with their hairy arms. Then all at once there rang forth a chorus of shrieks and howls such as Ru had rarely heard before. In it was a peculiar blood-curdling note not to be described, except that it had something of the growling menace of the cave-bear, and something of the yelping fierceness of the sabertooth— and Ru knew that it was this cry that had so terrified him last night among the tree tops.

But now the only effect of those screams was to make Ru push even more desperately away from shore. Such was his haste that once or twice he lost his balance and slipped into the water, and several times struck his own legs painfully with the paddle.

Recognizing that all their clamoring was gaining them nothing, the howling ones dropped suddenly into silence; and, picking up small stones and pebbles, began to hurl them furiously at Ru. Their aim was good, and the missiles went hurtling through the air at tremendous speed; but the fugitive was already out of range; and the pebbles splashed harmlessly in a little shower to his rear.

Angry mutterings now sounded from the throats of the stone-throwers. With deep-voiced growls and grumblings, three or four of them strode out into

the water after their fleeing prey. Ru's alarm grew
by leaps and bounds as the wavelets broke first over
their knees, then over their thighs, then almost up
to their sloping shoulders and bull-like necks—and
his dread turned to actual terror when he observed
them swimming, swimming toward him with rapid
and powerful strokes! Through the fast-diminish-
ing distance, he could watch their hideous round
heads bobbing up and down, could see the gleam
of the fiendish little eyes and the brutish lines of
the heavy eye-ridges.

On and on they came; their great arms clove the
water with the easy, regular strokes of accomplished
swimmers; their hairy, baboonish faces were twisted
into diabolical grins. And Ru, though he tugged and
pushed at his pole with all his force, could not
match the speed of his pursuers; the space between
them steadily grew less and less until it measured
but a stone's throw.

Like a pack of wolves upon a cornered deer, they
pressed nearer, still nearer, until he could see the
white glittering of their enormous teeth and make
out the clotted blood-streaks on their outthrust
arms. Then a sudden idea come to Ru. Abruptly
he ceased his paddling; carefully he balanced himself on the broadest and flattest part of the log.
And into his anxious face and pale gray eyes a
grim smile flitted as he stood there and waited.

But his pursuers seemed not to suspect that anything was amiss. An evil leer lighted the eyes of the
swiftest of the band as he drew near; he muttered

in savage triumph as he stretched out a massive black arm toward the log where Ru stood.

But his arm was never to reach the log. In a flash Ru had swung his paddle from its hiding-place behind him; and with a dull thud the heavy stick came down upon the head of his assailant.

The swimmer sank back with a low piteous moan. His form collapsed helplessly into the waters; there was a sudden floundering of arms, a gurgling, a few bubbles—and one man less was afloat upon the lake.

Still with a grim smile, Ru looked out across the waters. Not fifty feet away, two or three dark bobbing faces were peering at him hesitatingly. Ru held his place firmly on the log, shouted a challenge, and swung his club angrily. And the swimmers, after a moment's indecision, made unexpected response to the threat—of one accord, they turned and energetically splashed their way shoreward.

CHAPTER XI

The Return of Ru

TWO or three hours had passed before Ru would venture away from the shelter of the lake. And when finally he paddled to land, he chose a point a mile or more from the scene of the conflict—a secluded little inlet not far below the mouth of the Harr-Sizz River. Here, he knew, he was secure from the gaze of his foes, even had they been watching for him. But he could not be sure that others of their kind were not lurking in the woods; and it was with extreme caution that he took his way along the beaches and around the dense clumps of greenery, his club gripped in readiness for immediate action.

No sign of anything hostile appeared, however, save now and then a serpent squirming out of his path. Neither wild beast nor wild man seemed to be abroad; he gained the Harr-Sizz River unmolested; and, with tension relaxed, followed its turbulent course toward the spot where his tribe had crossed.

This point proved to be somewhat farther than he had expected. More than once, as he glided through the seemingly endless woods just above the river bank, he asked himself whether he might not be following the wrong stream by mistake. But he continued in spite of his doubts; and at last, shortly before sundown, his efforts were rewarded. Rounding an abrupt turn in the river, he recognized all of a sudden the scene of his recent misfortune, the fording place of his people.

After a few minutes' search, he found the clear marks of their passage. Innumerable tracks stared at him from the soft soil, as plainly as if made only that day—tracks of all sizes, which wandered from the river bank into the shadowy wilderness, trampling down the grass and underbrush and curving through the open spaces in long meandering loops.

It was with mixed feelings that Ru read these silent messages from his kinsmen. He had something of the feelings of an exile who beholds from afar the shore-line of his country; the full bitterness of his loneliness flooded back over him again, the sense of isolation and of loss, mingled with renewed anger that—through no fault of his own—he should have been subjected to such humiliation, suffering, and peril. But, above all, the remembrance of Yonyo the Smiling-Eyed came back to him. Useless for him to reflect that she was unworthy of his attention, that she would only laugh at his wretchedness, ridicule his misfortunes, and contemptuously forget him were he to die—the thought of her filled him at once with fury and with a deep but tender emotion.

Yet Ru lost no time in idle ruminations. Having

found his people's tracks, he followed them as far as the waning daylight permitted, then warily set about the business of finding a tree for the night.

This time he was to be disturbed by no mysterious screams. There were only the usual night noises— the cry of some nocturnal bird, the far-off call of some predatory beast, the stirring and the rustling of the breeze amid the foliage.

The following morning he awakened in happier spirits. Now, for the first time, he felt that he was actually on the way back to his people! He realized, to be sure, that they had preceded him by nearly three days; but, retarded as they were by implements and provisions, by women with babes in arms and by the younger children, they could travel no farther in two hours than he could travel in one.

For many miles he followed hopefully on their trail, which ran through the forest up a slope that ascended first gently and then with bold and difficult grades, until Ru realized with apprehension that he was climbing a mountainside. Enormous boulders littered his way, and there were places where he had to crawl on hands and knees up the steep and jutting rocks; a tumultuous stream ran at his side, foaming in loud rapids or plunging in cascades; above him, through rifts in the woods, he caught glimpses from time to time of appalling slopes of white. Had his people mounted straight into that snowy desolation? He could not believe they had; but that they had passed this way was all too evident, not only from their tracks where the soil was damp and leaf-matted, but from the clues they had left even in the rockier places—here a flint tool that had been unwittingly dropped; there the rib of a buffalo or wild boar, chewed and discarded; yonder the torn-off strip of a deerskin robe.

Once or twice, indeed, Ru did fear that he had lost the tracks, and for a while wandered about aimlessly amid a stony wilderness. But always, after a few minutes, he discovered some reassuring token, and continued on his way. The sun stood about midway in the heavens when at length, to his relief, the trail swerved and led him over an open shoulder of the mountain, then down toward a gently sloping wooded valley, so wide that the farther end was lost in a blue haze.

Not far below the divide, and just above the border of the woods, Ru paused in sudden consternation. His watchful eyes had detected a little reddened bit of stone in a crevice between two boulders—one of the flint knives used by his people! Stooping down eagerly and seizing the implement, he examined it in uncertainty—could the clotted blood on the edge be that of some slaughtered beast? There was no possibility of proof; but Ru remembered once more the man-eating savages he had encountered, and wondered with what bloodthirsty foe his tribe had clashed.

A few yards farther down the slope he found other signs to confirm his misgivings. From a clump of dense brush he observed a bit of fur protruding; and he pulled forth a long strip of bison hide

of the size of one of his tribesmen's robes! In the
center it was pierced as by some' half blunt implement; and on the ragged edge of the cut were
streaks and blots of crimson.

As if this evidence were not sufficient, the very
ground beneath him bore witness to a conflict. In
places the weeds and shrubs had been crushed or
uprooted, and lay torn and broken in withering
masses; in places even the stones seemed to have
been dislocated, and sharply outlined holes in the
soil testified to where large rocks had been; while
in one spot there was a blur of footprints, crowding on top of each other, and most of them half
obliterated—some pointing up-hill and some down-
hill, as though from the mad surging of a multitude.

Half persuaded that some dire fate had overtaken his people, Ru hastened on into the woods,
guided by a swarm of tracks, which might have been
those of his tribesmen and might have been those
of their foes. What terrific struggle had taken place
during his absence? he asked himself again and
again, as he glided noiselessly through those dim
winding forest spaces. In his mind there was no
longer a doubt that his people had battled some
strange tribe; but what the issue of the conflict had
been, and how many of his kinsmen had survived
to tell the tale, were questions for which he could
have no answers.

Nor did he expect an answer for several days—
if at all. If the Umbaddu had fled before some

marauding foe, they must already be many hours away. And what if the enemy barred the path between him and his people, so that he would have no way of reaching them?

But a great surprise lay in store for him. Approaching a break in the forest not half a dozen miles below the scene of the ominous footprints, he was startled by hearing a faint murmuring of voices, which gradually grew louder as he stole warily forward through the shadows, until it was recognizable as the gibbering of a multitude.

A shudder of fear shot through Ru's heart. Might he not again be approaching a settlement of the man-eaters? Halting abruptly, he stood as though petrified; his impulse was to flee while flight might still be of avail. Yet once again curiosity mastered him—curiosity, and a glad surmise which seemed too fantastic to be true. Cautious not to expose his presence by a sound or a gesture, he crept forward inch by inch like a prowling cat, his shoulders bent far toward the ground, his arms reaching down beneath his knees, his frightened gray eyes alert for the least suspicious sound or movement.

But there was nothing suspicious to interrupt his progress. And at length, after a few minutes that seemed interminable, he reached the final line of the bushes; at length he was able to push the concealing leaves gently aside, and to peer out upon the meadow from which the gibbering voices still proceeded.

At the first glance, he uttered a low exclamation of relief. And impetuously he rose to his full height—the need for concealment was over!

Sprawled in a rude circle by the banks of a river, were scores of familiar fur-clad figures!

Trembling with happiness, Ru strode forward to meet them. "My people! My people!" it was on his lips to say, when he observed that his arrival was creating a peculiar effect.

Immediately upon his emergence, some of the nearer tribesmen had sprung to their feet, startled and amazed—as well they might be! As if at an electrical signal, others followed their example, with little shocked and horrified exclamations, until, almost in a flash, the entire tribe stood confronting him speechlessly.

Overpowered though he was by his own astonishment, Ru could see that the eyes of some were distended with terror; that the limbs of others were quivering; that the lips of one were moving silently as if in frightened prayer.

Before he could find words to demand the reason for this strange reception, the explanation was shrilled into his ears.

"It's Ru! It's the Sparrow-Hearted! It's his dead spirit come back!" shrieked one of the younger tribesmen, taking to his heels. And the others took up his cry, "It's his dead spirit come back!" until those fearsome words echoed and reechoed in a terrified din, and on all sides the panic-stricken people were fleeing toward the woods.

For an instant the bewildered Ru did not quite grasp what was happening. Then, as full understanding came to him, his paralyzed tongue was loosened, and he shouted, at the top of his voice, "It is no spirit you see! It is I, Ru! It is Ru come back to you!"

But so thoroughly alarmed were the people that most of them continued full-tilt toward the woods, as if the shouted words only confirmed their belief that they had seen a ghost.

Yet two or three, less timorous than their fellows, did turn at the sound of Ru's voice. While he continued to cry, "It is only I come back! I will not harm you!" they seemed half convinced that he spoke the truth, and began tentatively and hesitatingly to approach.

By some peculiar chance, these audacious spirits were all women. And among them Ru recognized, with a tremor of delight, Zubu the Prattling Brook and Yonyo the Smiling-Eyed!

It did not now seem to matter that the tribe had fled. As Yonyo drew near, Ru entirely forgot his vanished kinsmen under the fascination of those glittering black eyes.

"So the Sparrow-Hearted has come back?" she called, striding ahead of her more cautious tribeswomen, and coming almost within touching distance of the supposed phantom. "For three days already we have believed the Sparrow-Hearted drowned." And half tauntingly, and with an admonishing smile, she added: "It is not right to pretend to pass the great mountains of the dead."

"Oh, Yonyo, I did not pretend!" he pleaded. And then, as she came within arm's grasp and halted, he felt once more the full fury of his loneliness and of his longing for her.

"Are you not glad to see me back, Yonyo?" he cried. "Do you have no word of joy for me? Is it nothing to you that I have been saved from the wild beasts, and from men more savage than wolves? Oh, Yonyo, do you not care?"

One of her most taunting, tantalizing smiles overspread her face; and he could not be certain whether she intended to reassure him or to dash all hope from his heart.

But her reply, although trembling on her lips, was never to be spoken, for at that instant Zubu the Prattling Brook came panting up to him; and, scarcely taking time to regain her breath, burst into a storm of questions.

"Ru, where have you been all these days? Have you not been drowned, as Kuff and Woonoo said? Have you not gone beyond the mountains of the sky, where those spirits live who can never come back? Or have you been there and escaped? Have you done that wonderful deed? Have you been dead, Ru, and walked down from the sky?"

"Yes, I have been dead, and walked down from the sky," he assured her, on an impulse that startled even himself. And as an awestricken light came into her eyes, he felt an audacious plan gathering form and power within him.

"I have been dead, and come back!" he repeated, with a boldness born of the effect his words had produced. "I am the only man who has ever escaped from the great wind-spirit that blows beyond the last mountains. Woonoo and Kuff spoke truth when they said they saw me drowned. For a whole day my body lay under the water, and I could not move nor speak; and in that day my spirit flew far, far away, and saw things that no man has ever seen before. But of all that I shall tell you later."

By this time two or three more women, observing that the apparition had not harmed Yonyo or Zubu, had approached and silently joined the group. They too gaped in wide-eyed wonder; but not a murmur of doubt or incredulity escaped their lips.

"Tell us more!" they begged, when Ru cut his recitation short. "Do not wait! Tell us more, Ru! We want to know what happened to you beyond the last mountains!"

"I cannot tell you until all our people are here to listen," declared Ru, with finality. "Go, call the people—and when they are all here, I shall speak of the strange things that happened to me."

And while several of the women hastened away to reassemble their frightened tribesfolk, Ru's imagination was busy constructing a story fitted to astound his kinsmen.

But even as he reflected, he took care to observe his surroundings; his eyes traveled appraisingly from detail to detail of the landscape. He noted that he stood in the midst of a small tract of grassland, bounded on three sides by the woods, and on the fourth by the river; and he was surprised to see how wide was the stream—wider than he had ever known any man to swim, so wide that the trees on the opposite bank made little more than a dim blur. Near the edge of the waters, whose current was so slow as to be barely perceptible, he beheld the ashes of three or four camp-fires, one of which was still smoldering feebly; while in several spots were unsightly piles of picked bones or of the discarded entrails of animals.

Glancing out across the broad reaches of the river, Ru could surmise the reason why his tribe had halted. But there was much about their recent adventures that he could not surmise—much that perplexed and troubled him, particularly since he saw several of his tribesmen returning with red gashes in their heads and foreheads, or with broken arms dangling limply from their shoulders.

Hence, while he stood awaiting his people's return, he asked Yonyo to relate all that had happened during his absence.

To his disappointment, it was not Yonyo that replied. A faint smile came into her eyes, though whether of acquiescence or refusal he could not say; but, almost before she had had time to speak, Zubu the Prattling-Brook—evidently thinking the question addressed to her—launched into an eager recital.

"Ever since we left the Harr-Sizz River," she said, "bad spirits have been with us. When we had gone as far from the stream as a man can run at top speed, an evil sign appeared: a strange beast, with great paws and growling lips, and two teeth as long as your arms. At this terrible sight, we all ran for the trees. But before we could get there, we heard a woman cry out horribly; and we saw the beast sneaking away into the woods, trailing the body of poor old Awoo.

"When Zunzun the Marvel-Worker heard about this, he looked very sad, and said that evil days were ahead. He thought that the good spirits were angry because we had left our cave; and he told us the bad spirits would come and take many more of us away. And he began to groan and grumble, and I heard him say we should all turn around and go back to our cave.

"But Grumgra the Growling Wolf swung his club very heavily, and there was no one that would cry out when he was near. For a while we all trembled and were much afraid, and there was nothing we could do. But Zunzun the Marvel-Worker was right when he said we should go back to our cave, for at last a terrible thing was made known. We had climbed a long mountain and were on an open space near the top, when we all stopped and Mumlo the Trail-Finder looked around him as if he did not know whether to go up or down. Then someone heard him say we had gone the wrong way! He did not think he had ever seen this mountain before! And no one knew where we were or where we were going!"

Zubu paused, and her tiny black eyes were softened momentarily with a sad expression. Then, while several of her kinsmen silently came up and joined the group, she continued:

"You do not know, Ru, what a bad time we had then. You should have seen the way Grumgra howled and swung his club, so that Mumlo had to keep hidden all the time. Nearly everyone was screaming like a frightened animal, but Grumgra's voice was the loudest of all. He cried out that we must keep on toward the noonday sun even if we did not know the way. And everyone was afraid to say no, until suddenly there came a yell from one corner of our camp—and we saw the beast with the teeth as long as a man's leg; and he ran away with another of our people.

"Some of us now cried out that this was a sign from the gods of the woods that we must not go on. And Zunzun said they would punish us, and turn us all into meat for the wild beasts; and then all the people were so frightened that they were like wild beasts themselves. Many of us shouted that we would not go on and let ourselves be eaten by the evil things of the woods; and we said that we wanted to go back again to our old cave. Then came Grumgra, swinging his club; and he roared that we must go on; but this time we were too frightened to do as he told us. Some of the other men swung their clubs and growled when Grumgra came their way—yes, growled and swung their clubs against Grumgra himself!"

"And what then?" demanded Ru, in breathless interest, when the Prattling Brook came to a sudden stop. "Did the Growling Wolf have to do as they wanted?"

"The Growling Wolf never does as anyone wants," pointed out Zubu; and her eyes shone with admiration of the leader. "There was a fight—but do we not know how any fight will end when Grumgra is in it? There was much swinging of clubs, and much throwing of stones, and striking of heavy blows, and shouting and hissing of oaths; and some were on Grumgra's side, and some on Zunzun's side, and some on neither side—they just fought for the fun of fighting. All the while half of us women stood watching, and crying out for our own men to win; but the other half did not want to watch, but left their babes and fought with the men—and very good fighters they were, too!

"When at last everything was over, two of our people lay bleeding on the ground, and could not rise again; and most of the rest of us were hurt on the arms or legs or shoulders. But those on Grumgra's side were not hurt so much as those on Zunzun's, for many a man had known the touch of Grumgra's club. And in the end we all cried out that we would do as Grumgra said, since one so mighty as he could not be wrong. And then Grumgra and Zunzun were friends once more, and the Marvel-Worker said we should go with Grumgra anywhere, for he was stronger than the beast with the teeth as long as a man's whole body.

"Yet"—here Zubu hesitated perceptibly, and her face was overspread by a rueful smile—"they have not been able to go with him past this river. It is very deep, and so wide we cannot swim across, and no man knows what to do, whether to go along its banks, or turn back, or—"

"Then did you meet no tribes of wild men?" interrupted Ru, unable to suppress the question that had been uppermost in his mind for hours. "You only fought with yourselves? You saw no men that eat other men?"

"Men that eat other men?" echoed several of the hearers, bursting into laughter. And, remembering the old discredited legends about human man-eaters, one of the women muttered to herself, "Ru has been hearing silly stories!" And one or two nudged their neighbors and murmured slyly, but loud enough for Ru to hear, "The Sparrow-Hearted is having dreams again!"

But before Ru could frame a retort, a great lumbering figure burst into view from a recess in the woods, and began to approach at a brisk pace. And a silence fell across the little assemblage, for who could be merry when Grumgra the Growling Wolf was drawing near?

CHAPTER XII

The Tale of the Wind-God

WITHOUT a word of greeting or recognition, Grumgra came shambling up to Ru. Then, while his people drew back before him and he brought his club with a thud to the ground, he burst into a bellowing query: "Where have you been all these days, O Sparrow-Hearted? Why have you left your people when they were in need of you? Woonoo the Hot-Blooded and Kuff the Bear-Hunter brought word that you were drowned. Is it that you have escaped from the great wind-spirit?"

"Yes, O chief, I have escaped from the great wind-spirit," replied Ru, now thoroughly determined upon his course. "When all the people are here, I will tell them how."

A hard light came into the black little eyes of Grumgra, and his heavy brows contracted into a scowl. "Tell them, then!" he assented, gruffly. "But let every word you speak be the truth! For if it be not truth, you will have to be punished!"

Here Grumgra lightly fondled his club. And Ru—for all his self-assurance—edged away fearfully as he beheld the hostile glitter in the eyes of the chieftain.

And it was not without misgivings that he began his recital a few minutes later. Standing in the center of a small open space, with his tribesmen squatting in a rude circle about him, he felt just a little disconcerted at finding himself once more the focus of the eyes of all his people. Vividly he recalled the last occasion—when he had received the brand that still disfigured his throat and chest; and he well knew that his failure today might incur another and even more painful penalty.

"Make yourselves ready to hear wonderful things, my people," he began. "It is very strange that I am with you now, for I was drowned in the Harr-Sizz River, and my body was taken far away by the waters. Woonoo the Hot-Blooded and Kuff the Bear-Hunter will tell you so, for they saw me drown. Is that not so, my brothers?"

With a smile, Ru turned and pointed to Kuff and Woonoo; and both growled unwilling agreement.

"Now do you want to know how it is I came back to you?" resumed Ru. "Ask the river-spirit, and he will tell you! I lay long under the water, and it was cold and wet and dark, and I could not cry out and could not even breathe. At last, after a long, long while, I heard voices speaking—strange and terrible voices as loud as thunder. One was the voice of the river-spirit, and the other was the voice of that great wind-spirit who blows beyond the last mountains. And the wind-spirit said, 'Let me have Ru! I want him! He is mine!' But the river-spirit answered, 'No! I will keep him! He is mine!'

"They argued and argued so long I thought many suns must have gone down and come up again while I lay there in the water. And the wind roared, and the river rushed and foamed; but they did not know which was to have me. In the end, they said, 'Let us each take half of him! Let his body stay here in the water, but let the wind have that part of him that thinks and feels.' And straightway this was done.

"Now I did not feel cold and wet any more, and it was no longer dark. But I flew through the air like a bird, and I felt the arms of the wind-god about me; and I went over wide forests and high mountains, until I came to a great cloud all bright with the colors of sunset. And in this cloud was the lair of the wind-god; and he led me in, up into a great cave whose walls were red and yellow like the falling leaves in the season of frost. And he bade me stay there and be happy, for I was with friends —and there I met Grop the Tree-Climber and Wamwa the Snake-Eyed and all our tribesmen that we lost long, long ago and shall see no more.

"But I could not be happy, for I remembered my people here in the forest, and I knew that they needed me. And I begged the wind-god to let me go, but he would not. He said, 'No one has ever left here yet'—and so I thought I must stay there more days than there are sands by the bank of a river. And it would have been thus, had I not done a wonderful thing for the wind-god. Soon after I came there, a strange beast walked into that cave—like a bear, but much larger, for his claws were the size of Grumgra's club, and each of his teeth was as big as a man. And his eyes were of fire, and his whole body shone like the sun, and when he growled I thought it was thundering. Even the wind-god was afraid and did not know what to do; and even he might have been killed, if I had not thought of a way to fight the beast.

" 'O wind-god,' I said, 'blind his eyes with your mists!' And this the wind-god did; and soon the great beast walked in a fog, and could not see any more. And it howled fiercely, like many wolves, and fell through a hole in the cave floor, and was killed on the rocks below!"

Ru paused; and two hundred pairs of black eyes gaped at him in unconcealed wonder.

"Tell us more! Tell us more!" came several eager cries, when the delay threatened to become protracted. And, satisfied with the astonished but not incredulous looks that greeted him on all sides, Ru continued blandly:

"When I told the wind-god how to save his cave, he was so happy that he blew all around me with a great glad noise, like that of waters falling in the forest. Then after a while he grew quiet again, and came over to me so gently that I could hardly feel him blowing upon my cheeks. 'A man like you,' he said to me, 'is very much needed by your people. You would do great things for them. If the river-god will let me, I will reward you by sending you back to them.'

"And then suddenly I had left the cave, and the wind-spirit was lifting me throught the air again; and I crossed back over the great forests and tall mountains, until I saw the Harr-Sizz River running like a snake beneath me. And I was very glad, for I knew that I was coming back home. But soon I felt myself go down into the river again; and it was cold and dark and wet, and I lay on the bottom once more, and could not move or speak.

"But I heard the wind-god talking to the river-god. 'Let Ru go!' he said. 'His people need him! He will do great things for them! I will give up my half of him, if you will give up yours.' But at first the river-god did not want to give up his half of me, for it was hard for him to get someone he liked so well. And the wind-god had to blow very hard and get very angry and stir up big waves before at last the river-god let me come up from the bottom and walk once more on the land.

"And that, my people, is my story. For two days already I have been out of the river; and all that time I have been coming back to you, so that I might be with you when you needed me. The wind-god has shown me how to find you, and will always be at my side and help me."

Ru ceased, and dropped to a seat among his fellows. For a moment an awed silence held the audience; then, as the spell was gradually dispersed, a torrent of questions burst forth; and Ru was showered with innumerable inquiries as to the wind-spirit and the river-spirit, and what they looked like and how they acted, and how it felt to be under the river and how terrifying it was to see the shining monster in the cave of the clouds. Although sometimes hard-pressed, Ru answered every question with great seriousness; and, in so doing, he added vastly to his descriptions, and supplied much detail of a sort to make his hearers stare and marvel.

Meanwhile many of the people sat about in small groups, chattering among themselves, discussing Ru's miraculous story. "What do you think? Is it true?" one would ask another; and brows would be contracted and grave heads would nod sagely: "Yes, it must be true, for did not Woonoo and Kuff see Ru drown?" But in other quarters the opinion would run in a different vein, although to much the same effect: "How could Ru think of such a story if it was not true? Besides, he spoke like one who tells the truth. . . . Do you not remember the tales our mothers told of how the wind-god takes dead spirits to his cave in the clouds?"

Yet, despite the general acceptance of Ru's story, there were still one or two skeptics. In most cases the doubters dared not even express their views, for fear of being overwhelmed instantly by derision and laughter; but soon it developed that there were some dissenters to whom all must listen respectfully.

After most of the questioners had flung forth their queries and been silenced by Ru's resourceful tongue, a more formidable adversary stood up suddenly amid the throng. It was Zunzun the Marvel-

Worker; and the sullen glow in his dark eyes seemed not to bode well for Ru.

"My people, do not let yourselves believe lies!" he urged, as he pointed a bony finger malevolently at his adversary. "Is it that you are all becoming like the Sparrow-Hearted, to listen to such foolish stories and think them true? No man has ever come back from the cave of the wind-spirit, and no man ever can come back. Let Ru show us that he has been in the cave of the wind-spirit! Let him show that we have need of him, as he says! Come, let him give us something more than empty air and words!"

And shaking his grizzled right arm menacingly while his eyes gleamed hostility and wrath, Zunzun slumped back to his seat on the grass.

Even while Ru opened his mouth to reply, and the throng waited gaping-eyed, a larger and more redoubtable figure towered gravely in their midst. And little murmurs of excitement traveled from end to end of the assemblage as the bellowing voice of Grumgra broke forth.

"Zunzun speaks rightly," he began. "The Sparrow-Hearted has been telling us nothing but lies. If he has been to the cave of the wind-god, he must give some sign, so that we may believe him. He must show what he can do for our people! He must call his friend the wind-god to help him!"

With a sneer that was half a snarl, Grumgra paused momentarily. Then, lifting his club high in the air and bringing it down with a thud upon the grass, he resumed: "After the sun has gone down and come up, and then gone down and come up again, Ru must show us that he speaks truth. If he cannot show us, he will be punished! And this time his punishment will not be such as we give to a child!"

And, turning to Ru with a sudden mildness that was almost genial, the Growling Wolf inquired: "But maybe you do not want to wait so long, O Sparrow-Hearted? Maybe you can show us now some sign from the clouds."

"I do not need to show you any sign from the clouds," replied Ru, slowly and thoughtfully. "But listen to this, O chief. The wind-spirit told me that he has blown past the caves of strange wild men, who wander in these woods and kill and eat other men. Be careful, O chief! For some day we may meet these beast-men! And you may find them more terrible than wolves or bears! And then you will know that I spoke truth!"

Grumgra, merely. grinning incredulously, did not reply. But from scores of throats came a rippling laughter of unbelief. Many of the people—they who had not doubted Ru's word about the wind-spirit— turned to their neighbors, and murmured: "This time the Sparrow-Hearted tells us lies! The Sparrow-Hearted only wants to frighten us!" And prolonged and hearty was the merriment at Ru's incredible report.

CHAPTER XIII

Ru Accepts the Challenge

ON the day following Ru's return, a badly needed hunt was held—for the tribe was running short of provisions, and many were the complaints that there was not meat enough. Several hours were occupied in digging pits in the rough earth by means of rude flint spades, and in covering these cavities with grass and the green limbs of trees. Since this was unfamiliar territory, however, much more than the usual time was necessary for stationing the men in a circle about the snares before the howling dash upon the prey. Yet even after the most careful precautions—and Grumgra, wielding his club, saw that the precautions were careful indeed—the hunt was a failure; all that the men gained for their efforts was two small deer and one half-grown boar.

But there was one who took no part in the hunt. While his tribesmen set off in pursuit of the game, Ru started away by himself along the bank of the river. In his gray eyes, as he ambled slowly upstream, there was a contemplative glow; while his ample brow was contracted in thoughtful furrows. He realized that he must do something spectacular before another day had passed; otherwise, his story about the wind-god would be disbelieved, and the torture of the branding would be as nothing compared to that which awaited him.

But what was he to do? He did not know; and in his mind was merely the vaguest idea about floating logs propelled by long poles . . . an idea so indefinite that it flashed into his consciousness and flashed out again as something alluring, provocative, and elusive as a dream.

He had strolled perhaps two or three miles before a lucky chance—coupled with his own quick perception—offered a solution of his problem. Rounding a turn in the river, he found himself on the shores of a placid little lake or pond opening into the stream. It was so small that he could have passed around it in two or three minutes; and no doubt he would soon have left it behind him had not his eyes been caught by that which filled him with sudden gladness. Here, in truth, was a lucky find! Half covered by the shallow water, half stranded on the sandy beach, were not less than six or eight trunks of dead trees.

It was not a minute before Ru had renewed his experiments in navigation. Using his club as paddle, he launched himself toward the middle of the pond; while, standing on a huge log, he balanced himself precariously. Or—to be more precise—he hardly balanced himself at all; time after time the log rolled and he toppled into the water, and before long he realized that it would be wiser to seat himself, as formerly, astride the log.

This he was about to do when a second log, released by his efforts, chanced to brush gently against that on which he stood. For a minute the two floated side by side, moving almost as one across the calm surface of the pond. And Ru, hoping to gain a better foothold, stationed one foot on each log—with the result that the two glided abruptly apart, and he was precipitated once more into the water.

But this time he emerged a wiser man. A sudden idea had come to him—an idea so simple that he could not understand why he had not thought of it before, and yet so amazing that at first he could only hold his breath and wonder if he were not dreaming. Suppose that he found some way of holding the two logs together!—would he not have a craft on which he might stand without fear of being plunged into the pond? Would he not be able to ride as he pleased across the waters, propelling himself by his pole, and so winning a might that even the river-god could not challenge? And would he not thereby surprise and dazzle his people? make them believe that he had indeed wonderful powers, powers that proved him especially favored by the spirits of the wind and waters?

So Ru reflected—but he did not spend much time on fruitless reveries. The problem before him was a practical one; and, with all the practical sense at his command, he set about to solve it. In constructing his new craft, the one important step would be to lash the two logs firmly together—and how could this be accomplished? Fortunately, Ru re-

Ru walks the waters

called how members of his tribe, in carrying fagots from the woods, had long been accustomed to bind them together with the tough stems and tendrils of creeping plants; and, moreover, he had long ago learned just what plants were most useful for such purposes and where to find them. So it was a matter of but an hour to go browsing through the woods, and, with the aid of flint implements, to cut off fibers enough to bind as many logs as need be.

Late that afternoon, as the Umbaddu huntsmen, laden with their meager trophies, returned gloomily from the chase, they were startled by an extraordinary sight. Coming out through a clump of bushes onto the river bank, they paused with exclamations of wonder and fear—in the midst of the waters was a spectacle such as no eye had ever rested on before since the world's beginning. Was that a man standing on a little platform in the center of the river, standing in one place and yet moving slowly down-stream, while pushing and pushing with a long pole? Was it a man, or was it a god? For what man had ever been able to stand on the waters without being drowned?

"The bad spirits of the river! The bad spirits of the river are coming after us!" cried some of the more superstitious. Hysterical with dread, they flung themselves down on the ground, and began to pray frantically. At the same time, some of their fellows fled shrieking back to the woods, and some merely watched and trembled—and all the while that terrible figure on the river kept drawing nearer, nearer.

At length it was no longer a vague black blur, but had taken on definite outlines. And, strange to say, those outlines were familiar! The watchers were amazed to see the hairy limbs and deerskin robe of one whom they recognized.

Or, if their eyes bore false reports, could their ears also deceive them? Was that not a well-known voice crying out, faintly and from afar, and yet clearly and in their own tongue: "My tribesmen, my tribesmen, look what the river-god has given me! Come, and see what the river-god has given!"

And while scores of gleaming black eyes stared out across the waters in consternation and wonder, Ru the Sparrow-Hearted rode by on his way down the river.

Half an hour later an excited group had gathered on the bank by the tribal camping-place. Men were shouting, women gibbering and crying, children racing back and forth with tumultuous exclamations; and all eyes were fastened upon a solitary form in midstream. But Ru, while he could not but know of the uproar he had caused, seemed in no hurry to come to land. He appeared not to hear his people calling, but by turns allowed himself to drift slowly down-stream, and then paddled energetically up-stream until he had regained every lost inch.

Never before had he been so much admired. "It is magic! A wizard's magic!" murmured the people; and many were the prayers offered by frightened lips and awestricken minds to Ru and the river-

god. Even Zunzun the Marvel-Worker—he for
whom magic was a daily affair—watched in a sullen
silence that made his amazement only too apparent.
Even Grumgra the Growling Wolf—he who believed in the might of clubs far more than the
might of spirits—stood staring open-mouthed and
gaping-eyed toward that wonder on the river. Whatever he may have felt, he expressed himself only
by an occasional growl; and it was not anger or
contempt that shone from those glittering ferret
eyes, but rather bewilderment tinged with what
may have been a hint of fear.

Not the least astonished of the party, and not
the least interested, was Yonyo the Smiling-Eyed.
She stared out toward the waters as intently as any
of the others, and her cries expressed as much of
wonder and awe; yet, after the spectacle had lasted
for some minutes, she succeeded in veiling her surprise, and went so far as to chaff her two companions—Kuff the Bear-Hunter and Woonoo the
Hot-Blooded.

"See! There is a real man!" she cried, pointing
to Ru. "He stands on a log—and it carries him
out across the waters! It is really nothing—any of
you could do the same—but none of you are brave
enough! No, neither you, Kuff, nor you, Woonoo,
are such a man as Ru! You could not go walking
on the river!" And long and scornful was the laughter of the Smiling-Eyed.

"I could do it! It is easy!" pleaded Woonoo,
stung by her contempt.

"I too!" chimed in Kuff, not to be outdone.

"I do not see you do it!" she flung her challenge.

For a moment Kuff and Woonoo stared at one another in uncertainty; confusion and fear shone in their eyes.

"I do not see you do it! I only hear your words!" taunted Yonyo. "Are you going to let the Sparrow-Hearted laugh at you?"

This gibe was more than Woonoo could endure. With an angry cry, he pointed to a fallen tree that lay near the river at the verge of the forest. "Come!" he growled, and, with Kuff at his heels, started hastily away.

By means of a tremendous straining and tugging, the two men pulled the log into the water. Before they had succeeded, a crowd had been attracted by their noise and exertions, and had gathered shouting about them. Among the onlookers, the gigantic form of the chieftain was conspicuous.

It was Woonoo that made the first attempt. Mounting the log, while his watchers murmured in astonishment and delight, he pushed with his club against the bottom of the stream—and for a moment he seemed to be emulating Ru, for a moment he too seemed favored of the river-god, and balanced himself securely on the surface of the gliding log.

A proud and envied figure he was as the distance between him and the land gradually widened—one pace, two paces, five paces, until he seemed to be doing all that Ru had done!

"Look at Woonoo! Woonoo is walking upon the waters!" cried the excited people. "The river-god does what Woonoo tells him to!"

Even Grumgra, forgetting his club, seemed to be mightily impressed; he yelled and clamored with the others, exclaiming in a thundering bass: "Look at Woonoo! Woonoo is an enchanter! Walk all the way across the river, Woonoo! Walk all the way across the river!"

But, just when the applause was at its highest, something happened. Just what it was that happened, Woonoo himself could never say, for it was all over too quickly for him to know. Perhaps the log struck a snag in the stream, perhaps it merely rolled and turned over, perhaps Woonoo was so overwhelmed by the cheering that he forgot to keep his balance. At any rate, all that he knew was that one moment he was standing like a conqueror on the log, and the next had gone plunging through space and felt the cold waters closing over him.

But as, wildly sputtering, he arose from his unpremeditated bath, tumultuous laughter came to his ears. And, turning his eyes shoreward, he be-held scores of amused faces shining derisively.

A sobered and much meeker man, he waded slowly to land, while the unoccupied log went drift-ing away with the current.

But his misfortunes were not over, for no sooner had he reached the bank than he was confronted by the irate Grumgra.

"You are more foolish than the Sparrow-

Hearted!" bawled the chieftain. And the great club was lifted, and came down with a resounding smack.

Howling with agony, Woonoo clutched a bruised shin and limped away toward the woods, while after him rang the mocking laughter of his people.

Not the least contemptuous was the laughter of the Smiling-Eyed. "Is there no man among you?" she ridiculed, as she pointed to the retreating form of the abject Woonoo. "Must you let yourselves all be laughed at by the Sparrow-Hearted?"

So saying, she turned again to the river bank, and bent her eyes upon that lonely figure, far out in the stream, who was now beginning to propel himself slowly landward.

CHAPTER XIV

The Treachery of Yonyo

IT was an excited audience that made way before Ru as he steered himself to land. Heedless of the waiting throng, he jumped into the water as soon as the head of his craft struck the river bottom; then, by means of strenuous straining and tugging, he pulled the catamaran up upon the bank, lest it be borne away by the current.

In this task he was greatly impeded by the people that swarmed about him, gibbering and shouting, gabbling incessant questions, staring at the raft in wide-eyed curiosity.

"Do not touch it!" Ru felt forced to cry, in exasperation. "If you do, the river-god will strike you down!" The threat proved effective; the people at once backed away to a respectful distance, and stood regarding Ru and his handiwork with a reverence that was a compound of wonder and fear.

"Now do you not believe the river-god is my friend?" exclaimed Ru, when at last the raft was safely beached. "Do I not speak truth when I say that the river-god and the wind-god have done great deeds for me?"

Not a person had a word to say in reply; and,

in the midst of an impressive silence, Ru started away. There was none who raised a hand or spoke a word to stop him; even the glowering Grumgra and the glaring Zunzun seemed not less impressed than the others, and gazed after him in a sort of stunned respect.

But there was one who did make bold to follow the retreating Ru. She pursued him not directly but in a wide ambling curve, and her course was not apparent; yet it was not many minutes before Ru, approaching the edge of the woods, heard a light voice calling behind him, and turned to find himself confronted by—Yonyo the Smiling-Eyed!

Truly, she deserved her name now if ever, for her face was like a burst of laughter. Her large black eyes burned with brilliant fires beneath beetling ridges; her gleaming white teeth shone merrily by contrast with the tan of her face and the black of her dense, loose-flowing locks; her manner was as simple and ingratiating as that of a child who comes to crave a favor.

Ru, although he still felt anger against her, could not but be impressed. He thought that he had never beheld anyone quite so beautiful before; once again a strange, unaccountable feeling, half tender and reverential, took possession of him; and he experienced vague stirrings of a longing which he could not understand, and which could be at once fierce and sweet.

"So the Sparrow-Hearted has worked wonders!" she exclaimed, not waiting for the preliminary of a greeting. "Soon we will call you Ru the Marvel-Worker! Zunzun will envy you—he has no marvel like yours! Tell me, Ru, how did you do such great deeds?"

"I have told you already," he returned, eying her questioningly. "Have I not told all the people about it?"

"But there are things you have not told them!" she cried. "I know there are things you have not told them! Let me hear those things, Ru!" And she flung herself down upon a clump of grass, and motioned to him invitingly.

Therefore what was Ru to do but obey?

"Tell me all that you did!" she urged, smiling her most ingratiating smile as he took a seat beside her. "Did the river-god and the wind-god show you how to walk upon the waters? Or did you find out all by yourself?"

"Do you not believe it was as I said?" he asked, regarding her gravely. "Do you not believe I spoke truth?"

"I know you spoke truth!" she assured him, with what may have been a trifle too much emphasis. And the smiles rippled across her face as she proceeded: "But I wish the gods had not helped you so much. I wish you had found out all by yourself how to walk upon the waters. That would be a much bigger deed!"

"I did find out all by myself!" Ru found himself admitting; then stopped suddenly, fearing he had said too much.

"Did you? Did you?" exclaimed Yonyo, clapping her hands delightedly. "Tell me about it! Tell me!"

Confused and embarrassed, Ru did not know what to do except to confess everything.

And so, beginning with how he had been saved by the drifting log in the Harr-Sizz River, and how he had propelled himself across the lake and later rescued himself from the man-eating savages, Ru gave Yonyo a full account of his experiences as navigator. He dwelt at greatest length upon the way in which he had made a raft by lashing two logs together; and he spared no details in his description, particularly since Yonyo hung eagerly upon his every word, questioned him when she did not understand, made him repeat when she was in doubt, and all the while regarded him with such wondering and admiring eyes that he felt his adventures had been worth while merely in order to make this moment possible.

When he had finished, she beamed upon him genially, and told him that surely, after all, he was favored by the gods, for without the gods' help no one could have done all that he had done. Her manner was so affable that he felt again the old curious impulse to put his arms about her and draw her close. But perhaps she did not know what was in his mind, for just when he was about to act upon his desire, she rose abruptly to her feet, and started tripping merrily away across the fields.

"Let us go back to camp!" she called; and though he cried out his objections, she danced away all the more swiftly. Not to be daunted so easily, he set out in pursuit; but she increased her speed; and all the way back she led him a gay chase, for women in those days were fleet-footed and skilled in saving themselves by flight.

Immediately upon his return to the camp, he was waylaid by tribesmen, who deluged him with questions; and while he was busy attempting to answer, Yonyo disappeared among the crowd.

That evening, while Ru sat with his kinsmen before the camp-fire, chewing at his scanty portion of meat and at some tough, uncooked roots he had gathered, there occurred an event that brought Yonyo back to his mind in no pleasant fashion. While scores of men and women munched and munched contentedly and the sound of busy jaws mingled with that of the crackling fires and jabbering tongues, the tall form of Grumgra was seen to arise; and the thunderous voice of Grumgra lifted itself above that of the multitude.

"One of our people has been telling us great lies!" he proclaimed, wasting no time about coming to the point. "He has said that the wind-god and the river-god showed him how to walk upon the waters. But the wind-god and the river-god did not show him anything at all. One of our people heard him say that he only tied two logs together, just as we sometimes tie fagots. There is no magic in that at all. Is it not so, Yonyo the Smiling-Eyed?"

And Grumgra nodded significantly toward Yonyo, before continuing: "After the sun comes up again, I myself will show you how to walk upon the waters. I will tie two logs together, and then one of you may go across the river just as the Sparrow-Hearted has done. Who wants to be the first to do that?"

Grumgra paused. . . . An utter silence fell across the assemblage.

"You may do it!" pronounced the chieftain, designating one of the most stalwart-looking of his followers. "You, Kimo the Hairy Mammoth!"

Kimo shuddered; a frightened light flashed from his tiny black eyes. But he answered not a word.

"Kimo will show you that the Sparrow-Hearted has learned no magic at all," concluded the Growling Wolf. "He will walk across the waters very easily—and after that we will punish the Sparrow-Hearted for telling us lies!"

Titters and loud guffaws greeted this speech; and, from the scornful glances in his neighbors' eyes, Ru perceived that his prestige had dwindled toward the vanishing-point.

But it was not his prestige that troubled him now, nor even his impending punishment—it was the treachery of her whom he had adored. Could she actually have told Grumgra the secret he had confided for her ears alone? If so, she was not to be forgiven! Without being able to say why, he felt that a great wrong had been done him. And anger, proportionate to his very helplessness, flamed to life within him. He was gripped by a passion that was almost murderous, and he would have been glad to strike out violently to relieve his overburdened mind and wounded feelings.

Fortunately, it was not possible to strike out violently just then; he had to content himself with clenching and unclenching his fists furiously and kicking savagely at the unoffending soil. That night he could not sleep, but stared out wide-eyed through the long hours at the pale twinkling stars and the weird flickering firelight. When morning came, his frenzy had spent itself; he felt little besides a great weariness, and a disgust that was made up in part of his resentment at the world, and in part of an insatiable vague melancholy. Yet he did find the energy to move his lips in a whispered prayer—and, had one drawn close, one might have heard an invocation to the river-god to bring down vengeance upon his betrayers.

The last star had hardly been extinguished when the camp was astir. Among the first to rise, Ru observed that gigantic figure which he loathed above all others. He noticed apprehensively that Grumgra appeared unusually cheerful this morning, and that, accompanied by two or three of his henchmen, he set off toward the woods with a jauntiness which bespoke no good design.

It was two or three hours later when Grumgra returned. His arrival created a consternation equaled only by that which Ru had caused the day before. Wading through the shallow water near the river bank, he and his helpers were pulling a raft similar to that which Ru had made! Similar, but not quite the same, for it was longer and the logs were thicker, which made it more impressive and also more unwieldy; and the vines and creepers that bound it were fastened in two places instead of in four.

Mounting the bank, the Growling Wolf stood regarding his handiwork with every sign of pleasure, while the vociferous multitude pressed close to see. "Grumgra's magic is better than Ru's!" they cried, jubilantly. "The river-god does great deeds for Grumgra! He has made a bigger wonder than Ru can make!" And many were the exclamations of awe and admiration at the cleverness of Grumgra.

"Now I will show what big lies the Sparrow-Hearted tells! Kimo the Hairy Mammoth, you walk upon the waters!" ordered the chieftain, pointing to the bulky form of the chosen one, who stood cowering in the rear.

Urged by his companions, Kimo came slowly forward, although his knees seemed unsteady beneath him, and terror shone from his eyes.

"Take this club," Grumgra continued, thrusting the long, straight limb of a dead tree into Kimo's hand. "Take it, and push yourself to the middle of the river! It is very easy—even the Sparrow-Hearted can do it!"

But, at the crucial moment, the Hairy Mammoth stood hesitating, and casting desirous eyes toward the forest. Had not strong arms restrained him, he might have been tempted to make a dash for liberty and life. "O chief," he pleaded, "the river-god wants to take me. I cannot swim farther than a strong man can jump. Let some other—"

But Grumgra's club was raised like a challenge,

and a foreboding scowl came across the chieftain's face.

Understanding the strength of this argument, the unlucky one stepped toward the waiting logs.

In the moment that elapsed before he had mounted the raft, the throng was startled by an unexpected voice.

"Anger the river-god, and he will strike you down!" came the warning of Ru, whose clear tones rang with the courage of desperation. "Terrible is the punishment of the river-god!"

There was a moment's silence; several of the people shuddered; Kimo again glanced longingly toward the inaccessible woods. But in an instant there came the deep reassuring voice of Grumgra. "What is this the Sparrow-Hearted says? Who would be stopped by the Sparrow-Hearted? He speaks only empty words! And he who speaks empty words shall be punished! Go, Kimo! Go out and walk upon the waters!"

Still trembling, Kimo stepped into the water, and hauled himself clumsily onto the raft. Then, standing with one leg planted on each log, he began to push his pole awkwardly and yet powerfully against the river bottom. And the raft, responsive, slid slowly out into the waters!

Eagerly the people crowded forward to see, until, in the excitement, not a few were shoved into the river. But no one seemed to notice; all eyes were fixed upon the retreating figure. And Kimo, finding himself perched safely upon the raft, appeared to

regain confidence; he began to push and paddle as
if accustomed to manipulating rafts all his life; and
once or twice he even paused to wave to his gaping
tribespeople.

Farther and farther into the waters he propelled
himself; farther and farther, until a stone thrown
by the strongest man could not have reached him;
farther and farther, until he became but a vague
and minute black blur, with features no longer distinguishable, with voice scarcely audible even when
he shouted. Now he was approaching the middle of
the river, and the current was carrying him slightly
down-stream, yet he still struggled toward the opposite bank; now the head of his raft was buffeted
and turned by the waters, and he was straining
to keep it straight; now he seemed actually past the
middle, seemed actually to be drawing near the
land beyond—when suddenly he was to be seen no
more.

There was a splash, a far-off, quickly muffled
scream—and two logs, bound together at one end
but disentangled at the other, were floating haphazard down the current. From just behind the
logs came a series of small splashes; then a hoarse
cry, then another hoarse cry, like a half-stifled call
for help; then still feebler splashes; then suddenly
only silence, and the undisturbed wide current, and
the two logs drifting slowly down-stream.

The people gaped in amazement. For a moment
they did not seem to understand what had happened; then, as realization gradually came to them,

they uttered low cries of fear and horror. Their glaring eyes were shocked and frightened; and first one and then another began to pray to the river-god, until all had joined in a distracted chorus, and there burst forth a tumult of pleas and groans and mutterings to the god of the waters not to punish them for their daring, and not to believe that they would willingly do him wrong.

CHAPTER XV

The Magic of the River-God

THE disastrous failure of Kimo the Hairy Mammoth had more than one interesting sequel for Ru.

Not least important was the change it marked in his relations with Yonyo. Only a few hours after Kimo's fatal effort at navigation, Ru encountered Yonyo at the edge of the meadow where the tribe was still encamped. She was obviously glad to see him; her sharp black eyes shone with pleasure; her broad dark face grew bright with sudden smiles.

."Ru, you have done wonders!" she commended him. "Only you are loved by the river-god! No other can do as you do! No, not one—"

Here she stopped suddenly short, for the look in his face was not reassuring.

For a moment he stood staring at her as a man might stare at the foe he is about to throttle. His nostrils were dilated; his breath came fast; his fingers were clenched significantly about his club.

"Ru, what evil spirit has entered you?" she cried, in alarm.

But her words seemed only to provide the spur he required. With an inchoate growl, he strode suddenly forward; and his club, clenched more tightly than ever, was uplifted as if to strike.

Yonyo screamed, and darted away. Too often had she seen women struck—too often not to believe Ru in earnest. Without even a backward glance to see if she were pursued, she raced all the way back to her tribespeople.

With a black scowl, Ru stood staring after her. He did not know whether he would actually have hit her; he only knew that a blow would have been small repayment for all she had made him suffer. And, strange to say, a feeling of self-satisfaction, almost of exultation, came over him as he watched her flee; he felt strong with a strength he had never known before; he was almost ready to swagger with triumph, for now at last he, the Sparrow-Hearted, was acting as a man should act!

It did not even occur to him to wonder whether, by his wrath, he might not have alienated Yonyo altogether. At the moment, he did not care. Moreover, had he not often watched beaten women come cringing back to their men?

But before the issue between him and the Smiling-Eyed could be decided, he was confronted with a second result of Kimo's unhappy experiment.

On the evening of the following day, Ru was surprised to find himself again the center of attraction before the tribal camp-fire. It was a time of general complaining and gloom, for another hunt had just been held in order to replenish the tribe's dwindling larder; and the hunters had suffered more heavily than the hunted, for while one small deer had been brought down, two of the men had succumbed before the charge of an infuriated woolly rhinoceros.

Among the women there were lamentations, and among the children cries of hunger, as the tribe engaged in its meager repast of roots and berries seasoned with just a sprinkling of meat. The only exception occurred in the case of Grumgra, who feasted abundantly on the day's catch of venison.

But Grumgra's right to a major part of the supplies was taken as a part of the necessary order of things, and occasioned no comment; and it had nothing to do with the cries of discontent that shrilled from all sides. "What are we to do? What is to become of us, what is to become of us?" mourned some of the more dismal-minded folk; and many were the complaints that they had left the safety of their cave behind them, and many the prayers to the fire-god, the wind-god, and the gods of the woods and waters.

Seldom had Ru seen his people in so despondent a mood. Here, sprawled in the long grass before the fire, a three-year-old was wailing, or a scrawny infant screaming for food its mother could not give it; yonder an old man mumbled and muttered about the plenty he had known in the old days; a little farther on, a haggard group sat chattering, with occasional groans and sighs audible to the entire assemblage; and now and then, from any corner of the encampment, there would come a series of growls and frightful snarls, when some man would snatch at a bone being chewed by his neighbor, and the two would fight like famished dogs. But no one paid any heed to such scuffles, nor to the lamentations of his neighbors; and the firelight, leaping and wavering like some menacing giant, illuminated only sullen apelike faces, and heavy brows contorted in dreary scowls, and lips that grumbled, and eyes that spoke in silent complaint.

"Grumgra, come help us!" pleaded many a voice that had tired of vainly invoking the gods of fire, water, and air. "Grumgra, come tell us what to do! Shall we not go back to our cave? If we stay here we shall starve, and our children will die; and soon there will be only our bones to be picked by the vulture and the hyena."

At first Grumgra made only brusk answer to these appeals. "Zunzun the Marvel-Worker will help you!" he snapped. And Zunzun, coming unwillingly to the rescue, took his place before the fire. With his most eloquent gesticulations, he begged and implored the god of the flames to rescue his people; but even after he had worked himself into a frenzy and puffed and sweated profusely, there was no sign that the god had heard him.

Then, with unheard-of temerity, one of the men began to shout: "We do not need the fire-god! We need the river-god!" And Zunzun, although apparently he had had enough of magic for one evening, was compelled to execute a series of new incantations addressed to the god of the waters.

After he had finished, and while a few of his followers still chanted the prayers devoutly, Zunzun was seen to approach Grumgra as if on secret business. For some minutes the two of them sat in a group apart, talking eagerly in low tones and lifting their clubs threateningly whenever anyone ventured too close.

At length Grumgra sprang up decisively, and stalked energetically toward the fire. "My people, I must have speech with you!" he declared, in his usual bellow.

A murmur of excitement trembled through the assemblage, and all drew close to hear.

"We must all go away from here very soon," he announced, after a moment's pause. "The land of the noonday sun still lies before us; and the river must not stop us, for if we stay here, we will all starve. Is it not so, my people?"

A chorus of groans and sighs signified the agreement of the tribe.

"But how shall we cross the river?" Grumgra continued. "The river-god must show us the way— and there is only one of us that the river-god loves. That one is Ru the Sparrow-Hearted. We must ask Ru to speak to the river-god, so that we may go across. Tell us, Sparrow-Hearted, will you speak to the river-god?"

And the chieftain lifted the club high above his head, as if to indicate that a refusal on Ru's part would be summarily treated.

Rising from where he sat among the shadows to

the rear, Ru strode forward until the firelight was full upon him.

"I will speak to the river-god," he began, while scores of serious little eyes, burning with a new eagerness, were fixed intently upon his slender form. "If you will do all that I tell you, I will find out how to take you across the river. But if you will not do as I tell you, the river-god will devour you! You remember what he did to Kimo the Hairy Mammoth, do you not, my people?"

Grumbled exclamations of fear and horror signified that the people had not forgotten.

"I am the only one that can speak to the river-god," Ru continued, severely. "I know a magic that will save you. But if I use that magic, what will you do for me?"

Ru paused; a hard glitter came into his eyes. "If I use that magic, what will you do for me?" he repeated, with the manner of one that strikes a shrewd bargain.

"What do you want us to do for you?" growled Grumgra, his thick lips twisting into a snarl. "There is nothing we can give. Would you have us throw you the meat we have not?"

"It is not meat I ask!" flung back Ru. "It is something I like better than meat!"

Scores of eyes were fixed upon him in uncomprehending amazement, while earnestly he continued: "For a long, long time, my people, you have not treated me as a brother should be treated. You have said bad things against me, and struck me with

sticks and stones, and burned me with fire; and there
has been evil laughter in your eyes when you did not
understand the things I did. And deep within me
there has been a great pain; but you could not see
it or know it was there. If I help you, should you
not try to take that pain away? Should you not
show me that you will treat me as a brother?"

"How can we show you?" grumbled the chieftain, fumbling with his club impatiently. "You ask
that which no man can do!"

"I ask that which every man can do!" insisted
Ru. "Always you have called me by a name which
does not belong to me, and which I do not like.
Take that name away, and call me by my right name
—and I will ask the river-god to do great things
for you. If not—" Here Ru paused, as if to indicate that, unless his request were granted, the gods
would avenge him.

"And what does the Sparrow-Hearted want to
be called?" sneered Grumgra.

"The Eagle-Hearted!" replied Ru, without an
instant's hesitation.

A little murmur of surprise ran through the assemblage.

"The Sparrow-Hearted cannot become the Eagle-
Hearted just because he asks it!" thundered the
Growling Wolf, glowering menacingly.

"And our people cannot cross the river just because they ask it!" countered Ru, retreating far
enough to escape the swinging club.

"Call him the Eagle-Hearted, the Eagle-

Hearted, the Eagle-Hearted! Only let him do as we want!" came a multitude of shouting voices.

Grumgra stood hesitating; it was easy to see that public sentiment was against him.

"What matter what we call him? Only let him take us across the river!" cried Zunzun the Marvel-Worker. "The Eagle-Hearted let it be!"

"Take us across the river, and you shall be Ru the Eagle-Hearted!" pronounced Grumgra, for once without his usual assurance.

And Ru, with an acquiescent smile, assured his people that they should not have long to wait before crossing the waters.

Early the following morning, Ru was observed to go gliding away into the woods. Toward noon he returned, but not directly from the woods; once more he astonished his people by "walking on the waters." Borne on a raft similar to that on which he had made his spectacular appearance a few days before, he first drifted slowly down-stream, then vigorously propelled himself landward; and, drawing his new creation to the bank by the side of the original craft, he paid no heed to the murmurs and exclamations of the watching throng, but burst at once into fervent prayer.

"O river-god," he cried, "I thank you for making me your friend and doing wonderful things for me. Take care of my people, as you have taken care of me; let them cross your waters, as you have let me cross; show them the way to the land of the noonday sun!"

Having uttered these words, Ru flung himself down on the ground, and began to mutter incoherently. No one could make out what he said; but the spectators gaped wide-eyed; and perplexity and fear were in their looks.

Suddenly breaking short his unintelligible mumblings, Ru leaped to his feet, and spoke in loud, clear tones: "My people, I have been talking with the river-god. Do you wish to know what he has told me?"

A loud-voiced chorus signified that the people did wish to know.

"He says that you may all cross the waters if you will let me show you how," Ru assured them. "But if you do not do as I tell you, the god will put an evil spell upon you all!"

"We will do as you tell us! We will do as you tell us!" the people avowed.

"First you must wear a charm," Ru continued— and in his gray eyes, as he spoke, was a sly twinkle, which no one appeared to observe. "You must each take a pebble from the river bank and tie it to you, so that the god may know who you are and use his magic for you."

Very solemnly every man, woman, and child— from Yonyo the Smiling-Eyed to Zunzun and the stern-browed Grumgra—reached down and selected a pebble, which they slowly and clumsily attached to their garments by means of strips of hide and the fibers of plants.

Following this ceremony, Ru again muttered a few meaningless phrases; then, having done everything necessary to propitiate the god, he declared: "Now I will show you how to cross the river. Who wants to be the first to find out how?"

A frightened silence greeted these words.

"Kori the Running Deer, you go with the Sparrow-Hearted," designated Grumgra.

"My name is the Eagle-Hearted!" corrected Ru, scowling a black scowl.

"The Eagle-Hearted," acknowledged Grumgra, also scowling.

Kori the Running Deer came slowly forward. He was an especially slender and wiry-looking tribesman; his muscles were stout and powerful, yet he had not the oxlike build of most of the Umbaddu.

He seemed to realize at once the uselessness of protest. "Tell me what to do, Ru, and I will try to do it," he declared, as he stopped within arm's length of the raft. And though his small black eyes showed more than a trace of fear, his limbs did not waver and his voice did not shake.

"Do as I do—and only that," directed Ru. And he climbed onto the farther end of the raft, and motioned Kori to take his place at the opposite extremity.

"Now push with your club," Ru ordered, after Kori had stationed himself on the raft. "And move it the way I move mine."

Whereat he gave a powerful shove, and Kori followed with another shove not less powerful. And the raft slipped away from the bank out into the wilderness of the waters!

Once again the people murmured in admiration

and surprise; once again there were cries of wonder
at the magic of Ru. And all eyes were riveted upon
that little craft which made its way slowly, slowly
out toward the center of the stream.

Loud was the splashing of the waters as Ru and
Kori pushed and pushed with their clubs; and still
louder the excitement of the people as the two
tribesmen made their difficult headway. At times, to
be sure, they made no headway at all, but would
paddle in opposing directions, and the raft would
merely swing round and round; at other times they
seemed to be drifting backward, and once Kori lost
his balance and fell into the river, but, with Ru's
help, quickly recovered himself. Yet, with all their
awkwardness, they did make some progress; and,
as they advanced, their movements seemed to become slightly more efficient and assured. At length
they had reached the middle of the river, at length
had gone beyond the middle, and, dwindling each to
a slender black line, were approaching the opposite
bank. Smaller and smaller they grew, until they had
disappeared entirely behind a projection of land
and not even a speck remained to mar the slow-
moving, muddy brown expanse of the waters.

Impatiently the people waited; the air rang with
their disappointment and forebodings. Could it be
that their tribesmen had vanished not to return?
Could it be that the river-god had been angered
after all, and had devoured Kori and Ru even as
he had devoured Kimo the Hairy Mammoth? A
period that seemed interminable went by; many a

voice cried out in apprehension, and many a prayer was murmured by frightened lips. Then suddenly there came a shout of relief; then a great roar of applause—the missing ones were returning!

But were they returning? Only one slender form was to be seen against the vague vastness of the waters. Had Kori too gone the way of the Hairy Mammoth? Horror and dismay glared from the eyes of the people as they stood muttering and waiting, muttering and waiting, while that single figure gradually drew toward them, until at last the tribesfolk knew that it was Ru coming back.

"Where is Kori?" they cried, tumultuously. "Where is he? Where is he? Where is the Running Deer?" And from one corner of the crowd there sounded the sudden wailing of a woman.

Many minutes passed, and still their doubts remained. Not until Ru had drawn his raft up to the bank and alighted did he attempt to answer the stormy questions of the throng.

"Kori is waiting on the other side," he explained. "Who wants to go next?"

No one appeared anxious for the privilege. "Targ the Thick Club, you go now with Ru!" Grumgra had to command, before another candidate could be found, and Ru undertook to ferry his second passenger across the river.

CHAPTER XVI

The Conflict

MORE than a week was consumed in the passage of the river. After the first day, Ru abandoned his work as self-constituted ferryman, which threatened to become endless; he found it simpler to train several of his young tribesmen in the task of ferrying, and to devote himself to the construction of new rafts. Even in this pursuit, he was not now without assistants; indeed, he became something of an overseer or director, while it was his fellows who did the actual work. With their aid, he produced a fleet of ten rafts—several of which were superior to the first two, since they were composed of as many as three or four logs lashed tightly together. It was these larger craft that bore what may be termed the "freight" of the tribe: the flint implements, and the scanty remains of the provisions.

As for the people themselves, they were transported one by one, some of the younger folk shouting with joy, some of the less reckless shivering and frightened, a few of the children shrieking and crying, one or two of the older women wringing their hands or beating their breasts at the thought of crossing to a land from which they might never return. Yet of actual casualties there were very few; now and then, indeed, a passenger did fall into the river, but never with fatal results; now and then someone was bruised or injured in the excitement of landing, but always the wounds were trivial and soon forgotten. And, on the whole, the people crossed confidently enough, for did not Ru say a prayer to the river-god every time a new raft was launched? and did they not know that his magic was powerful to protect them?

Yet, during the time of the passage, the fortunes of the tribe were fast ebbing. There was now an encampment on each side of the river, and on each side a daily hunt was held, although usually without result, except when one of the hunters chanced to slay some small creature with clubs, or with pebbles from his rabbit-skin pouch. And now the tribe dined mostly upon roots, herbs, and berries, supplemented by a sort of paste which the women made from the bark of a tree ground up with beetles, grubs, and grasshoppers. But these were the rations of famine—and as the days went by and no relief appeared in sight, the complaints and wailings of the hungry throng grew more desperate and louder.

Only in the words of Ru could they find any hope. "Do not be sad, my people," he would say. "The river-god has told me that after we have all crossed we shall go to a land of plenty." And his evident cheerfulness served as a prop for the people's drooping spirits.

But Ru, more than any of the others, had reason

to be cheerful. Was not this his moment of triumph? Did not the people look at him with wondering eyes, as they once had looked only at Grumgra and Zunzun? Did they not call him the Eagle-Hearted? and did he not overhear them murmuring that he was a magician, an enchanter more powerful than the Marvel-Worker himself?

Even Yonyo, he was not sorry to learn, seemed to share in the general awe at his deeds. Ever since that memorable day when he had threatened her with his club, she had kept at a safe distance from him, and he was still too angry with her to seek her as his deeper desires urged. Yet at times, when suddenly he would look up from some absorbing task and with quick gaze would isolate her from amid the throng, he would catch in her eyes a light he had never seen there before—a light almost fond, almost tender, yet tinged with just a little of distant admiration. And seeing that which surprised and delighted him, Ru pretended to have noticed nothing at all, but held himself more firmly aloof from her than ever.

Indeed, he found himself indulging in wiles that matched her own! When he beheld her strolling in his direction, he would turn aside and pretend not to have seen; when she called to him, his ears would be closed and he would not hear; when she stared in his direction, he would merely stare back as though through a wall of stone.

Thus matters continued for many days—continued, indeed, until the people had almost completed the passage of the river and only a score remained on the northern bank. Among these, in addition to Ru, were Grumgra and Zunzun; also Yonyo, who seemed determined to remain on the same side of the river as Ru; also Kuff the Bear-Hunter and Woonoo the Hot-Blooded, who had apparently made up their minds to stay where Yonyo stayed. Evidently the withdrawal of a majority of the people had meant a relaxing of restraints; for, before the last of the tribe had attempted to cross, there occurred a little drama that added unexpected variety and flavor to life.

Early one morning Ru was propelling himself down-stream on a small raft he had constructed for his own exclusive use, when he was startled by a series of shouts, groans and horrible oaths arising from a thicket near the river bank. Alarmed, he ceased paddling and stood still to watch. The shouts and oaths continued, in tones still more ferocious, punctuated suddenly by the shrill cry of a woman— a cry he could not fail to recognize!

Not a second did he waste. Leaving the raft to drift as it would, he plunged into the water and hastily swam the few yards to land; then, drawing himself up upon the rocky bank, he paused for an instant to listen again.

The cries had died down to a confusion of mutterings and snarls, like the grumblings of angered beasts; and through the intervening tangle of foliage a sound as of heavy breathing came to his ears.

Picking his way warily through the thicket while the muttering and snarling gave place to a savage howling, Ru found himself approaching a little open space where great shadowy forms were to be seen in violent motion. Cautious as a panther stalking its prey, careful not to rustle a twig or a leaf, he crept forward inch by inch. His thin shoulders were bent far down; his fingers at times touched the ground; his watchful eyes glittered with uncanny alertness. Meanwhile the shouts and screams grew louder and louder, each moment more frenzied and terrible—and again there came the shrill call of a woman!

As that cry rang forth, Ru stole forward to a tiny break in the bushes. Still unseen although able to see all, he peered out upon the grassy floor of a small glade—and what he viewed held him as speechless as if he had confronted a ghost.

Writhing and twisting furiously on the ground, two men were in deadly conflict. Their deerskin mantles had been torn from them; their clubs lay beside them on the grass; their huge hairy bodies were bent and convulsed in desperate battle. Gripping one another with a python-like hold, each seemed bent on tearing his adversary to bits; their long arms clutched and pulled at resisting sinews, their great jaws snapped, their stout legs frenziedly kicked and strained. Over and over they rolled, first one on top and then the other, a contorted, swift-moving mass of muscle and black hair; over and over, muttering and groaning, their hands and faces streaked with red, the ground beneath them dotted with red blurs; over and over, over and over, so fast the eye could hardly follow their motions as crooked fingers tugged at bleeding throats and chests, and wolfish crimson teeth cut and slashed.

It was long before Ru, staring out from his green hiding-place, had recognized the combatants. But finally, when there came a lull, and both contestants momentarily relaxed their efforts, he distinguished the blood-smeared faces of two of his tribesmen: Woonoo the Hot-Blooded and Kuff the Bear-Hunter! And seated at the opposite edge of the thicket, watching the fight with calm detachment, he beheld another whom he well knew—Yonyo the Smiling-Eyed!

Evidently she had not seen him, and he himself was so absorbed in watching the struggle that he scarcely noticed her. Even as he espied her, the fighters began to grapple with renewed energy, coming to a clinch that threatened a swift, fatal ending. Now, as the two men writhed on the ground, Kuff on top, Woonoo beneath, the long stout fingers of the Bear-Hunter fumbled for the neck of his foe; now they were closing over Woonoo's throat, closing and pressing down with fiendish fierceness. The little eyes of Woonoo were bulging out of his head, his tongue was lolling from his great, wide-open mouth, he sent forth a series of gasps and half-stifled groans, and his arms and legs twitched convulsively.

And, but for a timely interruption, the story of Woonoo would have been over.

Just as the murderous fingers were tightening about the doomed man's throat, Ru, forgetting himself, uttered a low excited cry.

Kuff, looking up in alarm, released his hands from the prostrate Woonoo. But Ru had withdrawn instantly into the thicket; and many seconds passed while Kuff stood staring at the shrubbery for sight of the intruder. During the interval, Woonoo clutched at his throat, and began slowly to recover; he groaned, stirred a little, and sucked in the air in long-drawn agonized gulps; then, casting blood-shot eyes at his adversary, he began to creep abjectly away, first crawling on hands and knees like a prisoner escaping, then rising and tottering toward the edge of the woods. But Kuff did not seem even to notice him; his attention was still concentrated upon the unknown foe among the bushes.

Yonyo, meanwhile, had sat watching with an air of utter indifference; neither when Woonoo was vanquished nor when he escaped did she show any sign of emotion. But as the gory form of the defeated one went slumping away into the bushes, she seemed suddenly to realize that she might be something more than an observer.

Convinced at last that there was no enemy in hiding, Kuff had turned to garner the fruits of victory; and with tiny eyes that twinkled wickedly, he stood gaping toward Yonyo. Never too prepossessing, with his huge squat figure and apish countenance, he was particularly hideous now; on his shoulder was a great newly healed scar that added to the natural ferocity of his aspect; on his face were long streaks of blood, while his thick black hair was blood-matted, mud-caked and disheveled, and little crimson patches stared from a hundred places on his unclothed body.

But evidently he had already forgotten his wounds. His thick lips expanded into an unpleasant grin; his eyes, staring from his head like two inky little berries, were fastened upon Yonyo with evil relish. Not a word did he speak, but slowly, as if under some irresistible fascination, he started toward the watching woman.

And slowly, as if she too were under an irresistible fascination, she began to back away. A little cry, half of repugnance, half of fear, trembled from her lips—then, almost before she could turn to flee, the great form of Kuff had come plunging toward her, and she was helpless in his devouring arms.

She felt herself clutched to the hairy breast; she felt powerful fingers tightening about her; to her nostrils came the acrid reek of sweat, and all things grew dark before her eyes. She scarcely heard the raucous breathing, scarcely felt the pain of the gripping hands, the terrible pressure of the huge convulsive body. Blindly, with an instinctive revulsion, she attempted to resist, but her efforts were the flutterings of a thrush in the talons of a hawk.

Yet all this took place in a second, perhaps in the fraction of a second—as suddenly as the great arms

were thrust about her, so suddenly were they released. Startled and bewildered, she went reeling
to the ground, while there came to her a glimpse
of an immense squat form whirling about, and she
heard an infuriated snarl. Even as she staggered and
fell, she saw two new adversaries ranged face to
face—Kuff and Ru the Sparrow-Hearted!

For a moment the two men stood confronting one
another like stags ready for combat. Angry fires
shot from their eyes; suppressed growls issued from
their curling lips. The heavy arms of Kuff were
spread apart as if to seize and crush his rival, and
the fists were clenched savagely; the left arm of Ru
was at his side, but in his right there hung
threateningly—a club! And with a howl of rage
Kuff recognized it as his own club—his own, which
Ru had snatched up from the grass!

Seconds passed. . . . The mutterings of the
rivals rose in a challenging crescendo. Then, with a
stride, Ru crossed half-way over to his foe. The club
leaped to the level of his shoulders; a yell of fury
came to his lips; there rang out a still more ferocious answering yell, And, in a blind frenzy, Ru
started forward again, while the club was lifted yet
higher and swung.

To Yonyo, watching from where she sat huddled
on the grass, it was not apparent just what had
happened. She saw the club descend; she heard the
scream of the smitten Kuff; she watched him lunge
violently for the weapon, and knew that his fingers
closed over it; then there seemed to be only two

figures frantically writhing. Each, she could see, was clinging to the club, each struggling to wrest it from the hands of his adversary. But, disabled though the Bear-Hunter was, Ru was still no match for him; he battled desperately, but in vain. . . . Slowly, slowly Kuff was winning his second triumph. At last Ru lay on the ground, convulsed and panting; at last he seemed to be crushed by the great bulk of his rival, and his fingers were releasing their feeble hold on the club—while into the beady eyes of Kuff there came a bestial light as one hand reached for the throat of the Sparrow-Hearted.

Why it was, Yonyo did not know, but at this crisis she screamed. Her cry was long-drawn and shrill as if she herself were in peril; the very forest seemed to stand affrighted, and the red dripping hands of Kuff were momentarily halted in their gruesome work.

As if in answer to her scream, there came an angry bellow from the woods. And before either she or the fighters could do more than gasp and stare, they heard a crashing in the brush, and saw a tall familiar figure glowering before them.

"Grumgra!" murmured Yonyo, in amazement.

For a moment the chieftain uttered not a word. He merely stood gazing with a half-scornful grin at Yonyo, at the two blood-smeared combatants, and at the disordered glade with the red-streaked grass torn up and crushed. But Kuff, like a small boy detected in a prank, released his grip on Ru, and, rubbing his bruised shoulder, arose to his feet with a sheepish grimace. Immediately afterwards, Ru also arose, while glaring at Kuff with eyes that were like a snarl.

Now there was heard another rustling from the shrubbery, and the stooping form of Zunzun the Marvel-Worker emerged. Disregarding the others, Grumgra turned to him, and, in a growling voice, declared: "It is as I said, Zunzun, when I heard the noise. They have been fighting. They have been trying to kill each other. It is all about a woman!"

A malicious light came into Zunzun's shrewd little eyes. "Fighting about a woman!" he muttered. "That is against your orders, O Grumgra!"

"It is against my orders!" echoed Grumgra, turning threateningly upon Kuff and Ru. "Who is it that started to fight against my orders?"

An awed silence greeted his words. "You, Ru," he thundered, after a moment, "why did you start to fight with Kuff?"

"It was not I that started it," pleaded Ru. "First there was Woonoo the Hot-Blooded—"

The very mention of this hated name brought fury to the heart of Kuff. "It is so! It is so!" he broke in, excitedly. "Woonoo the Hot-Blooded tried to take my woman! She would have been mine, but he wanted to take her! So we fought, and I tried to kill him! I won her from him! Now she is mine!"

"I am not yours!" flung back Yonyo, defiantly.

"Quiet!" howled Grumgra, turning hotly upon the Smiling-Eyed. "Can any woman say which man she belongs to? Is that not for me to say—me,

Grumgra, the father of the tribe? Can I not give any woman to any man I want?"

Utterly subdued, Yonyo went creeping away toward the shadow of the thicket.

"But she is mine! I won her! I won her!" insisted Kuff, glaring malevolently at the chieftain, while the hair upon his back bristled.

"I have said there shall be no more fights about women!" bawled Grumgra. "And you know how I shall punish you!"

There came a murmur of dismay from Kuff and Ru, and a low cry of fear from Yonyo.

"O chief, it is a wise rule you have made," said Zunzun, addressing the Growling Wolf in a mincing voice. "In the days when your father Rung the Roaring Cataract was our leader, there were many fights about women, and many of our men lost their lives. But ever since the day when your club slew Rung, you have had a better way. Not many of our men have fought about women since then. For it does them no good."

"It does them no good!" reiterated Grumgra. And for an instant he paused and leered hungrily at Yonyo, who shrank from his gaze as from a blow. "When two men find a woman worth fighting about, it is well that the woman should belong to me! Is it not so, Zunzun?"

"It is so," acknowledged the Marvel-Worker, nodding sagely. "Such, O chief, is the wise rule you have made!"

"Not too many women have come to me in this

way," recounted Grumgra, regretfully. "No more than there are fingers on one of my hands. But now it is time to find another."

And with eyes wickedly shining, he started toward his intended victim. "You are good to look upon, Yonyo," he muttered. "Good to look upon—"

Yonyo shuddered, and cried out again in fear. Like a cornered beast, she pressed far back into the thicket.

But her shrinking seemed only to whet Grumgra's desire. "Come here, O Smiling-Eyed! Come here!" he commanded, with a growl. "I will not hurt you!" And he darted forward with great strides, his hairy arms outspread to grasp his prey.

There could have been but one sequel, had it not been for Ru. "Stop, Grumgra! Stop! Stop! Stop!" came an imperious cry.

The chieftain turned about with an oath. And Ru, raising his right hand commandingly, solemnly declared: "The river-god will not let you touch Yonyo! If you do, he will punish you!"

And while Grumgra stood glaring at him in bewilderment and rage, Ru lifted both hands skyward and burst into fervent prayer: 'O river-god, punish Grumgra! Do not let him go near the Smiling-Eyed! If he does, you must not let him cross over your waters! You must sink him in the middle, down where the fishes fly about with their sharp little teeth and it is dark and cold. And you must never let him come up again—never, O river-god, unless he will not go near the Smiling-Eyed."

On and on in this vein Ru rambled, waxing more heated in his pleas, more furious in his demands for Grumgra's punishment. And Grumgra, still watching in bewilderment, seemed uncertain what to do. At first he growled and grumbled a bit, then fell into a staring silence; then, while Ru still importuned the river-god, his great lower jaw sagged and his mouth gaped wide; then by degrees an expression akin to anxiety crossed his face; and from anxiety he passed to fear, and from fear, by slow gradations, to actual terror, until at length his legs seemed to be unsteady beneath him and his frightened little eyes half bulged out of his head.

"I will do as you want!" burst forth Grumgra, as Ru reached an emotional climax. "Only ask the river-god not to take me when I cross!"

Whereat he mumbled a little to himself; then, without so much as a glance toward the cringing Yonyo, he reached for his club and went stalking away into the shadows of the wood.

CHAPTER XVII

When Wolf Meets Wolf

WHEN at last the river had been crossed, the tribe continued southward for many days. Although there was no trace of a path and Mumlo the Trail-Finder no longer knew the way, the people pressed on as best they could along a route selected by Mumlo and Grumgra. In a disgruntled, straggling group they pushed their way down the long corkscrew defiles of the mountains, through the underbrush of unknown forests, around the marshes of treeless valleys, and over boulder-strewn wildernesses where serpents hissed and the lone wolf slunk. Many a tongue cried out to complain that they did not know where they went; many a heart was filled with terror at the tracks of huge beasts, or occasionally at sight of some great horned form among the bushes. But, no matter how they groaned and grumbled and lamented, the people no longer thought of doing otherwise than to follow Grumgra as he led them on and on.

Of daily occurrence were the mutterings at the scarcity of food. Roots, herbs, and berries were of course still to be had, and these were supplemented by grasshoppers and grubs, and even at times by ants and butterflies; but very little actual game was captured, and day after day the people complained at their enforced vegetarian diet. Once, indeed, they did all feast, when, led by Ru and his firebrands, they drove the vultures and hyenas from the carcass of a newly dead mammoth; occasionally they slew some small bird or beast with their pebbles, or literally dug it out of its burrow; but such times were rare, and to waylay the larger animals was beyond their power. There were suggestions, to be sure, that they should pause for a day and hold a hunt; but Grumgra vetoed this idea with a single gesture of his club, and growled half under his breath that not even a day must be wasted.

And so, never actually starving and yet almost always hungry, the tribe trudged along a weary course that seemed endless. Scarcely a night went by but that the camp was disturbed by the wailings of some woman at the death or threatened death of her babe; and there was hardly a day when someone did not have a tale to tell of his close escape from the hoofs of a rhinoceros or wild bull or from the trap of quicksand, precipice, or lake. But where they were going, and to what end their sufferings and dangers led, the people had only the vaguest idea.

Now, by a curious irony, all their grumblings began to concentrate about a single object. If Ru and the river-god had not helped them across the waters, then their troubles would all have ended; they would have turned around and gone back to their abandoned cave—and they would now have been living as happily as of old. The fault was therefore Ru's for showing them how to cross the river. Thus, as the gathering days brought fresh discontent, the people began to reason; and now, when they muttered their complaints, the name of Ru was almost invariably spoken—it was he who had brought them to suffer and pine so far from home, he who had turned against them the spirits of the woods and caves and streams and those more terrible spirits in the hearts of the wild beasts!

And now Ru went about always with club in hand and with eyes alert. Wherever he walked, he was greeted with hisses and snarls, or with silent, unfriendly stares; sometimes, when he approached, his tribespeople would withdraw into little groups, whispering among themselves, with furtive glances in his direction; and the very children—they who had once been his particular friends—would echo the antagonism of their elders by shouting accusing names at him and flinging stones.

Even his prestige—that prestige which he had enjoyed as an ally of the river-spirit—was under partial eclipse. He was no longer Ru the Eagle-Hearted, as in the days of the river-passage; the contemptuous appellation "Sparrow-Hearted" had returned, despite Grumgra's promise to the contrary; and always it was by this term that his tribesmen addressed him.

It was Grumgra himself that had brought about the change. When the tribe was halting for its first night's rest after crossing the river, Ru had chanced

upon Yonyo in a secluded corner of the encampment; and, finding her face bright with smiles at
his approach, he had paused to speak with her. But
scarcely had he uttered the first word when a tall
shadow intruded. With a low cry, Yonyo flitted
away and disappeared—and Ru found himself face
to face with Grumgra.

"What is this? You dare to speak with my
woman?" bellowed the chieftain, in tones so loud
as to attract many of his tribesmen to the scene.

"She is not your woman!" denied Ru, with one
eye watchfully upon Grumgra's club.

"All women are my women!" growled Grumgra
the Omnipotent. "She is not yours—not yours, Ru
the Sparrow-Hearted!"

By this time a dozen hairy forms had gathered
near, and a dozen pairs of eyes were regarding the
contestants expectantly.

"I do not know Ru the Sparrow-Hearted!" came
the angry reply. "I am Ru the Eagle-Hearted!"

"No! Ru the Sparrow-Hearted!" Grumgra
chuckled evilly, and his laughter was echoed by the
crowd. "Ru the Sparrow-Hearted! Or should it be
the Rabbit-Hearted?"

Again Grumgra chuckled derisively; and again
his merriment found ready response among the auditors.

"Do you forget your promise to me and the
river-god?" demanded Ru; but his words were
drowned out by the roaring of the chieftain.

"We will see whether you are the Sparrow-

Hearted!" the Growling Wolf exclaimed. "We will see!" And his great club flashed high in air, and he started toward Ru as if with murderous intent.

At that crisis Ru did precisely as he was expected to do. He did not remain to meet the impact of the descending club; he sought the way of safety and of flight. In an instant, his fleeing form had disappeared behind a little rise in the land.

But after him rang the derisive howl of Grumgra: "See how the Sparrow-Hearted runs!" And from a dozen mocking voices there came gleeful screams and cries: "Sparrow-Hearted! Sparrow-Hearted! Sparrow-Hearted!"

But though once again Ru had to face the hostility of his people and of Grumgra, he found his hopes brightening in at least one respect. Between him and Yonyo things were no longer as they had been. Ever since that encounter in the woods, when he had fought for her and she had screamed in terror at his peril, they had been drawn together as never before. Forgotten now was Yonyo's treachery, her scornful ways, her callousness; it was enough for Ru that she had given some sign of a kindlier feeling. All the mysterious attraction she had exerted came flashing back upon him, so that he felt himself again at the beck of her sparkling glance, her self-willed nods and gestures, and roguish smile.

His enthralment was all the more complete since Yonyo seemed to be separated from him by an impassable bar—Grumgra still cast covetous eyes upon her, and she lived in terror of his approach. Hence all their little meetings were brief and fear-troubled; they saw each other at odd times and places and clandestinely as children dreading a parent's arrival; they were in constant alarm lest Grumgra should find them together, or lest some gossip-loving tribesman should bear him news of their rendezvous.

Yet in those stolen moments Ru found a joy beyond anything he had known before. Yonyo was gracious to him now as never in the past; she could still smile her tantalizing smile, but she would not jeer and mock; her face would at times assume a look that was almost gentle, and her tongue would murmur softly; she would peer at him with eyes in which he caught an admiration that had never been there before, and at the same time there was just the trace of a shyness that puzzled and provoked him. Again and again Ru felt the old unaccountable impulse to fold his arms about her and draw her close; and more than once that impulse was about to be gratified, when with a sly laugh she slipped away and led him a merry, hopeless chase through the forest. But, on each occasion, he seemed nearer to success; and no doubt the moment of victory would not have been long delayed except for the perpetual shadow of Grumgra.

Grumgra's attitude was still something of a mystery to Ru and Yonyo. Now that the chieftain had safely crossed the river and had no further dread of the river-god, he did not hesitate to taunt and

ridicule Ru, and even to assail him with his club.
But, at the same time, a little of the awe Ru had
inspired seemed to remain—and it was no doubt
this that restrained him from pursuing Ru relentlessly and from hunting down Yonyo as he would
have hunted down any other woman whom he desired.

Prayers to the gods of the waters and of the
winds were still frequently on Ru's lips, and on
sundry occasions were uttered within the hearing of
Grumgra; and while the chieftain perhaps doubted,
still he had more than once been heard to mutter
uncertainly to himself while listening to the Sparrow-Hearted's supplications; and in his tiny black
eyes Ru had beheld a glint of wonder which verged
upon fear.

Yet, at one of the tribal meetings, he had let it
be known that Yonyo was his woman, and that
none but him must lay hands upon her. And thus
by a word he had ended the courtship of Kuff the
Bear-Hunter and the possible courtship of all the
other tribesmen—with the sole exception of Ru.

But the days went by, and little happened. Sometimes Grumgra, casting greedy eyes upon Yonyo,
would start toward her with a growl that was perhaps meant for tenderness. But she would dash
away, screaming with fear, and he would turn aside
indifferently, as though she were not worth the
trouble of a pursuit. This was not like Grumgra,
and the people wondered; and still more they wondered when Woonoo and Kuff brought tales that
Ru had been seen with Yonyo, and the chieftain re-

warded the informers with a snarl and a blow from
his club.

Each day excited rumors circulated that Grumgra
was about to take vengeance upon Ru. Yet the expected outburst was long delayed—was delayed, in
fact, until the people had lost patience and almost
ceased to anticipate it—and when it did occur, the
results were totally unexpected. And the reason was
that, in the interval, Ru had gained an ally of a type
unique in the history of the Umbaddu.

It chanced one day that half a dozen men of
the tribe—Ru among them—came across some new-
made wolf tracks. "There may be some little wolves
in a cave," suggested one. "And little wolves are
good to eat. Let us find out." So curiosity and
hunger prompted the men to follow the trail
through the wilderness.

As they slowly advanced, the clubs of all were
poised alertly; the eyes of all gleamed warily; not
a murmur gave token of their excitement. At length,
to their delight, they came upon that which they
had hoped for—among a cluster of rocks there was
a little hollow, and it was from this retreat that
the wolf had evidently emerged.

Very cautiously, creeping on hands and knees,
they approached. The stench of carrion came to
their nostrils; confused low growls were borne to
their ears. For an instant they paused, then crawled
on again; actual pleasure was expressed in each
wily eye; the clubs were lifted a little more cautiously than before, but slowly and steadily they
still pressed forward.

At last the foremost of the party halted—not more than a yard from the cave entrance. Then, while the others gripped their clubs more firmly and a petrified silence held them all, the leader stole forward another pace, and peered anxiously into the hollow.

Straightway a whoop of triumph split the air, and the huntsman waved his arms exultantly. His comrades, crowding up to see, observed that the cavern was empty—except for six furry little forms huddled together against the farthest corner of the rocky wall.

Swinging his club with savage relish, one of the men crept in throught the entrance. The wolf cubs snarled, and their feeble jaws snapped; then madly they scattered in all directions. But the club swung, and then swung again, and then swung once more; and the air was filled with the squeals and yelps and baby wailings of the slaughtered.

Yet there was one among the six that long eluded his persecutor. After the last of his brothers and sisters lay blood-smeared and motionless on the cave floor, he still darted about as distractedly as a rat in a trap. Several times, when the smashing club descended, he escaped by the bare fraction of an inch.

Shouting with glee, the men pressed close to watch. But the sequel was not as they had expected. Just when the cub seemed to be cornered; just when the club was coming down to do final execution, the intended victim did a surprising thing. In a frenzy of terror, he gave a swift furious leap, as though to plunge straight through the waiting line of men. But his infant limbs were too feeble; he fell short of the mark, and came down in—the arms of Ru!

Ru never knew just why it was that his hands reached out and seized that desperate little living mite. But he did know that, once he had grasped the cub, he was thankful for his action. He could feel the tiny heart thumping fiercely upon his breast; he could feel the hot moist breath coming fast against his palm; he could feel the furry little form huddling close for safety—and a strange protective instinct came over him, the swift stirrings of an emotion that was all gentleness and pity.

Loud laughter convulsed Ru's companions as he caught the harassed cub; but in the heart of Ru there was no laughter. And his arms, once pressed about the little creature, were folded there as if not to be released.

"Come, Ru, give us the beast," directed one of his tribesmen, when at length their merriment was over. "We must make an end of it before the she-wolf comes back."

"I will not give it to you," refused the Sparrow-Hearted. "You shall not make an end of it."

New laughter racked the frames of the spectators. "What! Not give it to us?" they roared. "Do you want to eat it alive?"

"I do not want to eat it at all!" cried Ru, with a trace of anger. "I am going to keep it!"

"Keep it?" they all echoed, in unfeigned amazemen. "Keep a wolf? But it will devour you!"

"It will not devour me!" came Ru's vehement

denial. And after a second, while his fellows stood regarding him as though certain that his wits had fled, he added that he would work a charm over the creature to prevent it from harming him.

"It is not easy to work a charm over a wolf," commented one of the men, shrugging his shoulders, as he went to gather the carcasses of the slain whelps from the cavern floor. "You will want to kill it after it bites you!"

But the others, after enjoying some further laughter at Ru's expense, were tempted to try more forceful tactics—and were confronted by an irate Ru, who swore that if they so much as touched the cub he would bring down against them all the evil spirits of the woods and caves.

Hesitatingly and somewhat doubtfully, they decided to leave Ru to himself. "Only the Sparrow-Hearted would fight about such a little animal," they concluded. And so it happened that, when Ru rejoined the tribe, the young wolf still nestled safely in his arms.

Yet, having rescued the animal, Ru had no idea what to do with him. At first he had perhaps some vague notion of releasing him to find his way back to his kindred; but from the cub's quivering, frightened manner of huddling against him, he knew the creature was helpless—and, though he could not have said why, he had no desire to abandon him to the talons of some roving eagle or hawk. There was something in those timid, bright little eyes that awakened his sympathy, something that made him

Ru plays with Wuff

feel almost a sense of fellowship. And gradually—
since there seemed to be no other way—the thought
came to him that he might himself feed and care
for the cub.

And thus began the memorable partnership between Ru and Wuff the Little Wolf. The people
stared in amazement to see Ru sheltering a wolf
cub. They laughed merrily as they told one another
how the beast would bite and tear Ru for his
trouble. They crowded close to watch when Ru fed
him with bones and the skin and discarded remains
of slaughtered animals. They jeered and hooted as
Ru indulged in all sorts of games and queer antics
with his new-found companion, leading him a merry
race through the woods while the cub pursued in
puppylike glee, or wrestling with him for a stick
or bone, or merely holding him in his arms and
fondling him. Wherever Ru went, Wuff went with
him; at night the wolf huddled close at his side, and
during the day trotted contentedly at his heels. So,
in less than a week, Wuff had apparently forgotten
all about his lost home, and he became as devoted
to Ru as a dog to its master.

Ru meanwhile found himself increasingly attached to Wuff. Several times, with outbursts of
ferocious anger, he saved his young charge from
assaults by his tribespeople; and he threatened such
horrible vengeance upon anyone who harmed Wuff
that in the end the people were careful not to come
within touching distance of the beast.

Curiously enough, the cub throve under Ru's

treatment. He grew at a prodigious rate; and, as the days and weeks went by, his legs became long and scrawny, his jaw lengthened and grew heavier, and his teeth waxed dangerously sharp; while the shining little eyes gleamed ever more alertly. "Ru's wolf will devour him yet," prophesied the people, as they saw the cub daily assuming more of the characteristics of his race. When he snapped his jaws and snarled in harmless play, they foretold how he would soon snap and snarl in earnest—with Ru as the victim; and when Wuff began to go dashing eagerly although unavailingly after every stray rabbit, squirrel, and butterfly, they predicted that not many months would pass before the wolf's assaults would be more successful—and would be turned against his protector.

Yet with Ru, Wuff showed a gentleness that seemed to belie his savage ancestry—and never once did Ru receive so much as a scratch from him even in play. Toward most of the other tribesfolk, however, the cub exhibited a growling hostility. Yonyo alone he would endure, for Ru made him vaguely understand that she was to be tolerated; but upon the approach of any of the other people he would show his teeth and snarl. And—by some strange chance that delighted Ru—Wuff seemed to take an especial dislike for one man in particular. Whenever the wolf's nostrils would catch the scent of Grumgra, he would seem to go mad; his jaws would snap, his eyes shine with a light that was truly wolfish, his black hair would bristle, and low mutterings would issue from his throat. And more than once, had not Ru interfered, Wuff might have leaped to his death in the effort to set teeth in Grumgra's throat.

Grumgra, meanwhile, took little notice of the hatred of the beast. Once or twice, in his contempt for the creature, he went so far as to kick the cub with his enormous unshod foot—and, on each such occasion, it was only Ru's prompt interference that saved Wuff from striking back and ending with his skull crushed.

But thanks to Ru's watchfulness, Wuff survived the peril from the archenemy. And before finally the animal showed how fierce was his hatred of Grumgra, many a week had gone by and Wuff was no longer a mere cub but had attained the imposing proportions of a half-grown wolf.

Then, with amazing suddenness, the suppressed fires burst forth. One evening the tribe had paused to make its encampment in the glade of a hillside forest, when Ru, strolling with Wuff near the verge of the woods, was startled by a sharp cry from the thickets. Alarmed, he paused to listen; the cry was repeated, a distressed feminine cry that he recognized. Then there came a half-human grunt, followed by a groan that he thought he also knew, and the noise of a scuffle in the underbrush.

Meanwhile Wuff was sniffing significantly at a new-made trail. A low growl issued from his throat; his eyes shone angrily, and the hair upon his back began to bristle.

"Come!" commanded Ru. And, followed by the willing beast, he glided into the woods.

Not many seconds later he paused—directly before him was that which he had anticipated.

Clasped in two enormous brawny arms, with head bent back helplessly and long hair streaming, a woman was feebly struggling; while Grumgra, chuckling in evil glee, drew her to him tightly, then bent down and pressed his thick ugly lips to her reluctant ones.

Not an instant did Ru waste. "Go!" he muttered to Wuff, and pointed an angry hand at Grumgra.

Wuff, needing no second invitation, sprang with a snarl at the chieftain and buried his teeth deep in the flesh of the sinewy neck.

Grumgra, taken by surprise, was for a moment defenseless. His club lay on the ground, hopelessly out of reach; he could only release Yonyo as suddenly as if she had been a hot coal, and, howling with pain and rage, grapple instinctively for the throat of his aggressor. Meanwhile the sharp teeth cut deeper and deeper; a warm stream began to trickle down Grumgra's neck and chest; he could feel the fierceness of the living fury that was rending away at his flesh. . . . A madness such as even he had rarely known came over him as his hands closed about a hairy throat; with desperate power he pressed, squeezed and pressed with all the vehemence of hatred and the lust for life. And gradually the tormenting fangs were withdrawn and the body of his foe crumpled up in his grasp.

Then, while a murderous frenzy possessed him
and he was about to break the neck of his adversary,
a club came down violently upon his arm. Who it
was that struck him he did not know—screaming
with agony, he unclenched his fingers. As he did so,
someone behind him snatched the furry form away,
and his ears caught the patter of retreating footsteps. Blinded as he was by frenzy and pain, he
wheeled about a fraction of a second too late; he
saw no more than the foliage closing above two
dark, swift-moving figures.

That night, around the tribal camp-fire, Grumgra
was unusually sullen and morose. More than one
erring tribesman felt the chastisement of his club;
and it was noted that several times he started with
a growl toward Ru, and that Ru, followed by his
pet wolf, made haste to disappear amid the
shadows. It was also noted that Grumgra's throat
bore a great ragged new-made wound; and the
rumor circulated that he had received this injury
while wrestling single-handed with a bear.

CHAPTER XVIII

The Migration Ends

ON the following morning Ru overheard an interesting conversation. Seated in the hollow of a great boulder, he caught the muttered words of Grumgra and Zunzun as they conferred on the opposite side of the rocks. And unhesitatingly he crouched down so as not to be seen and not to miss a syllable.

"But why not kill him the easiest way?" Grumgra was saying. "One blow of my club—"

"That would seem better," came the suave interruption of the Marvel-Worker. "But would it be? I too want to be rid of him, for has he not laughed at my wonders? and does he not try false wonders of his own? But let us not be too much in haste. If you kill him now, the people will not believe our story about the bear. They will guess that you have been fighting with the Sparrow-Hearted, and will ask why you did not kill him at once. And how they will laugh then! They will whisper that the Sparrow-Hearted is stronger than you!"

"I will wring the Sparrow-Hearted's neck!" growled the chieftain, stung by Zunzun's hateful suggestion.

"Not yet. Not yet," cautioned the Marvel-Worker. "We will wait, and will think of some way. Maybe we can push him off the high rocks—or else the god of the fire or the storm may help us. Let me use my magic—it has broken the bones of bigger men than Ru."

"Go, use your magic!" muttered the leader, fiercely. "But use it soon! No man can strike Grumgra and live! The air I breathe is not sweet while Ru stays alive!"

"But do not forget," resumed Zunzun, in soft, persuasive tones, "the Sparrow-Hearted has his wolf to fight for him. I do not know what bad spell he has worked over it, but we cannot go near him while it lives. Why did we not kill it long ago?"

"I will kill it now!" vowed Grumgra. "This very day it will taste my club!" And his words were punctuated by low throaty mutterings and a gnashing of teeth.

"Grumgra speaks great wisdom," the Marvel-Worker approved. . . .

And that was all that Ru remained to hear. Fearful of detection, he slipped slyly away, and disappeared without a sound into a dense thicket.

All that day, while the tribe pursued its leisurely course through the forest, Ru watched cautiously for sign of some trap or ambush. But, somewhat to his surprise, he went his way unmolested. He did notice, however, that Grumgra seemed bent on keeping his promise with regard to Wuff; several times the chieftain approached the wolf with club dangerously poised. On each occasion Wuff showed his teeth and growled, yet seemed not unaware of his peril; he always managed to leap out of range of the descending club—and all that Grumgra succeeded in doing was to knock some holes in the earth, while Wuff, confronting him just out of reach, would derisively snarl and snarl.

Thus frustrated, Grumgra glowered with increasing fierceness as the hours went by; and the people, watching him at a distance, were secretly mirthful at his futile efforts.

But, except for the baffling of Grumgra, nothing happened all that day. It was not until late at night that the chieftain made his first determined effort at vengeance.

Long after Ru had fallen asleep, he awoke with a start. The night was clouded and starless; on both sides of him the camp-fires were smoldering to a crimson glow, and he could only dimly distinguish the huddled figures of the sleepers and hear their rhythmic breathing. All was as it should be— there was no sound or shadow to give alarm. Yet, for some reason, a shiver of fear shot through him. Without knowing why, he shuddered; and, as he did so, there came a low growl to his left—and he saw the two glowing eyes of Wuff. Vaguely he could make out the form of the wolf standing beside him, and as if by instinct he knew that the animal's hair was bristling.

At the same moment his eyes were startled by a sudden movement, and he saw a huge shadowy shape creeping along the ground. But he had no time to wonder what it was. Almost before he realized what was happening, Wuff had vanished. Ru was aware of a slim form catapulting through the air—then there came a howl that set the whole camp astir. And, with furious suddenness, the huge creeping shape sprang up, and towered to monstrous proportions. It lifted enormous arms, and swung a colossal club—and a small four-legged form, leaping through the air, nipped the giant on the elbows; then as suddenly withdrew; then once more darted forward and nipped the giant on the shins; then with lightning rapidity disappeared; then for a third time charged and slashed the calves of the giant's legs. The club-wielding one, thus assaulted, shrieked and bawled in leonine rage and thrashed madly at the air; but in the darkness he was half-blinded, and the strokes of his club were wild and uncontrolled; while his foe, gifted with better sight, continued to lunge and cut and then to vanish, with movements so incredibly rapid as constantly to elude the grasp of the huge clutching fingers.

In a minute, the struggle was over. The great figure disappeared at a run, to be lost among the crowd of his awakened fellows; while Wuff, slinking back to Ru's side, licked his chops contentedly and sank down to resume his interrupted sleep.

When morning dawned, it was observed that the body of Grumgra was reddened with half a dozen new-made slashes. But no one dared refer to the wounds in Grumgra's hearing; and there was much whispered comment that everyone knew better than to make public.

Meanwhile Ru noticed that the people kept at a greater distance from Wuff than ever before. As for himself, he looked upon Wuff with a new affection. Reaching down and stroking the wolf's fur, he murmured gentle words into the creature's ear: "Good Wuff! Good Wuff! You have saved my life! You would not let Grumgra come upon us in the night, would you, little wolf? You would fight for me as no one else would! You are the best friend I ever had!"

And Wuff, hearing these words, stood listening patiently and with eyes that shone steadily and brightly; and Ru swore to himself that his comrade understood.

From that time forth, Ru would never leave Wuff far from his sight; and his vigilance, both for his own sake and for that of his four-footed friend, was never for a moment relaxed.

But a day or two later there came a diversion of so exacting a nature that it required the full attention of Grumgra and Zunzun as well as of Ru himself, and left them little leisure for thoughts of vengeance.

By this time the tribe had been following the southern trail for possibly four or five months. No record, of course, could be kept of the days that passed, and it was impossible even to estimate the distance traversed; but when the people had left their cave it had been late spring, and now the

leaves on the trees had commenced to turn yellow
and brown; and the days, intensely warm for a
while, had begun to be varied by a refreshing cool-
ness at night and in the early morning. No one could
be sure as yet whether they had exchanged their
own land of bitter winter for a warmer region; but
there were those who whispered that it had been
colder than this in their old cave at the season of
falling leaves; and even the confirmed grumblers
admitted that they had entered a fairer country
than they had left. Not that the scenery was as
majestic, for there were not the same white-banded
glaciers and overshadowing mountains—but the
world about them seemed less harsh and unfriendly.
The storms that came trumpeting out of the
thunder-laden skies did not seem as severe as those
they had known of old; the woods, flowering with
vines and bushes unknown before, offered abundant
nuts and succulent fruits they now tasted for the
first time; while here and there were wide grassy
meadows through which they could travel more
easily and with greater safety than through the
forest.

Best of all, to their minds, was the fact that now,
for the first time since leaving the cave, they had
an abundance of animal food. Deer of a hundred
species browsed among the woods; bison and wild
boars and cattle were becoming plentiful; occasionally they would catch sight of a galloping herd of
horses, and the mammoth and the rhinoceros
offered tempting if inaccessible prey. There was the

corresponding drawback, of course, that dangerous carnivores were becoming numerous; not infrequently they crossed the tracks of bears, hyenas, and wolves, and once or twice they caught glimpses of the rare but dreaded sabertooth. Yet, perhaps because easier prey was to be found, the tribe was not much molested; it lost only two children and one old man to the wild beasts in the course of several months. And after they had held one or two successful hunts, and every member of the tribe had feasted and gorged to capacity, they were all in a more cheerful mood. They murmured that they had reached a land where they might halt and make their home.

Whether or not they remained permanently, it was necessary to find some resting-place before long. They could not wait until the last leaves had dropped from the trees, until the cold winds and the snow should overtake them; no man could say how severe the winter here would be. To delay too long might be to perish. So Grumgra had given orders that if anyone discovered a promising-looking hollow or cave entrance, they should all pause and examine it.

At first there was no sign of the hoped-for cavern. No retreat large enough to shelter even a bear could be discovered among the rocks; in vain the people searched the hillsides and the cliffs; in vain they hunted along the banks of rivers and in the heart of the woods. Dark prophecies could be heard from the mouths of the disgruntled, as the days went by

The Umbaddu hunters were successful

and the tribe was still forced to wander; and even the more cheerful grew silent again, and a somber expression would come into their eyes when they heard mention of the elusive cave. Slowly and relentlessly the autumn was advancing: brilliant red and yellow patches were springing up like gaudy reminders in the woods; the underbrush seemed all aflame; and from time to time there sounded the querulous calls of the southward-winging wild geese. Now the people were increasingly aware that winter could not be far behind. As if to lend fuel to their misgivings, Grumgra and Zunzun would hold whispered conferences every evening; and every evening, before the camp-fire, the Marvel-Worker would go through a series of furious incantations, and from his lips would come frenzied prayers to the gods of the flames, the woods, and the caves.

It was when the gold and scarlet of autumn were burning their fiercest that Wuff had his two encounters with Grumgra; and it was at about the same time, likewise, that the long migration of the Umbaddu came to an end.

A day or two after Grumgra's unsuccessful midnight attack, the people found themselves following the loops and meanderings of a narrow river that reminded them of the Harr-Sizz. Through deep wooded gorges, under beetling rocky cliffs and around the base of forlorn hills they kept close to the stream for many miles, until at length they went trailing into a ravine similar to that which they had left months before. On both sides of the stream, the craggy cañon walls shot precipitously to a height of hundreds of feet; here and there a scraggly bush or tree clung precariously to a limestone ledge, but for the most part there was no vegetation; and the innumerable successive strata, twisted and bared as before some gigantic dissecting knife, had a ruggedness that brought thoughts of home to the hearts of the people.

But what they particularly noted was a small ragged patch about a third of the way up the cliff. In excited little groups they gathered, all pointing up to it at once, and all exclaiming, "A cave! A cave! See! A cave!"

What cries of relief and gladness now poured from their lips! Some jubilantly yelled and shouted; some sank down upon the ground, and uttered fervent prayers; some flung their arms about the shoulders of their neighbors and thankfully embraced them; some merrily leaped up and down, executing fantastic dances of their own invention; some merely turned to their kinsmen, and eagerly chattered and chattered.

But, as of one accord, they all halted beneath the cave entrance and waited for Grumgra to give that all-important command which they knew he must give.

No sooner was all the tribe assembled than the chieftain, all the more impressive and hideous because of his crimson new-made cuts and gashes, shouldered his way sullenly to the center of the crowd. The people made haste to open a path before him; and an expectant silence overcame them all when, lifting his club regally, he signified that he was about to speak.

"We think we have found a cave, but we do not know," he began, in his characteristic bellow. "Maybe there is no cave at all. Or maybe it is not big enough for us to live in. Or maybe there are great rocks that will fall and kill us; or else the roof may be too low. Or wild beasts or wild men may be there already. And so we will have to send someone to find out. He who goes in may never come out again— but someone will have to go. Who will be the one?"

There was a moment's silence; each man peered furtively at his neighbors, and several deliberately squeezed out of sight amid the throng.

"Then I must make someone go!" decided Grumgra. And his eyes, scanning the crowd, chanced to fall upon a slim hated form.

A look of malevolent relish lighted his apelike face. He had the expression of one who had just hit upon some brilliant, sinister scheme. "Ru the Sparrow-Hearted," he bawled, "you be the one to go into the cave!"

Sighs of relief and titters of amusement issued from the throats of a hundred auditors. And Ru, coming forward with features compressed to a stoic rigidity, quietly declared: "I am glad, O chief, that you think me brave enough to go. It shows that you would do great honor to me."

Grumgra growled, and the club swung menacingly above his shoulders. "I do not honor the Sparrow-Hearted!" he snarled; then stopped short in confusion, for Ru, with a scornful laugh, had already slipped out of sight among the multitude.

CHAPTER XIX

Among the Labyrinths

HALF an hour later, Ru had commenced the ascent toward the supposed cave entrance. His only companion was Wuff, who scrambled willingly after him along the perilous ledges; his only equipment, in addition to the pouch of pebbles and the club that were slung at his side, consisted of a flaming torch liberally greased. From below, his tribesmen stared at him in a great crowd, shouting directions and by turns encouraging him and jeering; but he paid little heed to them, and picked his way as rapidly as he could among the crags and boulders toward the little black spot in the cliff wall.

As he approached, that spot widened promisingly; and when from time to time he caught glimpses of it through fissures in the rock, he became increasingly certain that it was indeed the doorway to a cavern. But what a cavern it must be! The opening was perhaps wide enough to admit half a dozen men walking side by side, and its coaly opaqueness brought visions of interminable depths. His imagination was not fully awakened, however, until he stood on a sort of rocky terrace or balcony directly facing the gaping hole. Then, when he saw the jagged aperture giving upon the tunnel-like recess, with the low roof that would barely admit his unstooping form, and the interior unillumined and blank as if here were the end of all things, a tremor of fear shot through him, and his horror-stricken mind conjured up all manner of fantastic terrors.

As if to lend some color of reason to his alarm, Wuff crouched down before him with bristling hair and eyes angrily shining; and from his throat there issued low growls and grumblings.

But Ru had no time for hesitation. His torch was already half burned away, and the cave must be explored while the flame lasted—and so, trying to forget his unreasoning dread, Ru forced his way into the blackness.

Reluctantly Wuff followed at his heels; but each second his growls grew louder.

Yet at first Ru was aware of nothing disturbing. There was only the bare floor and the shadowy walls dimly lit by the torch; and a new assurance came to him as he pressed farther into the gloom.

Then—not half a dozen seconds could have elapsed—he became conscious of a light that was not of his torch. From the darkness beyond, two phosphorescent eyes were staring out at him!

While he shuddered and thought of flight, and the mutterings of Wuff rose in a savage crescendo, the phosphorescent eyes lunged toward him, a sudden wind blew past, and a great body went bounding by. Ru screamed and waved his torch, and thereupon two more phosphorescent eyes emerged from the darkness; there came another puff of wind, and a second huge form went hurtling past. As it plunged into the rim of daylight and disappeared, Ru recognized the hideous spotted shape of a hyena.

For a moment he stood motionless, to make sure that no other beasts lurked in the shadows. Then, convinced that the routed pair had been the cave's sole tenants, he started slowly forward again; while Wuff, keeping close at his side, still growled a little and sniffed suspiciously at the cavern floor.

As he advanced, breathing the dank air that reeked with odors of dampness and decay, Ru observed that this cave was uncannily different from that which he had known. It twisted and turned confusingly; not for many yards anywhere did it keep a straight course; its roof was high in places, and in places so low that he could barely creep beneath; here and there huge stalactites, like gigantic tapering clubs, hung from the ceiling; and on the floor the pointed stalagmites bristled. And now and again he could hear the murmuring of invisible water—an eery murmuring, which sent queer little shudders down his spine and made him recall all the tales his people had ever told of evil spirits that dwelt in recesses of the mountains.

Yet, although he had a curious sense of things unearthly, Ru was fascinated. There was something enchanted about those great deserted shadowy vaults and galleries, illuminated only by the flickering of his torch; the silence, unbroken except by the sound of the unseen waters, acted upon him like a charm; and, as one in a magic spell, he wandered on and on, forgetful for the moment of the peril into which he was thrusting himself.

It was the discovery that his torch was nearly burned out that brought Ru back to reality. Without light in these dayless corridors, he would be helpless!—he would be worse than helpless, he would be lost beyond rescue! Like a dreamer suddenly aroused, he wheeled about, then turned back at a sprint, following the devious windings at reckless speed. The torch, fanned by the swiftness of his flight, burned threateningly low; the molten fat rolled down over his fingers, and he felt the searing heat of the flames. But with the grip of madness he clutched that life-bearing brand; and with the fury of madness he raced through those shadowy labyrinths. He could not be far from the entrance, he thought—another moment, and he should see the welcome light of day.

But the moment passed, and he did not see the light of day. Instead, he paused at last in utter bewilderment. Unexpectedly, the gallery branched in several directions—and he could not remember coming this way before! Was he lost? he asked himself in terror. Which way should he go? But there was no time for debating—choosing at random, he shot off down one of the corridors.

Another minute, two minutes passed—still no sign of the daylight. His alarm rose to an overmastering horror; his torch sank to a little sputtering point that his scorched hands could scarcely hold. Reason had left him utterly; his mind was a blur of blind passions, passion to escape, at any price to escape; his breath came by furious gasps; his legs sagged beneath him; but still he stumbled on and on, like a harried beast close pressed by the huntsmen.

Then suddenly, from somewhere ahead of him, there came a strange whirring, a murmur as of many wings. Abruptly he stopped; his heart gave a great leap—and just at that instant the torch went out.

As a blackness deeper than the blackness of midnight closed about him, there came a low whine from just beside him. Sinking down to the rocky floor, he pressed as if for protection against the huddled form of Wuff—his sole companion amid that appalling emptiness.

Only in the remotest recesses of his old cave had Ru known a darkness such as this. The gloom was absolute; a blind man could have seen as well as he. Yet never before had he felt so intensely the need of eyes. Out of the depths of the cavern that strange whirring still proceeded, a flapping as of great wings, as of gigantic birds. Louder and louder it grew, louder and louder although never less eery, until Ru could have sworn that the air was filled with enormous evil shapes, gliding back and forth in wide loops and circles through the thick cavern air.

For many minutes he sat hunched on the floor, his hands pressed into the thick fur of Wuff. He did not dare to move; he was afraid that his very breathing would betray him; intermittently the whirring continued, sometimes nearer, sometimes more remote, then gradually dying down altogether, until the silence seemed more terrible than sound, and he had visions of stealthy marauders creeping up on him in the dark. And still a mad eagerness to escape possessed him. Panic-stricken and yet helpless, he suffered all the torments of hopeless captivity—his whole being was aflame with desire for the free air, the open fields, the light of the sun.

At length the darkness and the silence became too oppressive to endure. With no plan in mind, with a brain too overheated to conceive a plan, he began to walk slowly away. Fumbling for his course like a sightless old man, he groped along the wall, sometimes cutting his hands on sharp projections of the rock, sometimes bruising his bare feet on unseen stalagmites. At his side Wuff trotted, as bewildered as himself—at times Ru could hear the heavy breathing or feel the bushy form brushing against his legs. Where he was going he had no idea; he only knew that he was curving in and about, bending and twisting and winding in a series of loops that merely added to the confusion in his mind. Perhaps he had a vague notion that, at some sudden turn, the longed-for daylight would greet him— but, if so, the hope died slowly in his heart. The blackness was everywhere unbroken, everywhere opaque and impenetrable, as if no sun or star had ever shone—and the farther he advanced, the more unlikely did it seem that he would ever regain the open.

Now, as he forced his way haltingly through the
invisible, his first frenzied desire to escape had given
place to a steadier but scarcely less horrifying emotion—a preying dread that would not leave him, but
that persisted and grew while he felt for his path
along dark passageway after dark passageway.
What unspeakable monsters prowled in these laby-
rinthine recesses? To his impressionable mind, accustomed from infancy to thinking of all places as
populated with evil beasts and still more evil spirits,
there could be no doubt that unseen eyes were spying
upon him, unseen claws clutching and preparing
to strike—and he expected each instant to feel the
stroke of rending talons or fangs, or to go writhing on the floor in deadly conflict with some unknown adversary.

Blindfolded though he was, he was not long in
realizing that he was wandering through sections
of the cave that were new to him. Time after time
the galleries divided into two or even three passages, and he had necessarily to select at random.
That he had chosen wrongly became more and more
apparent as he advanced and found himself even
more hopelessly entangled. The corridors had ceased
to run upon the level; now and then he was faced
with a sharp descent, and he would turn back sooner
than take the risk of falling; again, he was confronted with a steep rise, which likewise he would
seek to avoid; and once or twice he entered what
was apparently a blind alley, and paused in bewilderment before a wall through which he could find no

exit. He was impeded, also, by having occasionally to creep on hands and knees beneath a drooping ceiling, and several times he crawled through a slit in the wall so narrow as to admit him only with much crowding; while, by way of contrast, he had sometimes a sense of ample spaces and wide distances, as though the vaulted roof were high above and the walls far apart.

As the ascents and descents became more frequent, a new terror began to take possession of him—what if there were a hole in the floor, and he should go slipping down into bottomless vacancy? Once, with this fear foremost in his mind, he actually did slip, and, with a horrified scream, found himself falling into space! But he did not have far to go—there was a splash, and unseen waters closed over him. For an instant he floundered wildly in the cold depths, drinking in huge gulps while his bewildered mind vaguely apprehended that the end had come; then, groping by instinct, he found his way shoreward, grasped at an overhanging rock and pulled himself to comparative safety, while all about him the echoes of his sputtering and splashing sounded like the mutterings of evil spirits.

After this ordeal, Ru moved even more cautiously than before. To his mind it was not credible that he had slipped by natural means—the simple explanation was that some invisible watcher had shoved him into the waters. New panic seized him as he wondered how to elude the attacks of his silent persecutor; and it was long before he could summon forth the courage to venture on into the unknown.

Yet he had no choice; and for a time that seemed never-ending and a distance that seemed interminable, he groped through the blackness of the winding mazes. The only sound was the occasional murmuring of invisible waters, varied by the unearthly echoes of his soft footsteps or of his voice when he called to Wuff. For all he could tell, he might not have moved an inch since entering the cavern—in this lightless world, space seemed to have been blotted out.

At last, in utter despair that matched his utter exhaustion, Ru flung himself down upon the cave floor for a few hours' rest. It may be that in that hazy interval he found needed repose—certainly, he was long in a state of half-consciousness, in which confused visions trailed across his mind. First he would see an avenging demon with eyes like fire and a club as big as a mountain and an evil, sneering face like Grumgra's; then he would view a dark gallery from which a wolf the size of a bison would emerge, with long sharp teeth and blood-dripping tongue; then the scene would change and there would be a murmuring of soft voices, and he would feel the hands of Yonyo and peer into her sparkling eyes, and all things would grow comforting and kindly; then once more he would be alone in the darkness, and all about him would brood slinking demons with snaky arms, and vulturelike birds with wings wide as a spreading tree, and enormous bears into whose cavernous jaws he was forced to walk. . . .

From one such nightmare he was aroused with the consciousness that many hours had passed. Perhaps in the world above ground another day had broken—but here all was unchanged. At his side he could hear the rhythmic breathing of the invisible Wuff; but, except for that faint murmuring, the silence was undisturbed; and through the pitchy darkness there was still not a spark to be seen.

But now Ru was aware of a new and most unwelcome sensation, an emptiness within him that brought dreadful premonitions—the gnawings of incipient hunger. In a flash of terrible insight, he perceived that here was a foe more destructive even than the unknown horrors of the dark. What if he should be a captive for days within the cave, captive not only without food but without the means of finding food? In old times of famine he had known starvation and learned what a savage thing it may be; but never had he imagined so dire a fate as to starve in the darkness, with only a wolf for companion!

And as Ru recalled that his companion was a wolf, curious and horrible fancies flitted through his mind. What if, goaded to madness by the hunger pain, he should be plunged into a life-or-death struggle with Wuff—yes, even with Wuff, his protector and his friend? What if, in a fury of self-preservation, he should be tempted to slay Wuff for food?—or if Wuff, reduced to the ferocity of his kind, should pounce upon his master with murderous, slashing fangs?

So appalling did these possibilities seem, and so far from remote, that Ru could retain his sanity only by thrusting them resolutely from his mind. Springing suddenly to his feet, he called to Wuff, then set off once more down the lonely galleries at as determined a pace as the darkness would permit.

The hours went by, and still he wound around interminable curves—and still there was no relief in sight. His hunger had risen to the point of torment, his fatigue to the point of anguish; but there was nothing to do except to go on and on, on and on, lest the fate he dreaded should overtake him. His anxiety was all the greater because of the strange manner of Wuff; at times the beast panted heavily, at times whined in low complaint, at times querulously grumbled and growled, while once or twice —with a display of evil temper he had never shown before—he snapped angrily at Ru's hand.

It was after Ru had renounced his last hope that he beheld the first encouraging sign. Like one wearily trudging on the way to foreordained doom, he was plodding mechanically along the labyrinths, in such torment of mind and body that he had almost ceased to dream of escape—when suddenly, rounding a sharp turn, he was confronted by that which made him pause in mingled joy and alarm.

Not that he had actually come into the day! But his startled eyes at least beheld the light! Far from a bright light, scarcely even a dim crepuscular glow—yet a misty illumination, barely distinguishable from darkness, did indeed show the high-arching cavern walls in shadowy outline!

Instantly aroused to alertness, Ru advanced cautiously and with heart wildly beating. Could the light be a deception, a promise that soon must fade? Did it perhaps proceed from the goblin tenants of the cave? Was it luring him to the lair of some fanged monster? Or did it come from the camp-fire of some savage band of men? or of some festival of cavern spirits? or of some dancing circle of fiends?

But, no, it could not be a camp-fire! It shone too steadily, and did not flicker. After all, it must be the light of day!

Cheered by this reflection, Ru increased his pace. As he did so, he became aware once more of a whirring of wings, a singular buzzing and flapping as of great flying forms. Terror seized him again, and he stopped short, and thought of retreat—but this time his doubt was short-lived. Even as he paused and shuddered, the invisible became visible —several black-winged creatures went circling and whirling past, not like birds, for they had no feathers, but rather like flying rats!

Startled and yet relieved, Ru stood regarding these curious apparitions in uncertainty. They flitted about blindly as lost souls—veritably, they seemed shapes of evil! But they had done him no harm, and seemed to intend no harm—and, beside the mys-

terious horrors he had feared, they were insignifi-
cant.

At length, grasping his club firmly, Ru started
slowly forward again, while Wuff, plunging about
and growling with restored animation, made many
a vigorous but futile lunge at the flying creatures.

Ru's thoughts now returned to the unknown illumination. As he advanced, the light became a trifle
more distinct, although it did not increase beyond
the brightness of a vague twilight; then, when hopes
of early escape were burning warmly within him,
he made a discovery which at once answered his
questions and plunged him back into despair.

The light was indeed that of the sun, but it
entered from no accessible source! High in the
cavern roof, perhaps a hundred feet above, was a
hole like a skylight, and through this the sunlight
tantalizingly seeped!

But even while Ru stared up at that unattainable
opening, the light began gradually to dwindle. At
first the change was barely perceptible; then by degrees the aperture grew gray with the grayness of
the sunset-time. And, with a sense of renewed hope-
lessness, Ru realized that this must be the twilight
of the second day.

For many minutes he stood staring helplessly up
at the diminishing light. Then, before the inky
blackness was upon him again, he turned to more
practical pursuits. First he followed Wuff's example
by quenching his thirst from a little stream trickling
from the cavern wall; and after that, being faint

from his exertions and the lack of food, he sank down once again upon the cave floor, hoping for nothing except for sleep.

Before unconsciousness overtook him, he noticed vaguely that Wuff was sniffing the air significantly. He was even aware that the wolf, guided no doubt by his keen senses, went sneaking off into the darkness. But Ru's own senses told him nothing, and he was too weary to attempt to understand. And long before Wuff had returned, Ru was plunged into delicious dreams of bison roasts and sizzling joints of venison.

By degrees those dreams lapsed into other and less pleasant visions: it seemed to Ru that he was gnawing the bone of a bear, and that the animal returned suddenly to life and seized him in gigantic claws and slowly rent him apart. Now he could see his own flesh being torn and slashed, could feel his own bones being cloven and gnawed, could hear a crunching and grinding as his skull was crushed by teeth as long as his fingers. . . .

With a cry of horror, Ru awoke—awoke to consciousness that his dream was gradually merging into reality. The crunching sound had not ceased; through the intense blackness he heard it still, louder than before, insistent, rhythmic, like a splitting of huge bones. Terror came flooding back upon him, terror such as he had scarcely known even in this cave of fear—some unknown beast lurked in the darkness, chewing and tearing at bones! Scarcely daring to breathe, he lay as motionless as though feigning death, while a cold sweat burst out at every pore, and still from the invisible came that crunching, crackling noise. At times he even thought he could hear the sound of some monster breathing, and make out the gusty smacking of heavy lips!

In his overmastering dread, he did not dare even to call out to Wuff, lest he betray his presence and fall victim to the prowler. But as he thought of Wuff, it occurred to him to wonder where his friend might be. Instantly the explanation, terrible, all-sufficient, came flashing over him. It was Wuff's bones that he heard being ground to bits! The unknown beast was making a meal of Wuff!

At this thought he was ready to relinquish all hope. His turn would come next; he himself would be spied out and smitten! Lightning-like the slashing fangs would descend; the curving claws would rip his flesh to ribbons; the giant sabertooth or bear would tear him limb from limb!

Yet he had no way to save himself. There was nothing to do but wait. He could not attempt to creep away; the least noise would reveal his presence. And even if he could escape, might he not stumble into the lair of a second monster?

Still like an animal feigning death, he lay motionless on the cave floor, listening and listening. For a long, long time, seemingly for half the night, the crunching continued—then suddenly it ended. Surprised, Ru listened more alertly than ever. Now, surely, the dreaded moment had come! But the silence remained undisturbed, and the minutes went by, and still went by—and nothing happened. And slowly the hope grew within him that he was saved!

It was much later, certainly hours later, when he awakened from another dream-troubled sleep to find a dim twilight shining through the rift in the roof. The objects about him were once more vaguely visible, and to his amazement and relief his eyes rested instantly on the curled-up, slumbering form of Wuff!

Beside the sleeping wolf were a number of curious shapes, whose exact nature Ru could not at first determine. But, upon creeping close to examine, he discovered them to be the remains of bones —bones in every stage of decomposition! Some had been shattered as if by sharp teeth; some showed clearly the marks of gnawing; one or two had been chewed literally to bits.

The mystery of the night was now plain. Wuff had been feasting on the bones—and this it was that had caused Ru such unreasonable terror!

But one mystery only opened the door for another. Surely, none of the bones were those of animals recently slain. Whence, then, had they come? And how had Wuff discovered them?

Emboldened by the gathering light, Ru arose and started out to inspect. To his surprise, he did not have far to look—around a bend in the gallery, not more than a hundred yards away, he found a complete solution. And at the same time he observed that which filled him once more with misgivings.

In a little nook or side-grotto of the cavern, the bones of animals were strewn in bewildering profu-

sion. Cast one on top of another in a heap that towered above his head over an area great enough
to seat a hundred men, they stared at him with the
ghastliness of a graveyard dismantled—great bones
and small bones, bones straight and whole and bones
crushed and shattered, bones clean and white and
bones dirt-crusted and discolored, the skulls of birds
mingling with the broken jaw-bones of wild cattle
and bison, the teeth of wolves and bears, the horns
of rhinoceroses, and the curling tusks of the mammoth.

For many minutes Ru stood staring at that gruesome spectacle. He was not less fascinated than
alarmed; he knew that he had made a discovery as
meaningful as it was appalling. Beings of his own
kind had inhabited this cave—no doubt inhabited
it at this very moment! At any instant they might
thrust themselves upon him! Perhaps even now
they were peering out at him from unseen recesses!
But what sort of men were they? Were they to be
welcomed or dreaded?

To this question he received an early answer. As
he stood regarding the great mass of bones inquiringly, his attention was caught by a half-hidden
object with familiar outlines. And, reaching down
with a shudder, he drew forth—a battered human
skull!

Recoiling as if shot back by a spring, he cast
the hideous trophy from him—and at the same instant caught sight of another skull with leering
human eye-sockets!

A shiver came over him; the hair on his head and

neck prickled and bristled as if to stand up straight. All too well he understood! Sudden and terrorizing visions came to him of the man-eaters he had encountered among the woods; and he knew that once again he was straying into the haunts of cannibals!

CHAPTER XX

From Bad to Worse

FOR a long while Ru was uncertain what next to do. He knew that he must at last be approaching an entrance to the cave, for no tribe of men could penetrate far into the interior; yet just when escape was almost within his grasp, the hope of it was snatched from him. If he were to continue toward the expected exit, would he not encounter the man-eaters? and would it not be better even to die of starvation than to fall beneath their clubs?

Yet to return through the dark labyrinths was impossible. Almost any fate would be preferable to roaming again through those lightless mazes. Hence, after weighing and balancing the opposing perils, Ru decided upon the course of daring; and once more he took his way through the dim corridors, advancing with the manner of a spy in hostile territory, while after him Wuff trailed with a huge bone gripped between his jaws.

But of the expected exit there was no sign. As by degrees the illumination from the slit in the roof grew more remote, Ru found himself wandering back into the darkness. At length, rounding a sudden turn, he was plunged into total blackness once more—and again he wondered whether he had not taken the wrong passageway.

But the tormenting doubt had not been long with him when he reached a second turn—and suddenly all his horror and apprehension came surging back. Vaguely, through the gloom ahead, he beheld a light, a blurred yellowish light that shook and wavered eerily. At first it was so indistinct that he thought he might merely have imagined it; but, as he advanced, it grew slowly brighter, and gigantic shadows danced on the dim walls ahead, until he could no longer doubt that he saw the reflection of a fire.

At this realization, his impulse was to flee. Around those wavering flames, he felt certain, were crouched a circle of unclad hairy black forms, with brutish faces uplifted and enormous clubs ready to strike. These he did not care to confront. Yet he could not return to the dark mazes. Ahead of him—if by some fortunate chance he was spared—there would be light and rest and food, the only things on earth he now craved.

Cheered by this hope, he huddled more closely against the walls and still pressed onward, while each moment the danger increased. Each moment the flames leaped more vividly and more fantastically; each moment it grew more apparent that he was approaching the abode of man. Before long, his nostrils caught the acrid odor of smoke; not much later, he could hear the actual crackling of the fire; and at about the same time there came to him—enticingly and yet horribly came to him—the murmuring of human voices. The words were indistinguishable; he could not even tell whether it was his own language that was spoken; there was no more than a confused babbling, a sound as of many persons chattering. . . .

Because of a bend in the gallery, he could catch no glimpse of the strangers; and his chief desire now was that they should catch no glimpse of him. As he approached within hailing distance, accordingly, he crouched down to half his normal height, with head bent low and every sense alert; and for many yards he crawled through that unsteadily lighted passageway. Just behind him Wuff followed, with nose to the ground and eyes that glittered; but the beast was as silent as he, as though also aware that a sound might mean betrayal.

It is needless to describe with what trembling and what caution Ru moved when at last the turn was within arm's reach. The firelight had grown much brighter, and the walls shone with a redder glow; the air was thickly charged with smoke, and was hot as with the fetid breath of some great monster; the murmur of voices had become each instant louder although not less confused. From time to time, there burst forth a disquieting, raucous laughter that seemed vaguely familiar.

Hesitatingly and with limbs a-tremble, Ru stretched himself at full length upon the ground. Then, fearful of discovery and ready to flee at the first suspicious sign, he craned his neck forward and peeped at last around the turn in the wall. As he did so, his eyes bulged half-way out of his head, a low amazed cry escaped his lips, and like one bereft of his wits, he leaped to his feet and plunged around the turn, waving his arms and shouting in mad abandon:

"My people! My people! Look, my people! Here I am, come back!"

From around a great fire there sprang scores of hairy, stooping figures. Some started toward Ru with cries of astonishment, others stood still as though paralyzed, many withdrew with shrieks of alarm. For a moment pandemonium reigned, while something between mere bewilderment and panic possessed the surging, firelit shapes.

"Ru! Ru!" shouted some of the bolder, press·ing forward while the more timid still retreated.. "Where did you come from? We thought you were dead!"

Like a weird echo the others took up the cry, "We thought you were dead! We thought you were dead!"

In confusion that equaled their own, Ru stood regarding his tribesfolk. "I do not understand! Where do you come from?" he heard himself demanding. "How did you enter here?"

But before he could frame less excited speech, the torrent of their questions had overwhelmed him. The frightened ones, regaining their courage, had come crowding around him, all crying out simultaneously in such a storm that they were scarcely able to hear even themselves.

It was only by constant repetition that Ru managed to make himself heard. "Give me to eat, my people," was his insistent plea. "I am weak with hunger, for I have not tasted food since two suns have set. Give me to eat, and then I will tell you all you ask!"

"Give him to eat!" spoke a commanding voice; and Grumgra, edging his way through the mob, came glowering up to Ru.

"So the Sparrow-Hearted has come back!" he snarled. "He has come back, after leaving us when we needed him. He ran away when we sent him to find out about the cave—and now he comes creeping back like a hungry babe!"

Ru stood regarding Grumgra in puzzled hostility, but uttered not a word. And with a growl the chieftain continued: "But we will forget that now. The Sparrow-Hearted only remembers that he must eat —so let him eat. There will be time for other things later. But if he cannot tell us where he has been, his punishment will be such as no man can know twice!"

Whereat, with a significant flourish of his club, Grumgra went bristling away down the smoky corridor.

But the chieftain's threat passed immediately from Ru's mind. The next instant, provided with the juicy roasted hind quarter of a young wild boar, he was chewing and chewing with the gusto of a famished beast, while the meat disappeared at a rate that was truly astonishing. Meantime, at his side, Wuff ravenously gnawed at the head of a deer which one of the women, on a generous impulse, had flung to him; and on every hand, as though witnessing some extraordinary spectacle, the people hovered to watch the two feasters.

It was many minutes before, his savage hunger appeased, Ru began to observe his surroundings. But when his huge portion of meat had been cleared away almost to the bone and he was toying pleasantly with the few remaining fragments, he took careful note of the details of the cavern. The section occupied by his people was higher-roofed and far wider than the average, and reached for hundreds of yards without the usual turns and windings; while the proximity of the open air was revealed by a steady white light that shone in through an opening some distance beyond. Ru was surprised to see that the walls about him were blackened as with the smoke of many fires, and that on the ground was a fine gray dust as of accumulated ash.

But he was less interested in his physical surroundings than in the individuals composing the throng about him. Among them he recognized Woonoo the Hot-Blooded and Kuff the Bear-Hunter; but after a while he caught sight of more welcome features, and felt a great warmth rising within him as the sparkling glance of Yonyo the Smiling-Eyed fell upon him. In her expression there was a silent greeting, which he silently returned, and which filled him with more gladness than words could have done. She did not come forward to speak to him, nor make any demonstration; and he knew

that this was because of her fear of Grumgra and
Grumgra's terrible jealousy. Yet, when at length
he questioned the people, and again asked how they
had chanced to be in this cave, it was she who undertook to answer.

"We have not much to tell you, Ru," she said,
while she smilingly looked him full in the face.
"After we saw you go into the cave, all the people
stood waiting a long, long while outside, thinking
you would soon come out. But you did not come,
and at last it grew dark, and terrible things were
whispered among us, for it was said that the bad
spirits of the cave had taken you, so that you could
never come back. That night we camped on the
river bank just under the cave, but when the sun
came up you were still away, and we thought that
you were dead. . . . And that thought was like
a great pain, Ru.

"Only Grumgra did not believe you had died.
He said the Sparrow-Hearted had run away, and
should be punished. But not many of us believed
him, for had anyone seen you come out? And so
when Grumgra asked for someone else to go into
the cave, we all cried out that the cave-gods were
evil, and would strike down any man they could
catch. And no one could be found to go in; and at
last we had to go on and look for another cave.

"But we did not have to look far. The sun was
not yet in the middle of the skies when we saw
another opening high up in the rocks. Grumgra
sent Mumlo the Trail-Finder to climb into it; and

soon he came back and told us it was big and empty, so that we could all go to live there. And this we did, and the cave he saw was the one we are in now. We have spent one night here already, and Grumgra says this is to be our cave always."

Yonyo paused, and over Ru's mind flashed the explanation of his sudden reunion with his people. The cave had more than one entrance—possibly many entrances far apart and connected by long winding galleries; and he had entered by one of these gateways, and, without knowing it, had been making his way toward another.

But as this comforting solution came to him he recalled once more the pile of bones in the twilight grotto—and the battered human skulls. And the terror and mystery of the cave seemed as great as ever!

Yonyo's next words only confirmed Ru's apprehensions. "Many of our people think we should not stay in this cave," proceeded the Smiling-Eyed, while her auditors nodded agreement. "They say there are bad spirits here, who will bring great harm to us unless we go away. And they are right in saying this, for we have found some things which the spirits have forgotten and left behind them. On the floor we saw the ashes of the fires that the spirits have lighted, and the black bones from the feasts that the spirits have eaten; and we picked up the broken flint tools that the spirits have used, and a great club all colored and marked with dried blood. This is an evil sign, as Zunzun the Marvel-Worker will tell you. What do you think, Ru?"

"I think the Smiling-Eyed speaks wisely," declared Ru. "It is true—the cave is filled with bad spirits. And some of these look like men, but have the hearts of hyenas and eat other men. You shall see them soon, very soon—unless you go to some other cave."

Ru dropped into a frowning silence, and low murmurs of dread and horror shuddered through the assemblage. But almost instantly there sounded an authoritative bellow, which drowned out every other voice.

"Has Ru the Sparrow-Hearted eaten?" rang out the thunderous words of Grumgra. "If so, let him come here, that he may tell us where he has been! Come, let him tell us where he has been!"

"I shall tell you everything!" Ru shouted his reply, in tones that sounded like a challenge. And he arose and strode toward the fire and seated himself calmly in the light, while the people stationed themselves in a chattering circle about him, and Grumgra, grasping his inseparable club, crouched sullenly almost within arm's reach.

"Remember," muttered the chieftain, by way of final admonition, "you must speak truth! You must speak truth! If you do not—" Here he lifted his club, and sat glaring at Ru threateningly, but no further words were forthcoming.

"Why should I not speak truth?" demanded Ru.

Grumgra still maintained a morose silence, and Ru continued: "I have done deeds so strange they may not sound like truth, but that is not my fault. Even I would not believe them to be truth, if I did not know they had happened. You remember how once Woonoo and Kuff saw me sink in the water, and I was drowned and did wonderful things for the wind-god and then came back to you once more. I thought that would be the last time I would ever die and come back to you—but it was not so. Once more I have died, and this time the god of the cave has given me back my life."

Ru paused, and an awed silence held the audience.

He was about to continue when Grumgra, apparently less impressed than the others, burst into a snarling "You lie! You were not dead, Sparrow-Hearted! You ran away, and now you tell us foolish stories!"

"May the cave-god show you that I speak truth!" swore Ru, lifting his hands appealingly to the blackened ceiling. "May the cave-god strike me down if I lie!"

But the cave-god did not strike Ru down; and the spectators, after waiting horror-stricken for a blast of lightning, seemed already half convinced.

"You remember, my people," Ru continued, after he had allowed time to make his appeal effective, "that you saw me go into the other cave down the river, and that I did not come out. Now suddenly you see me in this cave. And I do not come from outside, but from deep down in it. How does this come to be, my people?"

There was a puzzled silence. The slow seconds dragged past, but no one would offer an explanation.

"This shows you," Ru at length pointed out, "that I must have been dead. While I was dead, a god bore me here from the other cave."

Again he paused; and this time not even Grumgra ventured a word in dissent.

"You ask me how I came to die?" he questioned, his manner growing constantly more assured. "You remember, do you not, that two hyenas came out of the cave just after I went in?"

A dozen voices grunted a ready affirmative before Ru continued:

"Those two belonged to a great pack, many in number as the men of our tribe. Bad spirits possessed them, and they fell upon me as soon as I went in, and cut and tore me with their sharp teeth. One or two I might have slain, but what could I do against a whole caveful of them? I struck hard with my club, and broke the skull of their chief, a terrible beast as big as a bear. But the others all jumped on me, and soon they were on top of me so thick I could not breathe. I could see their little eyes shining like blood, and hear their big jaws snapping, and feel myself being torn to bits; but there was nothing I could do. The next moment I lay silent and still, and could not move at all; and then I knew that I was dead.

"It is terrible, my people, to be dead, for then everything moves very, very slowly; and the time it takes a stone to drop from the cave wall to the floor seems like the time between two days. And so I saw very much while I lay there and felt the hyenas cut me to pieces. First there came something big and dark, like the shadow of a man, only as high as three men standing one on top of another, and it was the cave-god, and it looked at me, and said: 'This is Ru the Eagle-Hearted. He is a brave man; he has killed the chief of the hyenas. What shall I do to reward him?' And the cave-god seemed to think for a while and then he turned toward me, and said: 'I will make him alive again. That is the best thing I can do for such a brave man.'

"And the next that I knew I was standing on my feet, and all my wounds were gone. Then I felt big hands lifting me, and carrying me through the dark cave, far, far away. And I heard the god's voice in my ear, 'I will take you to another cave, where you will find your people. They are in need of you, for there are bad men about, who eat other men like wolves. For two days you will wander around without food, and after that you will find them. This I will do for you, O Ru the Eagle-Hearted, since you have killed my greatest foe, the chief of the hyenas.'

"And all this was done; and the cave-god left me to myself in the dark, and for two days I wandered without knowing where I was going, until I found you again, my people. That is all I have to tell you."

Ru ceased, and a long, long silence ensued. The people stared at him in fascinated wonder; they seemed stricken mute before the tale they had heard. Not a murmur of doubt stirred amid those shadowy scores; the apish, glowing faces expressed bewilderment and surprise, but not incredulity. Even Grumgra seemed impressed, and had forgotten his growling and his club.

But just when Ru's triumph appeared to be complete, there came a cry that was like a threat, and a stooping figure pressed forward with gleaming eyes. It was Zunzun the Marvel-Worker; and the malignant grin on his wily old face boded no good for Ru.

"Let me ask one thing more, Sparrow-Hearted!" he challenged, as he halted almost within touching distance. "One thing more—and if you can answer me this, I will believe that you speak truth."

"Speak then, and I will answer!" returned Ru, boldly.

"Tell me this," demanded the Marvel-Worker, in tones of ill-concealed malice. "Tell me this— where was your little wolf when you were dead? He is with us here now, yet surely the hyenas must have killed him too. Did the cave-spirit bring him also back to life?"

And, for the first time, it occurred to Ru that, in contriving his story, he had forgotten Wuff altogether. For a moment he hesitated, utterly taken aback; his faculties of speech seemed paralyzed. He saw the scores of eyes regarding him in wonder and with the first signs of doubt; he saw Zunzun's hostile grin, and a glitter of menace on the brow of Grumgra; he saw Yonyo's face contracted in a disappointed frown—and, in his confusion, all he could do was to stammer a few halting, meaningless syllables.

Before he could find coherent speech again, his sputterings were drowned out by the thunder-tones of Grumgra.

"You lie, Sparrow-Hearted! You lie! I told you you lie!" And Grumgra sprang to his feet, and the club flashed imperiously in air, and came down with a crash—where Ru had been. Leaping agilely from the attack, the intended victim had gone dashing away into the startled crowd.

But Grumgra was not to be deprived of his prey. Brushing past his bewildered people as though they had been sheaves of straw, he bowled over two or three of the more careless without so much as a backward glance; then, swinging his club viciously while wolflike snarls sounded from his throat, he started at a sprint toward the inner recesses of the gallery, where a slim figure was racing toward a black void.

In a yelling mob, the people gathered to watch. "Look at them run! Look at them run!" they cried. "Grumgra will catch him! Grumgra will catch him! He cannot beat Grumgra! Grumgra is a fast runner! Grumgra will strike him down!"

And no doubt Grumgra would have struck his victim down, had not a still more stirring event intervened.

Unnoticed in the excitement, a fur-clad figure had darted in through the cave entrance. Apparently he had not observed the agitation of his kinsmen; certainly, he gave it not a second thought. Coming forward by great strides and leaps, he shouted at the top of his voice: "My people! My people! Make ready! Defend yourselves! The beast-men come!"

Only a few turned to heed him. But while the echoes of his appeal still reverberated about him, he cried out a second time, in tones of unmistakable terror: "Hear me, my people! The beast-men come! The beast-men come! Defend yourselves! They will kill you all, will kill you all!"

This time a score or more wheeled about to observe the newcomer. "Mumlo the Trail-Finder!" they muttered, while frantically he repeated, "The beast-men come! The beast-men come! The beast-men come!"

Struck by the note of genuine alarm in his voice, the people forgot all about Grumgra and Ru, and shrilled with Mumlo, "The beast-men come! The beast-men come!"

Soon all the cavern rang with the echoes of that dreadful cry. Even Grumgra, hearing it, stopped short in terror, and abandoned the pursuit of the Sparrow-Hearted. A moment later, he was one of the shrieking, howling, fear-stricken mob racing furiously toward the cave entrance.

CHAPTER XXI

The Arrival of the Beast-Men

WHEN the multitude stormed and crowded out of the narrow rocky doorway, there was at first nothing to be seen. Just beneath them the cliff walls shot almost perpendicularly for perhaps two hundred feet. Above them the rocky ledges slanted for other hundreds of feet, with projecting crags interspersed with a few dwarfed trees and stunted shrubs. At their feet the river curved tortuously through a wilderness of reeds, bushes and dense woods, while not very far away the opposite cañon walls arose in bare and beetling magnificence. But not a living thing was to be seen in all those desolate expanses; and the beast-men that Mumlo had reported might have been the figments of a nightmare.

But so excited were the people that at first they did not observe how still and unperturbed was the scene before them. Surging through the cave entrance like stampeding cattle, they literally fell over one another in their eagerness for a glimpse of the beast-men; on and on they pressed, on and on in an insistent stream, those in the rear pushing so frantically to be first that those in front could not

244

remain on the narrow ledge, but were crowded off, and, with horrible screams, pitched into the abyss.

Not until five or six had plunged to their death did the madness of the mob begin to subside. Then by degrees the furious pressure subsided; the cries of the throng grew somewhat less tempestuous, the crowding slowly relaxed; several who had been clinging to an overhanging spur of the rock were rescued; and the people began to glance into the cañon a little in the manner of reasonable beings.

It was at about this point that Grumgra arrived. "Let me see! Let me see! Let me see!" he bawled, shoving his way to the front; and only by the exercise of rare agility were two tribesmen saved from toppling over the precipice at the chieftain's heedless approach.

Long and severely did Grumgra stare into the wooded wilderness, while his people watched expectantly, as though confident that his eyes would see that which none of them had been able to discern.

But apparently even his vision had its limitations. "There are no beast-men!" he growled, as he turned angrily back toward the cave. "Where is Mumlo the Trail-Finder? Why is it that he tells us lies?" And his little ferret eyes gleamed with a vengeful fire.

"If Mumlo had not told us lies," his kinsmen heard him mutter, ruefully, "I would have tasted the Sparrow-Hearted's blood!" There were none who wished to be in the Trail-Finder's place just then.

But as Grumgra went slouching back into the cave, low cries of surprise and fear burst from the watchers on the ledge. And before the chieftain had had time to wheel about and return, there rang forth from below a yell so blood-curdling and ferocious that the people could only shiver, and stare in blind consternation. At first Grumgra thought it was the call of some wild animal, so shrill and cat-like and altogether unearthly did it sound; but in a moment he had learned his mistake; for once more, as the people pressed close to the precipice, a terrorized chorus shook the air, "The beast-men! The beast-men! The beast-men!"

Now, as Grumgra strode again to the verge of the precipice, he forgot his anger against Mumlo. Certainly, here were the beast-men after all! At the edge of the woods, almost directly below, he could see them screaming: two or three huge thick-set stooping shapes, taller than his own people by nearly half a foot, and mantled—in place of clothes—in shaggy black hair as thick as the fur of a wolf.

As he watched, those two or three were increased to six or eight, then to dozens, then to scores, then to a rabble that seemed innumerable. Screeching and shouting with a fierceness that made even Grumgra shudder, they came pouring out of the woods: brawny club-wielding men whom Grumgra himself would not lightly have opposed; women borne down by great bundles of fagots and the limbs of slaughtered beasts; children of all sizes, rushing about like frenzied animals, and shrieking insanely. As if nature had not made them hideous enough, with their baboon-like furry faces dominated by bony eye-ridges, many of the men wore crowns of bears' teeth or of eagles' feathers, of the skulls of wolves or the horns of the aurochs; and, across their ox-like chests, not a few of the males had painted stripes and patches of a bloody red.

Directly beneath the cave entrance the multitude halted, while their howls and yells rose to a pitch of frenzy surpassing that of a chorus of hyenas. Meanwhile, with agitated, angry gestures, many of them were pointing upward, pointing significantly and menacingly upward.

At this evidence of the beast-men's wrath, terrified murmurs trembled from the lips of the watchers on the cliff.

"This is the beast-men's cave!" they whispered, confusedly, in excitement that was a compound of astonishment, fear, and rage. "This is the beast-men's cave! They come back from the hunt—see the meat they carry! They want their cave back! But we will not give it to them! It is ours! We took it! They cannot get it now! We will fight for it! We will fight for it!"

The watchers on the cliff had spoken truly. . . . Even while they stood gaping in expectant horror, the first stone was thrown in one of the earliest of all human wars.

The beginning was as much a challenge as an attack. One of the beast-men, taller and stouter even than his giant fellows, stepped out from the throng with defiant screams and howls, picked up a rock the size of a small apple, and hurled it toward the crowd on the cliff. His aim was good; the initial speed of the stone was prodigious; but the distance was too great; and the missile, stopping many feet short of its goal, did a graceful about-turn and plunged back to earth with such force that the beast-men scattered before it in terror.

And from the watchers on the cliff came a low cackling of derisive laughter.

But Grumgra, not content with such mild ridicule, shouldered his way to the edge of the precipice, flung both his great arms high in air, and let forth such a bellow as must have strained even his powerful lungs.

While the woods rang with the echoes of his wrath, there sounded from beneath him an equally loud bellow; then other bellowings in a chorus fit to rival a thunderstorm. Stones in a shower leaped into air, although always to fall back without reaching their mark.

As Grumgra watched these futile missiles, a new idea dawned in his mind. Seizing a huge rock, he flung it downward with terrible force; and it came to earth among the beast-men with a thud that might well have alarmed them.

But no one was injured; and the low-voiced laughter of the savages, evil-sounding and sibilant almost to the point of hissing, broke forth in a harsh and demonic chorus.

That laughter was soon to end. A second rock from the hand of Grumgra went hurtling downward, straight toward a dense little knot of men and women. This time the watchers heard no thud of the striking missile; but there came a frightful moan, followed by terrified shrieks; and one of the great shaggy forms was seen to slump to earth, where it lay in an inert mass.

While howls of rage and yells of dismay broke forth among the beast-men, the little band on the cliff joined voices in a tremendous shout, a long-drawn scream of exultation.

Profiting from the example of Grumgra, all the men now picked up stones and pebbles and flung them downward. Whether their aim was good they never learned, for the beast-men, hearing the missiles thudding and clattering about them, showed no desire to face the onslaught. Squealing and bawling in a panic-stricken mob, they made for the shelter of the woods. In less than a minute, the last of them had disappeared into the concealing foliage— and thus was the first round in the fight won by the Umbaddu.

From the cries of glee and the roars of derision with which they watched their fleeing foe, one might have thought that the contest was now over. Indeed, the Umbaddu did believe that the contest was over. Gibbering in the happy consciousness of victory, they strutted back into the cave, where they entertained their women with tales of how their bravery had frightened away the beast-men.

Meanwhile Grumgra, in a more amiable mood than before, returned to the pursuit of Ru. But he was without success; nowhere could he catch a sign of the Sparrow-Hearted, and nowhere find anyone who could tell him of the Sparrow-Hearted's whereabouts.

It was perhaps an hour later when one of the tribesmen, venturing down the cliff wall just below the cave, stopped short with a piercing scream. From beyond a projection of rock some twenty or thirty yards beneath, he caught a glimpse of two furtive black eyes staring from a face as hairy as a bear's; then of two other apelike eyes; then again of two eyes; until he was conscious of a multitude crawling beneath, crawling toward him slyly and silently up the precipitous ledges.

"The beast-men! The beast-men!" he cried, scrambling back into the cave. And once more his fellows rushed forward in a tumultuous mob to confront the foe.

They were barely in time. As the foremost tribesman dashed out upon the ledge before the cave entrance, two heavy gnarled hands were reaching above the shelf of rock, and a bulky form was projecting itself over the edge.

A vigorous blow from a club served to dislodge the intruder, who went plunging with a terrible howl to the boulders beneath. At the same time, two other hairy faces protruded, two other clubs came down with murderous intent—and hideous screams rent the air as the aggressors vanished, to be replaced by others, who likewise disappeared without being able to lift an arm in their own defense.

After five of the beast-men had thus been vanquished, the rest appeared to lose heart. At a greater speed than one would have imagined possible, the huge stooping forms began to slide down the cliff, while after them came rocks in a shower. How the Umbaddu yelled and clamored at their foes' retreat! How gaily and energetically they let loose the torrents of stones! The swift pebbles did far less execution than the boulders which the defenders rolled to the rim of the cliff, and which went roaring and rumbling down amid a cloud of dust, crushing the bones of more than one unfortunate.

How many of their foes were slain the Umbaddu never knew. But whether five perished or five score, it was at least certain that the victory had gone for a second time to the Umbaddu!

Torn and bedraggled, the surviving beast-men went rushing toward the woods as though beset by wolves; while from the successful little band on the cliff there came another concerted long-drawn scream of exultation, and the victors returned once more to report to their women how the enemy had fled before their prowess.

Not least conspicuous among the conquerors was Grumgra, who announced that the foe had fallen terrorized over the cliff at the very sight of him— and who saw to it that his fellows confirmed his story. Yet, though he gloated as warmly as any, the first ghost of apprehension began to stir in his mind. "The beast-men came, and then came again," he was heard to mutter to Zunzun. "What if they come once more? They are big and strong—their clubs could kill many men. Should we not watch to see that they cannot get near?" And after a hasty conference with the Marvel-Worker, Grumgra commissioned two of his followers to serve as sentinels on the ledge just outside the cave.

But the day passed without further sign of danger. The cañon depths remained unruffled and tranquil; no voice was to be heard from the thick, secluding woods, save the occasional grunt of a prowling beast or the querulous cry of a bird; no moving thing was to be seen except the waters that foamed impetuously from the gray rocks, and now and then an antlered shape that emerged shadowlike from the woods, and shadowlike vanished. By the time twilight fell, Grumgra was convinced that the beast-men had gone never to return.

And now, forgetting the foe altogether, he set about to look once more for Ru. But no Ru was to be seen among the throng by the fire, and no Ru could be detected even in the black cavern recesses; nor could anyone say where Ru had been seen; while of Wuff, likewise, there was no sign. Although the chieftain growled and grumbled a great deal, he could gain nothing by threatening Kuff and Woonoo and their fellow tribesmen; and finally, muttering that the following day should see the Sparrow-Hearted's end, he abandoned the quest and settled himself down to sleep.

It was sometime in the depths of the night that Grumgra awoke. About him on all sides sounded the rhythmic breathing of his people; between him and the cave entrance the fire, burning to a dull red glow, cast feeble shadows. Instinctively Grumgra reached for his club—although his alert eyes had beheld nothing suspicious, he was aware that not all was well. And as his fingers closed about the oaken cudgel, he caught sight of that which sent a howl of terror shivering from his throat. Just beyond the cave entrance there was a light—and the light was not that of the cavern fire!

In an instant, the place was in an uproar. Aroused by Grumgra's scream, the people staggered to their feet with confused cries. Then, panic-stricken, they surged without knowing why through the semi-darkness, stumbling over one another, shoving one another to the floor, blundering against the walls like lamp-dazzled moths.

Yet at first there was nothing to justify their agitation—nothing, except the mutterings of Grumgra. "I saw a light," he mumbled, "—a light as big as a man's hand." But the light had disappeared; and where it had been there was only blackness.

"There are bad spirits about!" Grumgra called out, when at last he had collected his wits, and the confusion had begun to subside. "There are bad spirits about! Listen to me, my people! If you are very quiet, you may see the spirits!"

Frightened cries burst forth anew; but Grumgra,

with a snarl, threatened whoever should speak again. Very quickly the threat took effect, and the people lapsed into silence.

A minute dragged by, a slow minute that seemed never-ending. The only sound was from the suppressed breathing of the multitude; among all those shadowy shapes, there was no movement. How long they would have remained thus petrified by terror no one can say; in another moment, someone might have broken down, and screamed out his fears; but before the moment could pass, there occurred the event for which Grumgra was waiting.

In the dark entrance of the cave, a flaring light burst forth, borne slowly at the height of a man's hand. And, by its sputtering, sallow illumination, a dim black form was vaguely visible.

For a second the watchers within the cave stood gaping in silence; then, as by an electrical impulse, the same horrible thought shot through scores of minds.

"The beast-men! The beast-men!" rang out a chorus of screams; and the echoes of that cry pealed and reverberated in a deafening din.

Once more the light withdrew. . . . Murmuring with fear, the people stood staring toward the point of blackness where it had disappeared.

"The beast-men are coming! We must not let them come! If they come, we will all die!" howled Grumgra. And, lifting his club pugnaciously, he started toward the cave entrance.

Encouraged by his lead, most of the men quickly

followed. Their clubs swung angrily; their shouts were threatening and furious. . . .

The sequel was never quite clear to the survivors. To the women, huddled in a terrified band in the shadows to the rear, all that was apparent was that pandemonium broke forth. Even as their startled eyes caught glimpses of new lights that flashed and flickered from the outer blackness, their ears were assailed by unearthly screams more horrible even than the bellowing of Grumgra. And while the screams shivered and died down, there came to them the sound of scuffling, the thunder and thudding of terrific blows; vaguely they saw dark shapes that whirled and twisted, heavy arms that brandished mighty weapons, a tumult of tempestuous forms. As the conflict advanced, with a confusion of growls and mutterings, and groans, and shrieks, and yells, it seemed to grow constantly more bitter and violent; and there came a time when some of the women, screeching and clamoring like the men, seized clubs and plunged into the affray.

It was not many minutes before all was over. The howls of the combatants died away, to be succeeded by a series of shrieks and wailings as of men in retreat; the blur of struggling figures resolved itself dimly into individuals; and from the black cave entrance came the shouts of the triumphant and the moans of the wounded. . . .

When the first pale light of morning made it possible to see clearly the results, it was found that five of the Umbaddu lay dead, their skulls shattered by the blows of clubs; while two were wounded so badly that their recovery seemed impossible, and Grumgra ordered them slain. As for the beast-men —they had left three corpses in the cave, great hideous corpses with monkeylike faces, bearlike mats of hair, evil black eyes, and ghastly blackened teeth all sharpened to a fine point.

CHAPTER XXII

The Beast-Men Score

A FTER the night attack, the beast-men disappeared as mysteriously as they had arrived. Except for the three that lay slain in the cave, no sign of them was to be seen on the following morning—the cañon lay quiet and apparently untenanted, and from the woods there came no suspicious sound. And once again the Umbaddu wondered whether their foes had not finally departed.

It was most necessary that they find out—and find out without delay. The people required water from the river, since that trickling from the cavern walls was not ample; they needed fagots for burning, roots and berries for food, and meat to replenish their dwindling supplies. How procure any of these essentials unless they ventured down into the cañon, where possibly the beast-men were lurking? For the first time, some dim inkling of the danger ahead began to filter into the minds of the tribesfolk; but, as yet, it was merely an inkling, and the men had no thought of possible defeat as they boasted of the exploits of the night and swore to spill their enemies' blood to the last drop.

It was sometime in the afternoon when three of

the tribesmen, wearied by the hours of waiting, decided that they might safely descend the cliff and quench their thirst in the river. Cautiously they began to slide down the rocky walls, while their people thronged the terrace above to watch; slowly, with eyes alert and clubs gripped in readiness, they released themselves from boulder to boulder, taking their way in single file down the steep, narrow ledge. As they advanced, they gained in confidence, for the stillness of the woods remained unruffled, and no suspicious murmur or movement startled their eager senses. From above, their tribesfolk cheered and shouted encouragingly, and the farther they descended the more uproarious grew that chorus from the cliff; and they themselves, reassured not less by the clamor of their comrades than by the serenity of the rest of the world, had little fear for the outcome.

At length they stood unharmed at the base of the cliff! At length, picking their way warily over a flat rocky space, they were pressing toward the brink of the river! Now they were actually at the river bank; now the foremost was bending down and sucking in huge gulps of water. And from his tribesmen there sounded an applauding chorus that was like a peal of triumph.

But with disconcerting suddenness that chorus snapped short. Shrieks of alarm and cries of warning shrilled from the watching throng, mingled with sharp exclamations of horror. Then, almost before the three daring ones could wheel about to face the peril, the woods behind them rang with savage whoops and ululations, and a multitude of club-wielding hairy forms swarmed forth.

Caught by surprise, with the woods and the cliff on one side and the river on the other, the three assaulted ones had no chance to flee. Except for a few random strokes as futile as a hare's resistance to an eagle, they had almost no chance even to fight —their foes bore down upon them in a throng that was overwhelming. In an instant one of the men, not finding time even to lift his club, was clutched in the grip of half a dozen iron arms, in which he struggled helplessly as a manacled child; the next moment, swinging their cudgels despairingly, the other two went down moaning before the blows of the beast-men, who pounded and pounded their prostrate forms with the fury of exultant fiends.

And now, while the angered throng on the cliff screamed out their hatred and flung rocks in un-availing showers, the beast-men proceeded to dis-play their true nature. Bearing the two corpses and their one living prisoner as the spoils of battle, they retreated to an open spot at the verge of the woods, within clear view of their foemen, although just out of range of the missiles. Then, building a fire while the howls of the Umbaddu still pursued them, they prepared for a pastime that made their enemies gape in amazement and horror.

At first the Umbaddu did not understand what the beast-men were about when, by means of huge flint knives and axes, they dismembered the bodies of the slain; and even when the severed limbs were placed above the fire to roast and sizzle, the ghastly meaning was not at first clear to the watchers from above. But, from the very beginning, the Umbaddu had little doubt regarding the beast-men's plans for their living captive. Bruised and bleeding, the unfortunate man was dragged to a resting-place near the fire, where he was held full-length upon the ground, each of his hands pinioned to earth by a grimacing foe, his legs helpless beneath the weight of a particularly bulky adversary. And while he lay there like a soon-to-be-slaughtered beast, at times pleading with a fury that awakened only screeches of derision and at times moaning so pitifully as to arouse a low hissing laughter, his captors proceeded to entertain themselves at his expense. All about him, in a jabbering crush, crowded the stooping, hairy rabble; men and women pushed one another fiercely aside for a glimpse of their victim; children were brushed to earth like dirt while their elders stared at the stranger with inquisitive apish eyes, pulling at his hair to discover whether it would come out, lifting up his deerskin mantle to find out what was beneath, poking him in the nose or face or jabbing him with sharp sticks for the pleasure of hearing him scream.

But evidently he was held for some graver purpose. After the people had amused themselves for some time and the captive had been prodded almost into unconsciousness, the sport was stopped abruptly by one of the tallest of the beast-men—

a particularly unsightly individual, with face painted red, and body covered so thickly with feathers that he looked almost like a walking bird. Certainly, he was a bird of ill omen—for, after a single scream from his powerful lungs, the mob began edging away from the captive as if from something pestilential, until there remained only the three who pinned the man to earth. Thereupon the feathered one began to speak in a loud and ceremonious drawl, while the others flung themselves to the ground before him; then, rising, they retreated still farther, and, as though at a given signal, burst into a tumult of horrible hoots and howls, leaping up and down with wild gesticulations, and dancing a swift vehement dance of triumph.

At the same time the leader, picking up a long, sharp piece of flint, held it poised and pointed toward the captive, whom he slowly approached with diabolical intent. The man gave a gasp of terror; his eyes rolled and bulged; he strained and struggled as never before, and for an instant had almost wrenched his right arm free. But all his efforts were unavailing—slowly, remorselessly, that pointed bit of flint drew near. When it was within a foot of the intended victim, the feathered one suddenly paused and flung both hands skyward as if in supplication to some unseen divinity; then, almost as suddenly, he emitted a scream that made his hearers' blood run chill, turned about, bent down, and plunged the flint—into the captive's heart!

Furious yells and shouts of rejoicing burst from

hundreds of lips. . . . But from the watchers on the cliff there came growls of rage and defiance blent with a low wailing of dismay.

That evening the beast-men made their camp at the verge of the woods, in full sight of the Umbaddu. Uncannily their fires blazed and flickered, while above the tree tops the skies glowed an angry red; uncannily the huge shadowy shapes flitted about the flames, surging back and forth vaguely, like a rout of festive demons; uncannily sounded their mutterings and cries, their babbling merriment, their hissing laughter, the crackling of bones and the crunching of the powerful jaws of unseen feasters. . . .

When morning came, they had not gone. The fires still burned, although now smoldering low; hundreds of shaggy forms were sprawled at every angle upon the ground. Soon after dawn they were all astir, quenching their thirst at the river or chewing at the few scattered bones that still told of the night's repast. But they showed no intention of leaving; and though a violent storm came up, and the wind blew and blustered frenziedly and the rain came down in torrents, apparently it never occurred to them to seek quarters elsewhere. They strolled about in the rain as indifferently as if it had escaped their notice; when it was over, they shook the water nonchalantly off their hairy bodies and seated themselves in the gathering sunlight to dry—but still they had evidently no thought of going away. And the Umbaddu, watching through the slow hours from their safe perch on the cliff, felt an impatience that gradually expanded into dread; for now at last, though they could not have stated the peril in words, they realized that they were besieged!

That evening a conference of all the tribe was held, attended by every member with the exception of Ru, who was still inexplicably missing. While four or five of the men kept guard with clubs at the cavern entrance (which was too large to be blocked with boulders), the others convened about the fire, not more than a stone's throw from the gateway. They were not quite so numerous now as when they had assembled in that other cave many months' travel away; not less than thirty-five or forty of their number had succumbed to the attacks of the beast-men, to wild animals, to accident and to disease; and the losses had in no way been equalized by the few babes born during the migration. Yet, as the people gathered near the flames in whispering, furtive-eyed groups, they seemed to understand that the losses they had suffered were slight beside those which threatened. And such was their apprehension that their usual lively spirits had deserted them; their chattering was low-toned and suppressed, their cackling laughter infrequent; they had scarcely the energy even to quarrel; and for the most part their feelings were expressed by low moans, plaints, and wailings.

Nor was their depression relieved after Zunzun the Marvel-Worker had opened the meeting and lifted his voice to entreat the aid of the fire-god. His supplications had little of the air of conviction; he had something of the manner of one who implores a favor that must inevitably be denied. And though the people joined him in his incantations, at times even reaching a pitch of fervor, yet their enthusiasm was short-lived; and, as soon as he had gone shuffling away from the fire, their faces resumed a look of half-understood fear, of blank and uncomprehending misery.

"My people, what would you have us do?" asked Grumgra, when, in a less aggressive mood than usual, he took his place in the firelight. "The bad spirits of the woods have entered the hearts of the beast-men, so that they want to kill us all. They will not go away—and they know that we cannot always stay here. We have meat enough till the sun goes down, and then goes down once more, and then once again. But that is all—after that, the black demon of hunger will be with us, and we will cry out, and there will be terrible pains within us; but the more we cry out the more terrible the pains will be. What would you have us do, my people? Would you have us all wait here till the hunger-pain comes?"

"No! No! No!" rang out a chorus of despairing cries.

"No! No! No!" shouted a hoarse, deep-toned voice. And Woonoo the Hot-Blooded, springing up from somewhere among the shadows to the rear, plunged forward with the earnest appeal: "Let us not wait! Let us take our clubs and go down the

rocks, and fight the beast-people and kill them all!
Let us kill them all, O chief!"

"Let us kill them all!" echoed scores of voices.

But Grumgra, unimpressed, stood regarding
Woonoo contemptuously. "And would you have
them kill us instead?" he flung back. "Would you
have them do to us as they did today to our tribesman? Hit us with big rocks, and then eat us like
wolves?"

Incoherent oaths and mutterings greeted these
words. And still mumbling, "Let us not wait! Let
us not wait!" Woonoo slipped back into the
shadows.

But, unexpectedly, Woonoo's cause found an able
sponsor. "The Hot-Blooded speaks wisely," declared Zunzun the Marvel-Worker, as he shambled
unsteadily forward. "What can we do but take our
clubs and go down the rocks in a great crowd to
fight the beast-men? The cave-spirits will do nothing
for us if we stay here. And we have seen what they
will do if we try to go down in small bands. So let
us go down all together! That is what the fire-god
told me when I prayed to him!"

"Yes! Yes! Yes! Let us go down all together!"
pleaded a dozen excited voices, led by that of
Woonoo.

"How can we go down all together?" demanded
Grumgra, his brow contracted in an anxious frown.
"The beast-men are as many as the hands of all
our people—and two clubs are stronger than one."

"Sometimes one club is stronger!" denied Zunzun. "The gods put more power in one crafty club than in two clubs swung by foolish hands."

Grumgra still glowered fiercely. "A big club is stronger than a crafty one!" he growled. And he brandished his own lovingly, as if by way of proof.

"This is what we should do," continued Zunzun hastily, in disregard of Grumgra's last remark. "If we fight where they can see us and when the sun shines, the gods of the big clubs will be with the beast-men. But if we come upon them in the dark, when they do not know how many we are and cannot see us, the gods of the big clubs will be with us. We will then make a noise like fighting wild beasts, and kill many of our enemies and frighten the rest away. This also the fire-god told me when I spoke to him."

"Let us do as Zunzun says! Do as Zunzun says!" the people began to clamor—and so insistent were their mutterings that before long even Grumgra felt obliged to bow to public opinion and commend the Marvel-Worker's plans.

Excitedly, with the enthusiasm of hope regained, the people commenced to scheme for that night attack which was to be the all-decisive test between them and the beast-men.

CHAPTER XXIII

By the Light of the Half-Moon

THE following day passed without event. The beast-men remained encamped near the river within plain view of the cave entrance, and still showed no inclination to leave; but neither did they seem disposed to launch another attack. Meanwhile the Umbaddu held carefully to their safe rocky fastnesses, and never once did any tribesman descend within a stone's throw of the enemy. So far as any observer might have judged, the contest was developing into a perpetual deadlock.

But although the day witnessed not so much as a hint of action, yet the approach of evening was the signal for unusual agitation within the cave. Men and women were bustling about in a thousand directions on a thousand eager errands; some were busily sharpening flint implements, some affectionately smoothing the edges of their clubs; some were fastening pouches of pebbles in convenient positions on their deerskin mantles; some were gustily eating, some industriously chattering, some merely pacing back and forth, back and forth in savage impatience; a few were praying silently to the gods of the woods and the fire, and one or two of the women were weeping; while over them all brooded an atmosphere of expectation, of apprehension, of hope tempered by a sense of impending peril and even of disaster.

The patch of light that marked the cave entrance had dwindled to the gray of twilight, and then been lost in the opaqueness of night before Grumgra, stalking out of the shadows with club portentously swinging, bellowed the signal that sent scores of hearts beating pell-mell. He looked unusually impressive this evening, with his circlet of wolf's fangs fastened conspicuously about his head and his wolf-skin robe hideously black against his black form; and never had his people been quicker to make way before him and to murmur obedience to his orders.

"Are all of us here?" he began, eying his followers not without satisfaction. "Is every tribesman here?"

"I am here!" volunteered Woonoo the Hot-Blooded, striding forward ostentatiously.

"I am here!" echoed Kori the Running Deer.

"I am here!" chorused Targ the Thick Club, Kuff the Bear-Hunter, and Mumlo the Trail-Finder.

"Does anyone look for any tribesman, and not find him?" thundered Grumgra, scowling his severest.

There was an interval of confusion, while each man turned to search inquiringly among his neighbors. "Where is Karv the Leaping Stallion?" "Where is Zuno the Wily Fox?" "Where is Ugwung the Wolf-Faced?" came the voices of baffled seekers. But always, after an instant, there would be a reply, perhaps from across the cave, "Here am I, Ugwung the Wolf-Faced!" or, "Here he is, Zuno the Wily Fox!" And so, after some minutes' delay, the roll was completely called, and it was found that every man in the tribe was present—with only one exception.

"Where is Ru the Sparrow-Hearted?" shouted Grumgra, after the whereabouts of all the others had been established.

But there came no reply.

"No one knows where Ru is," Zunzun at length reported, with a malicious smile. "No one has seen him since two suns have set."

"Ru the Sparrow-Hearted does not act like a man!" grumbled the chieftain. "Truly, he is like a sparrow! He runs away when we need him most!"

"Ru runs away when we need him most!" echoed a score of angry voices.

"He will not be able to run away from my club!" growled Grumgra, half under his breath. "He will not be able to run away from my club—when I see him next!"

And the tribesmen turned to one another, and muttered, "Ru will not be able to run away from Grumgra's club!" Whereat some tittered gleefully, and from the lips of others came suppressed chuckles.

But their merriment was interrupted by the voice of Zunzun the Marvel-Worker, who began solemnly to invoke the fire-god, entreating victory for his kinsmen in the hazardous undertaking of the night. And straightway the people forgot all about Ru and joined fervently in the prayers, crying out their hopes and their terror in tones so loud that the fire-god must certainly have heard.

Having duly summoned that powerful deity to their aid, the men began to follow Grumgra in a slow, cautious procession toward the cave entrance. All wielded their clubs as if to do instant execution upon the foe; many muttered audibly their defiance of the beast-men. But as that grim-faced, straggling band filed from the firelit cavern into the outer darkness, the murmurings of the men were almost drowned out by the lamentations of the women. "May the good spirits of the cave be with you! May you eat out the hearts of the beast-men!" cried the wives and mothers of the tribe; and many, flinging their arms about the shoulders of the departing males, screamed and wailed as though thus to detain the bold ones, until in the end their hands had to be disengaged by sheer force and they were left to voice their sorrow to their sorrowing sisters. At the same time some of the younger women, more given to action than to words, seized clubs and quietly trailed in the wake of the men.

It was a silent, crawling party of marauders that descended the face of the cliff by the light of the half-moon. With snail-like patience and slowness, the men and women moved through the night; with infinite caution they crept from rock to rock,

guided more by the sense of feeling than of sight.
Each warrior could dimly distinguish above him
the shadowy form of the next in line; each warrior
could see below him a warily retreating figure that
sometimes lay flat against the rocks, sometimes
seemed to mingle with the vague ledge and to
vanish, and sometimes did vanish to reappear again
around the windings of the precipitous trail. Not
a voice could be heard in that ghostly darkness,
though now and then the stillness was broken by a
pebble which, dislodged by chance, went plunging
below with unearthly rattling and clatter.

Down and down, on a common impulse that had
no need of words, that stealthy procession continued; down and down, with the alertness of mountain-sheep and the caution of prowling cats. When
at times they paused and the apprehensive eyes
wandered away from the rocks close at hand, the
vision of all was fastened upon a glowing red,
wavering patch beneath, from which the golden
sparks darted and flashed. . . .

At length, after a period impossible to compute,
the first of the band reached the flat, open space
at the base of the cliff. And there, without a word,
he waited, while one by one his companions took
their places at his side. Many minutes went by, and
each moment the party silently grew, until scores
of dim figures stood motionless in the moonlight.
But it was long before Grumgra, convinced that the
last of his followers had joined him, lifted his club
in token of command, and, still speechless, started

along the river bank in the direction of the crimson flames.

If the progress of the party had been by inches before, it was now hardly by half-inches. Crouching low beside the river, the warriors worked their way at a worm's rate among the rocks and through the underbrush, cautious not to disturb a pebble or rustle a leaf. At the distance of a dozen paces, one could have seen little more than a succession of vague shapes drifting phantomlike through the darkness. . . .

After a few minutes, the foremost of the raiders emerged from a clump of bushes into a boulder-strewn open space. Directly across from him, the red fires flashed and beamed, brighter and more vigorous than before, with angry leaping tongues of flame that illuminated dimly the ragged rim of the woods. With the exception of an occasional jutting rock, there was no obstacle between. The men now stretched themselves full-length upon the ground, and, still clutching their clubs, began to creep with serpentlike contortions and convolutions toward the intended prey. As they made their painfully slow progress, sometimes dragging their hairy bodies through patches of mire and sometimes tearing and scratching themselves on the sharp stones, they caught occasional glimpses of a huge squat form indistinctly outlined against the fire—a huge squat form brandishing a gigantic club and shuffling slowly back and forth after the manner of a sentinel.

As yet, no other living thing was to be seen; but as the marauders drew near, the sound of heavy breathing became audible, a stertorous breathing that seemed to issue not from one source but from a hundred. And the prowling ones realized that, strewn somewhere around the fire, among the rocks and near the borders of the wood, their enemies lay in unsuspecting sleep.

It was at about this time that one of the beast-men—he who had been observed stalking like a sentry near the fire—seemed to become vaguely aware of danger. He was not quite sure; but he ceased to shamble back and forth and stood rooted in silence to one spot, his eyes fastened intently before him. From among the confusion of shadows, he thought he beheld one shadow that had not been there before—a creeping shadow that glided slowly, slowly toward him. But when he paused to stare at it, the shadow ceased to move—was it really there at all? or was it but some fancy that the bad spirits of the woods had put into his mind? Perhaps it was only the moonlight shedding a pale reflection on the rocks; perhaps merely one of the boulders he had not observed before. Minutes went by, and still nothing stirred—the world seemed empty except for the wilderness of rocks, the faintly shining river, the ragged line of the cliffs and the still more ragged line of the woods, with the yellow half-moon poised in the emptiness above.

Yet to that lonely watcher came the thought that living shapes were abroad in the darkness. The suspicious shadow had not ceased to disturb him, although it was now still and innocent-looking enough. At last, tentatively and with the caution of the prowling panther, he began to glide forward, inch by inch, his club held defensively before him. He had not more than five or six yards to cover, yet many slow seconds dragged by while he crawled through the flickering gloom. Still all lay unmoving and calm; the shadow had not stirred but lay before him, dark and irregular in contour as any boulder.

Straining his eyes in a blackness that told him nothing, the sentry suddenly reached out his club and prodded the doubtful shadow. Simultaneously, a terrified scream started from his lips—the object was soft and yielding before his touch!

As the startled beast-man leaped back, a huge form sprang up from amid the shadows; and through the darkness a huge club swung. And the beast-man's scream gave place to a moan, agonized and swiftly passing; and the great shape slumped to earth, and stirred no more.

Then all at once the gloom was peopled. A hundred figures darted forward, with long clubs swinging; and, at the same time, pandemonium burst forth from the obscure depths behind the fire. A chorus of screams, responsive to the screams of the stricken one, pierced the stillness of the night; then came a tumult of voices crying out in bewilderment, terror, and rage.

Blending with that tumult, and almost drowning

The Umbaddu plunged to the attack

it out, there sounded the exultant shrieks and howls
of the marauders. Hooting and wailing in a din as
of charging demons, the Umbaddu plunged to the
attack. Straight toward the camp-fire they rushed
in a roaring mob, while their clubs, wildly swinging, dashed out the brains of many a startled foe.
Then, fiendishly yelling with the joy of triumph,
they started pell-mell toward the shadows behind
the fire, where the surging figures were gathering
in a turbulent swarm.

Now all was blurred amid the confusion of
battle. One could have seen little more than a jumble
of tempestuously swaying forms; one could have
heard little more than an uproar as of fighting
beasts. In that deafening racket, one might have distinguished at times the crash of club on club, at
times the groans and whines of the wounded, the
sighs and moanings of the dying; one might have
made out growls and snarls of challenge, snortings
of defiance, squeals and bawlings of terror, bellowings and thunders of rage; but one could not have
told whether defenders or assailants clamored the
louder, or which was defender and which assailant
amid that phantasmagoria of stormy, furiously
swaying shadows.

In darkness the battle was fought out—in darkness or semidarkness, for the fire cast a weird, vari-
able half-light upon the nearer contestants, showing
here two writhing figures clasped in a smothering
grip, and there two stooping forms confronting
one another watchfully with lifted clubs; while be-

yond, where even the half-light could not penetrate and utter blackness began, the hissing and muttering and screeching and shrieking of savage-voiced combatants gave proof of a contest that no eye could see.

As the conflict proceeded, and the noise and confusion grew and grew, the fire, untended, sank constantly lower and lower; the pale rim of the light constantly narrowed; and the moon, sliding behind a cloud, threatened to leave the scene in total gloom.

It was at about this point that the battle took a decisive turn. One of the fighters, on an impulse that no one ever explained, snatched a burning brand from the still-glowing fire; and wielding the flaming weapon, went dashing headlong toward the enemy. All, both friend and foe, gaped in terror and fled before this fire-swinging apparition; and for a few minutes he darted unchallenged wherever he would, while at his approach great shaggy forms went crashing right and left into the brush. Then, when the brand had burned low, the bold one thrust the still-flaming remains into the shrubbery, and went slouching away in search of other weapons.

Without knowing it, he had made the end imminent. Through his unwitting intervention, the culmination was to be sudden beyond all expectations.

Almost without warning, the darkness was overspread by an unearthly yellow illumination; and a row of bushes along the river bank burst into bright flame. The nearer fighters turned and gazed in consternation, muttering to themselves and staring like

men whom the power of action has deserted. And
while, stupidly bewildered, they gaped and gaped,
the fire leaped higher and higher, till it was taller
than a tall man, and the sparks flew like meteors,
and glowing spirals of smoke soared to the skies.
Then, as the screams of battle gave place to screams
of terror, and fresh combatants forgot their clubs
and crowded close to see, the blazes spread and
spread, till in places they filled the cañon from the
river to the cliff.

Encouraged by a rising breeze, they sprang from
the shrubbery to the overhanging branches of the
pine trees, which began to burn and sparkle gustily.
And enormous flames, greater than any of the fighters had ever seen before, began to roar and crackle
among the trees. The bright streamers leaped far
heavenward, licking their greedy lips rabidly; with
amazing rapidity they grew, even vaulting across the
river, until from cañon wall to cañon wall there was
a glaring, brassy-yellow, wavering bank of fire,
which cast an unearthly, sultry illumination over the
black knots of watching men. The air was filled with
the acrid odor of smoke; great black cinders darted
through the gloom; and high above the flames,
where the red sparks vanished, all the heavens were
discolored with an angry crimson glow.

Now, above the sizzling laughter and the howling of the conflagration, there arose the voices of
men in mortal agony. All thought of the fight had
been forgotten; each was bent only on saving himself. Some, trapped in pockets of the woods, shrieked

and yelled in futile anguish before they gasped their last; others, with hair shriveling beneath the intense heat, cried out furiously and dashed for refuge into the river. "The fire-god! The fire-god! The fire-god comes to kill us!" wailed the panic-stricken Umbaddu; and mingled with their voices were the still ruder, more blatant ones of the beast-men. But friend knew not friend, and foe knew not foe, in that clamorous dash for the safe, cool waters. Side by side the combatants crept into the stream, side by side without so much as a hostile snort; and, once within the river, no man had any thought except to stand submerged with nostrils barely above the surface.

And while the survivors felt the refreshing waters roll over them, the hissing and roaring of the fire gradually grew less distinct, its heat a little less unbearable, its illumination dimmer and more remote. When at last the less timorous ventured out of the river, they beheld that same ghastly red glow reaching high in air and far along the horizon; but they could no longer see the shooting tongues of flame, and they knew that the fire-god had withdrawn and that it was safe to seek their people once more.

The following morning, in the cave of the Umbaddu, there was much weeping and wailing. Distracted women paced back and forth with prolonged sobs and lamentations; some tore furiously at the hair on their arms and chests; some beat themselves insanely upon the legs and thighs; some merely lay in a corner, moaning and moaning. As the survivors of the night's encounter trailed one by one up the cliff walls and back into the cave, it became apparent that the tribe's losses had been irreparable. The misfortune was not that those who came back were much bedraggled or disabled; that Kuff the Bear-Hunter limped grievously, while Woonoo the Hot-Blooded dangled a broken arm; that the throat and shoulders of Mumlo the Trail-Finder showed the red mark of teeth, while half the hair of Grumgra's back had been singed away—such injuries were of minor account. The real misfortune was that, of those who had gone forth the night before, nearly half had not returned. "Where is Targ the Thick Club? Where is Gurr the Stone-Flinger? Where is Ulu the Long-Armed?" rang forth the despairing cries of searching women—but none was ever to bring an answer to their appeals.

Most disturbing of all was the absence of one who had been thought immune to danger. "Zunzun the Marvel-Worker—where is he?" cried scores of anxious voices. But there came no reply; and the people groaned that their gods had indeed deserted them, for all the arts of Zunzun had not sufficed to save him from the beast-men.

CHAPTER XXIV

The Wonder Stick Strikes

WHILE the battered remnants of the attacking force were reassembling before the cave fire, one of the women made her way quietly out of a wailing group of her sisters, and slipped unnoticed toward the inner recesses of the cavern. In a moment she had been lost from view among the shadows. Rounding a turn at the end of the main gallery, she found herself in a blackness so absolute that her eyes could tell her nothing and she had to rely absolutely upon her groping fingers. Yet she took her way, not without assurance, even along the inky corridor, and her pace, while not rapid, was far from snail-like. It was only a few minutes before, passing another turn, she could make out a faint grayish radiance ahead; and toward this she proceeded at increased speed, while the light, although never approaching brightness, grew constantly more distinct.

At length, in the vague twilight, she found herself passing a side-grotto filled with an enormous pile of split and broken bones. At the base of this gruesome mound, crunching one of the bones with noisy gusto, crouched a half-grown wolf; but the creature did not deign to give her so much as the

280

greeting of a growl; and she continued around still another turn, and entered an enormous chamber illumined by the sunlight that shone in through a slit in the roof.

At one corner of this gallery, bent industriously above a mass of broken and denuded tree branches, squatted the slim, short figure of a man.

Disturbed by the sound of an intrusion, he looked up with a startled expression.

"Yonyo!" he cried, springing to his feet with every evidence of joy.

"Ru!" she returned, and came to him, and let him fold his arms about her.

"Why were you away so long?" he demanded, reproachfully, as he released her. "The sun has gone down, and then gone down again, Yonyo, and the spirits of darkness have twice taken the world, since you were here before. And last night—it must have been in a dream—I thought I heard terrible screams and howlings, as of beasts that fight. Why did you not come to tell me what befell? There must have been evil winds abroad in the dark."

"There were evil winds abroad," she assured him. "Our men all went down to fight the beast-people. And the evil winds blew against us, and many of our men were lost."

Surprised and dismayed, Ru stood staring resentfully at her. "Why did you not tell me?" he burst forth. "Why did you not tell me, so that I might go down with my brothers to fight the beast-men?"

But Yonyo merely shrugged in disdain. "I was not

silly enough to tell you. It would have done no good. Grumgra is very strong. He would have killed you with his club before you could throw one stone at the beast-man. You know how you have hidden here ever since Grumgra chased you. If he learned where you are, you would not live to see the sun go down again. I alone have found out where you are, for did I not follow you after Grumgra gave up the chase, and did you not show me where you were coming to live?"

"I showed only you, Smiling-Eyed! And I shall show only you until the gods make me as strong as Grumgra!" vowed Ru, hopefully eying the mass of leafless branches at which he had been working.

"Not even the gods can make you that strong!" sighed Yonyo.

But, disregarding her remark, Ru continued enthusiastically: "I can live here now as long as I want. I need no one to help me. You remember that at first, Yonyo, you brought me herbs and meat; but since then I have found a way to creep into the light through a long dark trail that leads out between two rocks. And so every day I go out, and Wuff goes with me, and sometimes he catches little wood creatures, but always I get many roots and nuts. And also"—here he hesitated, then continued with emphasis—"I get that which may yet make me stronger than Grumgra!"

The Smiling-Eyed looked at him uncomprehendingly, and he hastily proceeded: "Have you forgotten, Yonyo, that once, long, long ago, in our old cave, I told you of a weapon that would strike like lightning and kill at a distance?"

"I have not forgotten," she replied, without enthusiasm; but in her manner there was no trace of her former mockery.

"The gods have shown me how to make that weapon!" he announced. "They have shown me how to make it stronger than any club. Soon I will kill all the beast-men—and none will dare to come near when I am angry!"

Observing that she still eyed him questioningly, he pointed to some strips of hide and bits of flint that lay on the ground beside the denuded branches, and continued with assurance: "I did not use to know how to make that weapon—but now I have learned, I have learned! See, Yonyo, I will show you!"

And while Yonyo stood staring at him curiously, Ru picked up a long, straight shaft of wood, fastened a narrow strip of hide through a hole at one end, bent it with great difficulty, and strained and struggled to fasten the strip of hide through a hole at the other end.

"Look how tight it is, Yonyo," he explained, holding it out for her to feel. "At first I tried to use the stems of plants, but they were not strong enough and always broke. And so I thought of using this strip of animal's skin. I cut it with a piece of flint from my robe. It was hard to make the holes in the wood, but I have a very sharp flint borer—"

"But what is the use of it all?" interrupted Yonyo. "I do not see . . ."

"Here, I will show you," volunteered Ru. And he took up a second and shorter shaft of wood, one end of which was conspicuously dented. This end he applied to the center of the taut strip of hide, straining till his breath came hard and his eyes began to bulge out of his head. The bow bent forward many inches; it seemed that either it or the strip of hide would break. Meanwhile Yonyo gaped dumfounded, as if wondering what mad spirits had entered Ru's head.

Suddenly the bow snapped back with such force that Ru almost lost his balance; there came a whizzing sound—and the dented shaft of wood was to be seen no longer.

"Where did it go?" asked the Smiling-Eyed, more bewildered than ever.

"Let us see. I think we can find it," suggested Ru. And, followed by Yonyo, he started slowly into the shadows, inspecting the ground with painstaking care.

"Here it is!" Yonyo at length exclaimed, gleefully picking up the shaft of wood some twenty or thirty yards from its starting point.

"See! I told you I could make a weapon that would strike at a distance!" Ru reminded her triumphantly, while Yonyo, now completely convinced, had no more to say. "I cannot make it strike far enough yet, but the gods will show me that. And they will show me how to make the stick sharp and terrible, so that it will kill a man! Then we need not fear the beast-men any more!"

"Ru the Sparrow-Hearted will be stronger yet than Grumgra!" prophesied Yonyo, looking up at him with an admiring smile.

"Yonyo the Smiling-Eyed will make him strong," acknowledged Ru. And, coming close, he began to murmur gentle-sounding words that had no relation to the fashioning of bows and arrows.

But with a commanding gesture she repelled him. "No, Ru, you must not say pretty things now," she remonstrated. "First you must finish your wonder stick. We need that very, very soon. Then you can talk of softer things. But not before!"

And, despite all his protests, she started back into the dim recesses of the cavern. "When the sun has gone down and come up once more," she promised, "I will be here again." With these words for farewell, she was lost amid the shadows.

Returning to her people, she found that her absence had not been observed. The women were still wailing and lamenting; the wounded warriors were muttering and groaning querulously. Mingled with the oaths and curses of the men and the sobs and sighs of her sisters, she could hear occasional frightened murmurings about the beast-men. But no one paid any heed to her inquiries, or even seemed able to answer. Consequently, she was soon on her way to the cave entrance, to observe the latest happenings for herself.

It was with difficulty that she crowded her way onto the narrow terrace that fronted the cave, for dozens had preceded her, gaping speechlessly at the scene beneath. And how amazingly that scene had changed! Where yesterday there had been thick clusters of bushes and long stretches of woods, there was now a blackened waste, with here and there a pile of brush feebly smoking, here and there the charred and dismantled trunk of a tree standing as a lonely sign-post of ruin. Down-stream, as far as one could see, there was only desolation and ashes; up-stream, however, a chance turn in the wind had spared the woods—and the contrast between the still green expanses and the flame-swept desert was ghastly beyond all words.

But the destruction of the forest was not what disturbed the watching people. That which alarmed them was that the fire had not rid them of their foe. Many of the beast-men must have been slain, for did not every returned warrior boast of killing his scores? Yet, to judge from the throng that collected by the river bank, one would have thought that the dead had all come to life again. Swarming up-stream from the devastated areas to the fringe of the remaining woods, the beast-men had made camp serenely beneath the very eyes of their rivals, although well beyond range of stones.

It was a doleful tale that Yonyo brought Ru on the following morning. "The beast-men will not go away," she reported. "We pray and pray to the fire-god and the gods of the woods, but our foes will not go away. And so none of us can leave the cave now, for fear of the beast-men's clubs. We cannot go down to fight them any more, for many of our men have been lost, and the bad spirits have hurt the others so that they cannot swing a club. And so what shall we do, Ru? What shall we do? Our meat gets less and less, and we cannot go out to hunt for more. Soon there will be none left, and no berries any more, nor even any roots or nuts; and the women will cry out, and the men will grumble and complain, and the babes will die. Soon, soon after that, we shall all die!"

"No! We will not die!" denied Ru, fiercely. "We will not die! The cave-god will not let us!"

Then, snatching several slender shafts of wood from the ground, he thrust them before her eyes. "See, Yonyo! See! Our enemies will be the ones that die! These sticks will kill a man!"

Yonyo, astonished, observed that the sticks were tipped with little pointed bits of flint.

"How did you do that, Ru?" she gasped.

"At first I did not know how," explained Ru. "I tried to make the flint stay on the stick, but it would not stay. Then I split one of the sticks at the end without meaning to; and I found that I could push the rock in, and keep it there. And so I have split the other sticks with my cleaver, and filled them all with flint. If one of them strikes a man, it will be mightier than Grumgra's club."

"But can you make them hit hard enough?" inquired Yonyo.

"They can hit very hard." And Ru, picking up his bow, sent the arrow with a sharp thud against the cave wall.

Whereupon, in the sheer exuberance of her joy, Yonyo leaped up and down and shouted. "You will save us all yet! You will save us all! Your wonder stick will kill the beast-men!"

"All day I have worked to make the strip of hide tighter," Ru confided, after Yonyo's wild outburst had died down. "I do not know whether it is tight enough yet, but it is very tight." He held forth the bow as if to examine it, and dangled the end of an arrow playfully against the bowstring.

But suddenly his playful mood gave way to one of intense alertness.

"What is that?" he gasped. "What is that—" Without warning, the hoarse growling voice of Wuff had sounded from around a bend in the gallery; then a series of angry snarls, as though Wuff were at bay before some foe. And, mingled with the mutterings of the wolf, came the familiar grumbling of a heavy voice.

"Grumgra!" Ru murmured. And before he and the startled Yonyo had had time to turn and flee, a huge familiar figure shuffled into view, monstrous against the dark cave wall; and through the shadows a great club swung threateningly.

For a moment there was silence—a silence of paralyzing terror on the part of Ru and Yonyo—a silence of evil triumph on the part of Grumgra.

"So you thought to escape me!" the chieftain at length bawled, in tones of malicious relish. "You, Yonyo the Smiling-Eyed, thought to escape me to go to him—to him, the Sparrow-Hearted! But you are not wise enough for me. I watched you—and I followed! And now you cannot get away! I will take you! You belong to me!"

Leering at Yonyo with eyes that shone bestially in the half-light, Grumgra lifted his club yet a little higher, and took a step forward. But he was halted by an unexpected voice.

"She does not belong to you! You shall not take her!" challenged Ru, with a boldness that startled even himself.

"Does the Sparrow-Hearted then tell me what is mine to take?" bellowed Grumgra; and the echoes of his wrath sounded weirdly through that dim, vaulted chamber.

Then, striding forward still another step, he thundered: "Sparrow-Hearted, you and I have a fight to finish! Let us finish it now! After that, I will take the Smiling-Eyed!"

The club was lifted to its full height above Grumgra's head; a snort of defiance came from the lips of the chieftain, mingling with the shrill scream of Yonyo. Ru, with limbs trembling, pressed back against the cave wall; he clutched his bow hopelessly, without thought for its usefulness; all power of action seemed to have deserted him as he cowered against the rock, waiting for the end. . . .

Then came an instant's precious respite. Wuff, who had been skulking among the shadows to the rear, sprang with a snarl toward Grumgra. Grumgra, wheeling about, swung his club not at his human foe but at the beast. He missed by less than an inch.

Frightened by the crash of the descending cudgel, Wuff went scurrying out of reach as if at the sound of an explosion; while Grumgra turned once more to the chastisement of Ru.

But in that swift interval something had happened to the imperiled man. His quivering limbs had ceased to quiver; his fingers had taken a steadier grip on the bow; he had remembered how deadly was the weapon in his hands. Quickly, fiercely, and with something of a savage delight, he pressed the arrow to the bowstring, forced it far back with a vehement bending and straining of the heavy shaft, and then —for the desperate fraction of a second—waited.

Grumgra, gloating in the rout of Wuff, halted for an incalculably brief period to see Ru confronting him with a pointed stick. But he took little note of this queer device; striding forward with a roar of triumph, he lifted his club for the devastating stroke.

That stroke was never taken. As the club prepared to descend, something smote Grumgra furiously in the chest. Suddenly all things went black before him; he stopped short, dropped his club, staggered, and clutched with both hands at a long stick projecting from above his heart. The blood spouted in a torrent down his side, his black hair was matted with red, his eyes rolled and twisted crazily, a ferocious howl issued from his lips; then, almost instantly, he reeled, pitched forward, and plunged heavily on to the cavern rocks.

CHAPTER XXV

The Ascension of Ru

AS the huge form of the chieftain crashed to earth, Ru leaped warily to the farther side of the cave, half expecting Grumgra to rise and return to the attack. But Grumgra did not rise; the great sprawled shape lay stiff and motionless where it had fallen. And as the terrible slow seconds dragged by, there came to the two watchers an appalling realization of what had happened.

"He is dead!" muttered Ru, under his breath.

With spylike caution, he stole over to the prostrate figure, and prodded it with the tip of an arrow. Still Grumgra did not stir. Nor did he make response when Wuff, waxing bold again, came sniffing near with low, contented growls. A slow stream of blood was trickling from beneath his outstretched body—but there was no sign of life.

"He is dead!" Yonyo repeated after Ru, in incredulous tones. And, like one walking in a dream, she slipped across the cave to the smitten chieftain, stood hesitating an instant, then reached down her hand, and timidly touched the shaggy form.

As she did so, a piercing scream burst from her lips. "He is dead, dead!" she cried, as though the knowledge had now come to her for the first time. "Grumgra is dead! The Growling Wolf is dead!"

Then something like an hysterical sobbing racked her frame. "The Growling Wolf is dead, is dead!" she kept repeating, in tones of passionate relief, as if only repetition could lend truth to the incredible words. "Ru has killed the Growling Wolf!"

And, like one in need of every assurance her senses could give her, she reached down once more to touch the lifeless shape. Newly convinced, she seemed filled with a sudden fresh energy. Before Ru could stop her or even understand what she was about, she had gone dashing around the turn in the gallery and through the dark passageway toward the cave entrance.

"My people! My people!" her maddened voice shrilled. "Ru has killed Grumgra! Ru has killed Grumgra!" And again and again her words rang out, fainter and fainter as she recklessly retreated; again and again, and fainter and fainter still, until the cries came back thin and eery amid a chorus of echoes: "Ru has killed Grumgra! He has killed the Growling Wolf, has killed the Growling Wolf!"

After the sound of her calling had died away, Ru stood regarding the corpse of his foe with the startled air of one who has just seen a tree blasted by lightning. "I do not know how I did it. I do not know how," he kept muttering to himself. Reaching down and prodding the body of the fallen leader, he mumbled over and over again: "He is dead! He is dead! He will never strike me now! He will never take Yonyo!"

Then, as by degrees his bewilderment cleared away, there rose in his heart a great joy, a pride in what he had done, mingled with a contempt for the stricken man.

"Grumgra, you were not so strong, after all!" he murmured. "You were not so strong, O Growling Wolf!"

To lend his words emphasis, he picked up Grumgra's club, and violently pounded the unresponsive mass of flesh and bones that had been the chieftain.

Having thus expressed his feelings, he began to pace gleefully about the cavern, gripping the club —though it was far too heavy for him to swing with ease—and repeating to himself: "I am Grumgra now! I am Grumgra!"

It was while he was thus occupied that his attention was caught by a din of excited voices, a confused din borne to him far down the dark galleries. Not at all apprehensive, he paused to listen; rapidly that tumult of voices grew louder, until he thought he could recognize the shrill tones of Yonyo. A moment passed; then Yonyo herself, still wildly agitated, came dashing into view, with a shouting rabble at her heels.

"See! There he is!" she exclaimed, jubilantly. "There he is! I told you! I told you, and you would not believe me! See! Ru has killed Grumgra!"

And triumphantly she pointed to the lifeless body of the chieftain.

"Ru has killed Grumgra!" echoed the awestricken people. And, howling and gibbering, the dusky scores pressed close to view. Directly before the body of the slain one they paused, staring and gaping in horror; then, almost instantly, their amazement and dismay were drowned out by a low ripple of delight. And the uproar of the people was like that of a band of children at some incredible show. Some, to assure themselves that the chieftain was really dead, poked sharp sticks into his neck and back; others gently kicked or pummeled him or pulled at his hair; one, bolder than the rest, lifted the huge form onto its side, until a broken, bloody shaft was observed projecting from between the ribs.

"Ru the Sparrow-Hearted has killed Grumgra! Ru the Sparrow-Hearted has killed Grumgra!" Yonyo kept repeating, as though she could never tire of announcing the marvelous news.

"Ru the Eagle-Hearted!" corrected the slayer.

"Ru the Eagle-Hearted!" the people duly acknowledged, staring at him with a reverential wonder.

"How did Ru the Eagle-Hearted kill Grumgra? How did he kill Grumgra?" came a clamor of inquiries, once the people were convinced of the glorious truth. "He is not a big man! But Grumgra was so strong he could choke a wolf to death!"

"Ru killed Grumgra with his wonder stick!" announced Yonyo, eager to plead the cause of her hero. "He made the stick himself—the gods showed him how. It is stronger than a big club—and Ru can throw it so hard it will hit like lightning."

"He can throw it so hard it will hit like lightning!" repeated the thunderstruck people in chorus, while they began to edge fearfully away from Ru.

"Grumgra was going to kill him, but Ru was not afraid," Yonyo explained, enthusiastically. "He would not be afraid of a whole caveful of Grumgras. He just took his wonder stick, and threw it hard at Grumgra. And Grumgra fell down—and he was dead!"

"Grumgra fell down—and he was dead!" echoed the mob, unable to find any other words to voice their amazement.

"See how I use my wonder stick!" illustrated Ru. And before anyone realized what he intended, he had slipped an arrow into his bow and sent it crashing against the cave wall.

"The wonder stick is bewitched!" cried one of the people, aghast at this exhibition. And tremblingly he flung himself down before Ru. "O Eagle-Hearted," he begged, "do not hit me with your wonder stick!"

As though on an electrical impulse, the others all followed his example. "O Eagle-Hearted, do not hit us with your wonder stick!" sobbed and resounded through the cavern in a piteous chorus, while scores of shadowy figures groveled before Ru.

"I will not hit you with my wonder stick!" promised the Eagle-Hearted. "Only those who do bad things will be hit by the stick—as Grumgra has been hit. The others will be spared."

But seeing that the people continued to grovel on the cave floor with mumbled entreaties, Ru hastened to add: "The gods did not give me the wonder stick to use against my own tribe—not unless my tribe does evil things. The gods gave me the wonder stick to drive away the beast-men. The wonder stick will kill them all!"

"The wonder stick will kill them all!" chorused the marveling people.

Then, observing the reassuring smile in Ru's face, they rose one by one to their feet, while murmuring hopefully: "The Eagle-Hearted will kill the beast-men! He will save us from our foes!"

Five or six hours later, the body of the chieftain was borne to its final rest. In a dark, secluded corner of the cave, not many yards from the scene of the fatal encounter, a little hollow had been hastily scooped out with flint shovels and cleavers; and hither Grumgra's bulky frame was carried on the shoulders of three tribesmen. At his side, according to the age-old custom of the Umbaddu, his club was conveniently placed, along with a variety of flint implements and a handful of fruits and nuts; while his wolfskin robe was wrapped about him, and the circlet of wolf's fangs fastened about his head. Then, convinced that their chieftain would be equipped with everything necessary when the great wind-spirit came to take him away, the people began to pile earth and stones high above the recumbent form.

Owing to the absence of Zunzun the Marvel-Worker, there was none to lead in the prayers; yet

a multitude of voices began to pray simultaneously
in a babbling confusion, and each in his own way
invoked the gods of the cave, the fire, and the air.
Loud and ever louder they clamored, each striving
to drown out the voice of his neighbor, until the
uproar became like a tumult of madmen. But clearly
over all, in a wailing crescendo before which the
other voices stopped as if abashed, there rang forth
the sobs and lamentations of a woman. And more
than one man turned to his companions, and murmured: "It is Mog the Long-Faced! It is Grumgra's
first woman!"

Long and bitterly Mog cried out, while beating
furiously with her fists against the rocks that were
piling up upon the chieftain's vanishing form.

And while she screamed and wept, and the familiar, dreaded figure disappeared beneath the heap of
stones, a tardy regret seemed to awaken in the minds
of the people. It was as if they now realized for the
first time that Grumgra was no longer with them—
and as if they found the thought too terrible to
endure. "What are we to do now?" they moaned,
after the sobs of Mog had begun to die down and
they had caught their last glimpse of the black hair
of the slain one. "What are we to do now? Who is
to be our leader? Who is to tell us what to do? Who
is to say when we shall go out on the hunt, and how
we shall build our fires, and how we shall share our
food? Who is to watch over us and care for us in
Grumgra's place? Who? Who? Who?"

"Who but Ru the Eagle-Hearted?" came the

eager voice of Yonyo. "Who but him with his wonder stick?"

"Ru the Eagle-Hearted will watch over us!" cried a chorus of voices, responsive to the suggestion. "He will be our leader! He will guide us with his wonder stick!"

And since there was no one to venture a word in dissent, Grumgra's successor had apparently been chosen.

It was not long before Ru commenced to exercise the powers of his newly won office. The last stone was barely in place on the grave of Grumgra when he began to assert himself. Striding to the center of the gathering while his people withdrew awestricken before him, he proclaimed: "The Growling Wolf is dead now—so let us forget him. We have a great and terrible work to do! We must make ready to fight the beast-men!"

Here he paused a second, while regarding his tribesmen speculatively. In a moment his eyes fell with a twinkle upon a certain two, and he continued: "Before we go down to drive the beast-men away, we must be sure they cannot come up here to fight us in our cave. Kuff the Bear-Hunter and Woonoo the Hot-Blooded, you go out on the rock in front of the cave and watch to see that the beast-men do not come. And stay there till I tell you to come in."

Kuff the Bear-Hunter and Woonoo the Hot-Blooded muttered, but did not move.

"Go!" commanded Ru, starting with an imperious gesture toward his former rivals. And menacingly he lifted his bow. "Shall I hit you with my wonder stick?"

"No! No!" protested Kuff and Woonoo, shrinking back as far as the walls would permit. But Ru still strode toward them threateningly; and in another moment they had swung about and fled toward the cave entrance.

"Bru the Scowling-Faced, go and see that they do as I told them!" Ru ordered.

As Bru sullenly left, Ru turned to his people, and announced: "I have only one wonder stick now, but the gods will show me how to make more. First I must say some prayers before the gods, and none of you must listen, for the gods would grow angry and strike you down. But after I have made the wonder sticks, I will show you how to use them, so that you may help me kill the beast-men. Who would like to help?"

For a moment Ru waited. Each man eyed his neighbors fearfully, but no one replied.

"The gods will not let you all help," Ru stated, as though taking their willingness for granted. "Zuno the Wily Fox, you may help; and Kori the Running Deer; and Blab the Big Voice—" And Ru continued until he had named ten of the ablest and most easily managed of his tribesmen.

Several did, indeed, mutter audibly in protest, and one or two even ventured a gesture of defiance; but those who had not been named prodded on the chosen ones; and a few threatening motions with the flint-headed arrows sufficed to silence even the most fractious.

CHAPTER XXVI

Ru the Eagle-Hearted

RU'S ascension to leadership was followed by six or eight days of intensive activity, during which the cave buzzed with excitement.

First of all, Ru solved the food problem by showing the people the secluded cave-entrance which he had found; and through this, unobserved by the beast-men, they passed daily into the woods, returning always with roots and nuts enough to ward off immediate starvation. Meanwhile Ru labored assiduously at the construction of bows and arrows, which he made in an isolated little nook of the cavern, while Yonyo kept watch to see that no tribesman approached. And several hours each day he devoted to training the chosen ten in the use of the "wonder stick." He found not only that he had eager and imitative and hence capable pupils, but that his own skill vastly improved with practice, so that he was soon able to direct an arrow with accuracy to almost any desired spot. This art his followers, likewise, were not slow in acquiring, and he knew that the time for the encounter with the beast-men could not be far off.

The interval between the burial of Grumgra and

the battle of the "wonder stick" was marked by two important events. To begin with, there was the disappearance of Wuff. The young wolf, who had been growing manifestly restive of late and at times distinctly ill-tempered even toward his master, at last found the summons of his kind to be stronger than the appeal of human companionship. Standing with Ru one evening near the rear cave entrance, he started forward with sudden alertness and with wildly gleaming eyes as a long-drawn, doleful call sounded from far away out of the twilight. The next moment he had answered that call in high-pitched notes of his own—and then suddenly he vanished. Ru waited for a while, whistling softly to the animal, but Wuff did not come back; nor did he come back on the next day, nor on the day that followed. And Ru sighed regretfully, and realized that he had lost a friend.

The second event was of a more personal nature. It concerned his courtship of Yonyo—and its successful culmination. Standing proudly before the tribe in Grumgra's old place beside the fire, he announced one evening: "Yonyo the Smiling-Eyed is my woman. Is it not so, Yonyo?"

Yonyo came sedately forward, and admitted that it was so—and there was no one who had anything more to say, although Woonoo the Hot-Blooded and Kuff the Bear-Hunter did scowl furiously and mutter angrily under their breath. Ru, however, did not heed them, but proceeded forthwith to perform a little ceremony which the tradition of the tribe made necessary. Taking a sharp bit of flint, he cut a sudden gash in Yonyo's left arm; then, while the blood gushed forth and she bit her lip to keep back a groan, he made a similar wound in his own arm, muttered a prayer to the god of the cave, and let a drop of his blood flow into the released blood of Yonyo and mingle with it. And thus was their marriage solemnized.

Then, with Yonyo's hand tucked in one of his hands and his club gripped in the other, he led his bride away with him into their secret nook among the shadows.

After they had disappeared, an excited chattering burst forth among the tribespeople, for never had so quiet a wedding been known before. The older and more experienced folk predicted that not many days would pass before Ru would be beating Yonyo with his club and taking another woman.

But soon they forgot all about Ru's marriage in contemplation of a more momentous event.

Curious throngs would gather daily to watch their chieftain and his chosen ten at practice with the "wonder stick"—and an atmosphere of dread anticipation filled the cavern, gradually rising to a pitch of apprehension that compelled prayers from the lips of the more fearful-minded and put the others in a constant state of shuddering excitement. For the people realized that the "wonder stick" was to be the ultimate test not only of Ru's power but of the tribe's chances for very life.

Ru himself understood this fact not less clearly

than any of the others. He knew that the failure or success of the weapon would decide his own future and that of his people; and he looked forward to the approaching conflict with something of the sensations of a general who knows that a single defeat will mean disaster, a single victory win him an eternal crown.

Recognizing how much was at stake, he planned his campaign with the most careful forethought. When at length the chosen day arrived, he led his ten followers down the cliff in the early dawn, when the first tinge of gray was barely beginning to touch the cliffs. All had been carefully trained in the use of the "wonder stick"; and each man carried one of the weapons and eight or ten flint-tipped arrows. Confidently they stole from the cave, while the other men stood by in a glowering silence and the women poured forth encouragement, advice, and tears; stealthily and without a sound, each a shadow against the dark rocks, they made their precarious way along the ledges and to the base of the precipice.

Having reached the floor of the cañon, they crept forward a few dozen yards with Ru at their head; then, following orders which had been drilled into their heads beforehand, each concealed himself behind a boulder. And, until the daylight shone full upon them, not a sound nor a motion came from any of that watching band.

The beast-men meanwhile were unaware of their presence. The invaders could see the hideous black forms swarming about the brink of the river, could see them dipping into the water with hoarse gibbering and hissing laughter; they could watch some sucking in long thirsty draughts, some chewing greedily at great bones, some casting logs into the blazing fire, and some snarling and quarreling like embattled dogs.

Suddenly, leaping up from behind his rock with waving arms, Ru let forth a shrill and blood-curdling scream, the battle-cry of his tribe—"Oo-ow, oo-ow, oo-ow!" And at the same time his followers darted into the open, brandishing their bows high in air and joining in Ru's ferocious howl. And the watchers on the cliff above took up the call, so that it seemed like the roaring of a multitude.

The beast-men, startled, ceased their screeching and jabbering, and stared as if thunderstruck at their unexpected foes. For a moment they seemed unable to utter a sound; then confused low cries of surprise and fear broke from their lips.

Headed by Ru, the assailants were meanwhile striding forward. And the hairy, growling throng, unorganized and terror-smitten, appeared uncertain whether to charge and overwhelm the intruders or dash for safety to the woods.

But when Ru and his followers were within a hundred yards of the nearest beast-man, a tall befeathered individual stalked forth from the crowd, beating his chest and growling pugnaciously. In his enormous right hand was a club nearly as tall as himself; above his thick eyebrow ridge was a ghastly painted streak of red; his teeth, chiseled to a point

and stained black, gaped like the fangs of some gruesome monster. At his side, encouraged by his boldness, shambled a dozen of his fellows, their forms
gigantic and stooping, their evil little eyes staring
out from thickets of black hair. All snarled and angrily swung their clubs, while behind them their
people pressed, gibbering at a distance, as if expecting Ru's tiny band to turn and flee.

But they did not turn and flee. Some, indeed, did
tremble and draw back a pace; but there came the
reassuring, commanding voice of Ru: "Now, now is
the time!" And instead of taking flight, they hastily
adjusted the arrows to their bows.

Still the feathered one stalked onward, side by
side with his mighty companions. The space between
them and Ru had been cut in half; in another instant
the invaders would feel the touch of their clubs.

"Now, now is the time!" repeated Ru. And the
bows were drawn back by powerful hands, then
furiously recoiled. There came a sudden whizzing
sound—and an amazing thing befell.

Howling with agony, two of the beast-men
stopped short, clutched at long sticks protruding
from their chests, staggered, and fell to earth while
the blood spouted from new-made wounds.

Their fellows, startled and aghast, halted and
turned with bewildered cries to the smitten ones.
But even while they gaped and hesitated, there came
another whizzing sound, and one of the men
screamed, dropped his club, and wildly clutched a
crimson wrist; while another, reeling as the blood

burst from the split arteries of his neck, gave out a series of horrible gasps and gurgles, and toppled helplessly to earth.

Again came the battle-cry of the Umbaddu—"Oo-ow, oo-ow, oo-ow!"—taken up by the watchers on the cliff, and repeated in a long-drawn, furious chorus.

And while the uninjured beast-men, rooted to the spot by terror, gaped stupidly at their foes, they heard once more that mysterious whizzing sound—and still another of their number shrieked with pain, and fell to earth with a long reddened stick protruding from between his ribs. And this time the stricken one was the feathered giant!

A low moan of horror and dismay sounded from the watching ranks of beast-men. And rising to a deep-toned dreary monody, it seemed like the mourning of a multitude.

Simultaneously, louder and more insistent than before, there rang forth that terrorizing battle-cry, "Oo-ow, oo-ow, oo-ow, oo-ow, oo-ow!"

Then came another ominous whizzing, and another beast-man fell with a scream. And brandishing his bow high above his head, Ru started forward with a great leap; while after him dashed his followers in a yelling band.

The beast-men screeched with terror. Those nearest the charging squad dropped their clubs, wheeled about, and dashed pell-mell toward their frightened fellows.

It was as though they had touched a spark to dry

straw. The flight turned into a panic; in all directions the beast-men began to scamper, howling and bellowing with fear, tumbling over one another in mad haste to escape, scattering and running like stampeding sheep. Into the concealment of the woods they vanished, men, women, and children in an insane mob, until in a moment the last of them had been lost to view.

And Ru, following with hoots and screams of triumph, knew that the battle had been won. The beast-men would not return; the "wonder stick" had made the new cave secure for his people. . . .

High above him, from the throng on the cliff, there still sounded that tremulous, victorious chorus, "Oo-ow, oo-ow, oo-ow, oo-ow, oo-ow, oo-ow. . . ."

CONCLUSION

FOR many generations the legends of the Umbaddu told of the deeds of Ru the Eagle-
Hearted. From father to son, and from father to
son, and then again from father to son, passed the
stories of the great chieftain who had brought his
tribe to the warm lands and the cave above the river,
and who had driven out the beast-men and given his
people the "wonder stick." It was known how he
had twice died and come back to the world; how
he had made friends of the wind-spirit and the spirit
of the waters; how he had tamed even the wild
creatures, so that a great wolf, whom none other
dare approach, would come out of the woods to lick
his hands. And it was said that he had led his tribe
through many bold hunts and many brave wars;
and that always at his side walked his woman, Yonyo
the Smiling-Eyed.

Mothers, whispering by the light of the cave fire
when winter nights were long, would counsel their
half-grown lads to try to be like Ru; fathers would
murmur how tall he was of limb, how firm of arm,
how noted for his courage from his childhood days.
. . . Thus the years and the centuries went by, while
the Umbaddu tribe throve and multiplied, and sent
out its children to occupy caves near at hand and

then caves many days' travel away. . . . And as the waves of migration spread, and the people wandered into strange hills and woods, and sowed the seeds of that which was one day to transform the world, they bore with them always one prized and reverenced name, the name of him who was not as other men but was kin to the spirits of the air and the fire—the name of Ru the Eagle-Hearted.

THE END